DARK VISIONS
OF TORMENT

A DCI Will Blake Thriller

J.E. Mayhew

Obolus Books

ISBN-13: 978-1-9998407-2-3

Cover design by: Meg Jolly
Cover Photo: Dave Mort

For you, the reader!

Although the story is set on the Wirral, the names of some establishments and roads have been fictionalised to protect the unloved and godless...
but you can have fun guessing...

Eternals I hear your call gladly,
Dictate swift winged words, & fear not
To unfold your dark visions of torment.

(Preludium To The Book Of Urizen)

WILLIAM BLAKE

CHAPTER 1

The darkness was complete. Jayden New couldn't even see his hand in front of him. All he knew was the dark and the ankle-deep cold water that soaked his tracksuit bottoms. Apart from his ragged, sobbing breath and the steady drip of water from above, it was silent. Jayden wasn't sure how he had ended up here or where 'here' was. He tried to control his breathing, to calm it down like they'd taught him to do at school when he lost his temper. "One. And two. And three," he whispered, his voice echoed above his head. "Four. And five. And six..." He stopped; the sound of his lonely voice bouncing off the walls and water just increased the panic he felt. He wanted to shout for help, but he knew it would just come out as a scream of terror.

Finally, he put his arms out, testing the blackness for any barrier and found empty air. His head thumped and he could taste blood on his lips. Numerous little cuts stung on his arms and legs. He ached all over. What had happened to him? He felt like he'd been beaten up.

Whimpering, he shuffled forward a couple of steps. The cold water dragged at his trouser legs, and something slithered over his feet. He froze. It had felt slimy and cold. In Jayden's mind, snakes and lizards twisted around each other and between his ankles. Blood pulsed around his head, and he bit his lip, wishing his grandad was here. Grandad Dave would know what to do. But Grandad Dave was gone. A tear trickled down Jayden's cheek. Grandad would tell him to be brave. He'd say that God was watching over him.

Jayden took a breath and scrubbed his hand across his cheek. The slimy thing had stopped moving and slowly, Jayden lifted his foot. The air filled with the sound of water splattering back into the puddle but whatever it was, it slid off. From the crinkly sound, Jayden thought it might be an old plastic bag. He shuffled a little further, moving sideways, with his arms outstretched. His knuckles grazed something hard and rough.

Spreading his hands out, he ran them over bricks and cement. A wall. Where was he? Jayden sifted through the fragmented memories of his morning, having his breakfast, playing on his video games, leaving the house for school and stuffing his tie and blazer in his bag as he ran away from the bus stop. He'd had to run away from someone. There'd been a row, but Jayden couldn't remember what about or who with. Then he woke up here, sitting in a pool of water in the dark.

Jayden rummaged in his jacket pocket and pulled out his mobile, a flame of hope flickering in his heart. The screen flashed on, illuminating his surroundings.

He stood in a tunnel that stretched beyond the dim bubble of his phone light. The ceiling was high and curved, hewn out of solid rock. Some of the walls were stone, too but here and there, red bricks patched and held them up. Graffiti plastered the bricks; names and tags scrawled over each other in vivid white and black paint. Bricks, old cans and plastic bags littered the floor too, poking out of the water.

Ignoring the 'no signal' warning on the screen, Jayden pressed his dad's number again and again, sobbing as he realised no help was coming. Then he noticed that his battery was low. Soon, he'd be plunged back into total blackness. With a groan of despair, he fell back against the wall and felt it give under his weight. He jumped out of the way, stumbling and tripping as the bricks collapsed with a deafening clatter. Surely the whole roof would collapse. What if he was buried alive in this dump?

Staggering back from the tumble of bricks and masonry, Jayden held up the phone and his blood froze. The weak light deepened the shadows in the hole left by the falling stones and brought anything that caught it into stark relief. This time Jayden New couldn't crush the swell of terror that forced itself up out of his gut. He screamed louder than he had ever screamed before.

***

Eileen Rapino scurried along the street, her coat pulled tight around her neck. She'd told Father Lanigan what had happened and he hadn't batted an eyelid. "I'll pray for the child's safe return," was all he'd said.

"He'll do more than pray," she muttered to herself. "He'll bloody well pay. If he can't look more upset about it. It's not fair..." She stopped dead in the street and stared off into some distant past. "Not fair. Like my Peter. He went to that church, too. What good did it do him? What good does it do any of us? Where is God?" Licking her lips, she started her lurching half-walk, half-run. "I'll find a policeman, that's what I'll do. A policeman. They'll know what to do with him."

***

There was no request for money. No demands of any kind. Just a bald statement:

'*I know what you done.*'

It was written on thick, old-fashioned notepaper, the kind you used for job applications or if you really wanted to impress or maybe letters of condolence. It smelt slightly perfumed too. He wondered where you'd buy such paper these days and somehow, he knew it had been in someone's possession for a long time, lying in a cupboard

4

or desk drawer. Weirdly, there was a sticker of a daisy in one corner, as though the writer had started to embellish it. Maybe it was some random kid's idea of a joke. The handwriting didn't look childish, though. It was neat and slightly slanted, the loop of the 'y' swooping down beneath the 't' in 'what'. The word 'done' gave away the level of the writer's education, too.

'I know what you done,' he said and allowed himself a wry smile; he'd done lots of things. If whoever it was who sent this wanted to blackmail him, they were going to have to be a lot more specific.

Of course, there was one incident that he thought about every day. One moment in time, when he'd been faced with a decision, and made the wrong call. Just like the age of the paper, he knew that was the event to which the writer referred.

He'd had the letter for several weeks now and there had been no follow-up. Obviously, he'd expected something else; a second cryptic letter alluding to the incident or laying out the terms of payment. To hear nothing was even more disconcerting.

It could have been a hoax but somehow, he doubted that. If it was about that incident, then it could only be one of three people. But something about the paper and the weird daisy sticker didn't fit with any of his suspects. The vagueness of the letter might suggest a lack of detailed information, too.

He'd bide his time and see what unfolded. If there was a follow-up, with demands or more specifics about what it was he had done, then he would take action. For now, he'd just watch and wait. Then he'd pounce. Sammy was good at that.

CHAPTER 2

An unholy wailing dragged DCI Will Blake to consciousness. At first, he thought he was at work, being bombarded by the sound of police sirens. It took the warmth and weight of his duvet to make him realise that he lay in bed. What the hell was going on? The yowling was loud, continuous and almost supernatural.

"Serafina?" Blake muttered, squinting into the dark. The big Persian cat stood at the foot of his bed, her orange eyes glowing in the blackness. She growled again and padded on the covers, her claws catching and releasing the threads. Blake sat up. "What're you playing at?" Serafina just growled again and raised her tail in the air. Blake's eyes widened as he heard a quiet squirting sound.

"Jeez!" he yelled as a musky, urine smell filled the room. "Serafina, what're you doing?" he jumped up and the cat sprinted for the bedroom door. Blake stood in the middle of the room, his hand over his mouth. Outside the yowling continued but it couldn't be Serafina. Even she couldn't move that fast. From the kitchen, Charlie his Jack Russell terrier was answering the racket with a fusillade of yaps. Blake staggered to the window and pulled back the curtain.

Although it was November, the sky was clear and the moonlight made everything look icy blue. Blake's room looked out across the River Mersey to the twinkling lights of Liverpool, but he focused on his front lawn. A ginger Tom cat crouched in the middle of the grass, shivering and twisting round its own tail. Blake rubbed his eyes. This was the third night in a row that he'd been awakened by this caterwauling, and he'd had enough.

Calling for Charlie to hush, he strode downstairs and pulled the front door open. Serafina had obviously reached the ginger Tom first and sat glaring at Blake from the middle of the lawn, her ears back. "Oh for goodness' sake," Blake muttered, taking a step forward. Serafina showed no fear, but the Tom leapt from her back and scurried into the bushes. With an indignant meow, Serafina took off after her beau into the undergrowth.

Blake, suddenly alone in the garden, shivered at the cold breeze that blew up from the river. The bushes gave a little shake but there was no sound. He could feel Serafina's angry eyes on him, though. Shaking his head, Blake went back to his front door and found it shut.

"Jeez," he muttered. "Locked out of my own house in just my boxies." He turned back and stared at the bush. "I hope you're satisfied."

Serafina, however, made no reply.

CHAPTER 3

To say that Ian Youde, Blake's near neighbour, looked surprised to see Will shivering on his doorstep dressed only in a pair of boxer shorts would have been an understatement. He rubbed his eyes and muttered something about having a bad dream, then squinted at Blake again. "Will, what the hell are you doing? Do you know what time it is?"

"Yeah, I'm sorry, Ian, Serafina locked me out…"

Ian looked at Blake steadily. "The cat locked you out." It was more of a statement of incredulity than a question.

"Yeah," Blake said. "I didn't approve of her new boyfriend…"

"How could the cat lock you out of your own house, Will?"

"I went to see what she was making such a noise about on the front lawn. Sounded like she was being skinned alive."

"And you locked *yourself* out," Ian said, suppressing a smirk. "What are you like, Will? You need a holiday or something. Let me get you the spare key. Do you want to borrow a coat or something?"

Blake shrugged. "I'll be okay once I get back into bed."

Ian vanished back inside his house. Blake felt a flush of gratitude; Youde had literally saved Blake's life once and since then, they'd been firm friends. He lived just up the road from Blake in Rock Park, a small complex of Victorian villas on the banks of the River Mersey. The houses had experienced varying fortunes over the centuries, falling from their exclusive status into dereliction or being broken into flats, then back to luxury dwellings. Some had collapsed completely or had been bulldozed to make way for the dual carriageway that effectively cut the rest of the houses off from the urban sprawl of New Ferry and Rock Ferry.

Ian returned with a coat and the keys. "Stick this on," he said shoving the coat into Blake's arms. "At least you won't get done for indecent exposure on your way home."

"I can't imagine anyone else would be up and looking out of their windows at this time, Ian," Blake said, pulling the coat on anyway.

Ian rolled his eyes. "Who'd be daft enough to be awake now, eh, Will? Are you sure you're okay, mate?" there was a light of concern in Youde's eye that Blake had never seen before."

"Yeah," Blake muttered. "Just cat trouble, that's all."

"Only since all that business with the yacht and…"

"Honestly, mate, it's fine," Blake said, trying to keep the irritation out of his voice. Youde was right to be concerned. Only a couple of months ago, Blake had taken quite a battering and nearly drowned whilst investigating the murder of a local crime boss. Now that the shock of being woken so suddenly had worn off, he could feel his back and legs grumbling in protest.

Shivering, Will shuffled back to his house. Despite the dark, the day would be starting soon enough and there was little point in trying to get back to sleep with the fragrant gift Serafina had left at the end of the bed. Things could only get better, Will hoped.

***

Of course, Blake should have known that things were on a downward spiral the moment he was summoned to Superintendent Martin's office before he'd even had a chance to sit down at his desk.

Martin was a severe, hawkish-looking man with a sharp tongue. He didn't suffer fools gladly and, although he was fair, he didn't really 'get' Blake. He was suspicious of Blake's time working as a police liaison in a TV programme called 'Searchlight.' For a few years in the early noughties, Blake had been the handsome face of

UK policing, introducing CCTV footage of various crimes and asking for the public's help. It was a role that had earned him something of a cult status and he was still remembered by members of the public. Blake was tired of it if he was honest; some senior officers used it as a stick to beat him with, others made fun of him because of it. Martin couldn't get past the notion that Blake still craved some kind of public adulation despite demonstrating an aversion to publicity frequently during cases.

As Blake shuffled into the room, he could see the Superintendent looked slightly uncomfortable, as though he had bad news. "Is everything okay, sir?"

"Yes, Will," Martin said, trying out a smile that made him look constipated. "Sit down."

Jeez, Blake thought, that settles it, something terrible has happened. "Thanks. Not bad news, I hope?"

Martin made a couple of false starts and then launched into the speech he'd obviously been rehearsing for some time. "Look, Will, I'm worried about you. To be frank, you look terrible..."

"Cat trouble... sir," Blake said, lamely.

But Martin carried on. "Ever since that unfortunate incident with the yacht and the storm, I can't help thinking you're not at full strength. You took the minimum sick leave allowed..."

"It was all I needed, sir…"

"You were still recovering from injuries sustained in your last escapade… and then you're almost drowned. You aren't looking after yourself, Will and there are youngsters snapping at your heels."

"Kath Cryer, sir? I thought she was all for resigning not long ago," Blake said, he felt awful the minute he'd said it, but he didn't like where this conversation was heading.

"She's at a crossroads, Will and I think a little experience of acting up would nudge her in the right direction. I don't want to lose talent like hers. Or yours for that matter. I've organised a secondment for you, serious case reviews, cold cases, that kind of thing. You don't have to move offices or anything for now…"

"Cold cases, sir?"

"I know it might be a bit of a backroom job but just for a few months, eh? Just until you're on a bit more of an even keel. It's all very unofficial," Martin said, his face hardening. "I don't want to formalise anything. Of course, the way you limp around the office, I could ask you to have a chat with Occupational Health…"

Blake ground his teeth, partly because he recognised the truth in what Martin was saying; he hadn't fully recovered, and a few months of quiet desk work would certainly help. But he distrusted Martin's motives. That comment about it being a 'backroom job' as though Blake wanted to be front and centre, rankled. "I really don't think it's necessary, sir…"

"I know, Will but maybe that's why I'm the Superintendent and you aren't," Martin said. "It's not forever, just while you give your body a chance to heal a little more. There's a missing child over in Birkenhead. A cause for concern. I want Kath to head that up. You can be there for guidance but don't get involved, okay?"

***

The Major Incident Room was buzzing with the news that Kath was acting up. Adding to the gossip was the return of DC Alex Manikas. He was a tall and confident young man with dark, Mediterranean good looks but he seemed uncomfortable and almost shifty as he wove his way around the desks to where Blake stood. This didn't surprise Blake; Manikas had been suspended after it came to light that he'd gone undercover on a case when he had no authority or training to do so. It was touch and go whether or not he would stay in his post but as he'd owned up to disobeying orders and it hadn't actually jeopardised the case, he was allowed to return to return. Blake knew Alex would spend a good while living it all down though, no matter how many of his colleagues greeted him brightly and patted him on the back.

"Welcome back, Alex," Blake said. "Just in time to pick this case up with Kath."

"Thanks, sir," Alex said, glancing round at the team.

"Hi, mate," DC Andrew Kinnear said, giving him a gentle punch on the arm. "Good to have you back."

Acting DCI Kath Cryer narrowed her eyes. "Where've you been, Alex? Infiltrating the Russian Secret Police? Or masquerading as an assistant at Asda, trying to catch shoplifters?"

Alex looked deflated. "Very funny, Ma'am," he said. Kath Cryer was a big woman, larger than life, some would say. She had a sharp tongue and rarely worried about people's feelings. Blake liked her straight forwardness, but tact wasn't always her strong point. That was something she would have to work on.

"We all make mistakes, Kath," Blake said. "We're moving forward now."

"Just joking," Kath said with a shrug. She turned to Alex. "Sorry, mate. No offence intended."

"None taken Ma'am," Alex said, but Blake could see the haunted look in his eye.

Better get used to it, Blake thought, *there'll be plenty of banter like that in the next few weeks and months.*

DC Andrew Kinnear peered at Blake. "Are you okay, sir? You look done in already," he said.

"Cat trouble, Andrew," Blake muttered. "I'm fine."

Kath looked at Blake for a cue to start the meeting. He shrugged and nodded. "What have we got, Vikki?" she said, quickly to move everyone's focus away from Blake.

DS Vikki Chinn pointed to a photograph of a young boy with a tangle of brown hair, large ears and a lopsided, toothy grin. "Ten-year-old Jayden New left his home in Bidston for school yesterday morning and never made it to school, Ma'am. He didn't come home last night. We're considering him high risk because he has attention deficit disorder and is on medication for type one diabetes. Uniform have checked with his close friends, and he wasn't with them. They haven't seen him for a couple of days.

"Family Liaison?" Kath said.

"Tasha Cook, Ma'am," Vikki said. "She's over there now."

Kath nodded. "Does he have a history of running off? I mean if he's got attention whatsit, he might be impulsive..."

"That's true, Ma'am but Mum and Dad say he suffers from anxiety over his injections for diabetes. He never forgets and always makes sure he's home in time for them."

"So, what are the parents' thoughts? Is he bullied at school? Did something happen at home that might have made him run?" Kath said.

"Hopefully, Tasha Cook will have more detail soon, Ma'am," Vikki said, "but we do know that Jayden had been playing truant recently."

"Maybe he just got lost," Kath Cryer said. "I mean he doesn't sound the full shilling, does he?"

"He knew his way around and was quite capable of getting to school, Ma'am," Vikki said, an edge to her voice. "I don't think the level of his ADHD meant he had no sense of direction."

"Whatever the reason, he's missing and we're concerned," Blake said before Kath Cryer could retort. "What resources do we have?"

"We have uniform and a helicopter searching Bidston Hill and the surrounding area, sir," Vikki said. Bidston Hill was the highest point on the Wirral, a plateau of woodland, gorse and scrub. It was considered a local beauty spot and a place of interest with its windmill and observatory, not to mention ancient Viking carvings and views of the Wirral and beyond. But the hill had a darker side too and attracted other, less desirable elements.

"Biddy Hill, Alex," Kath said, giving Manikas a

nod. "Didn't your Viking friends used to party up there?"

Manikas winced. The case he'd almost blown involved a gang of self-styled Viking bikers who met frequently on the hill.

"The Sons of Sol took their name from the carving of the Viking sun goddess up there, Ma'am," Andrew Kinnear said, drawing Kath's fire away from his friend. "It is a weird place, but I don't think you could get lost up there for long."

"Plenty of weirdos lurking in the bushes of a night-time, though, Andrew," Kath said, looking archly at him.

"Okay," Blake sighed, rubbing his face. Maybe a quiet desk job would be just the ticket. He could easily just crawl under the desk, curl up and go to sleep after Serafina's early morning call. "Kath, keep me abreast of any developments. Hopefully, he's just lost and will turn up in one piece."

"Will do," Kath Cryer said, relishing not having to say 'sir.' "I'm conscious of the time limit on this, given that Jayden needs his insulin injections. Vikki, have a word with Hannah Williams, our media consultant, see if we can't get a call out on local radio…"

"Okay, people, let's get busy." Kath said clapping her hands together. It was a clumsy impression of Blake and a habit in himself that he deplored as it made him feel like he was patronising his team, but he fell for it every time. He gave Kath a wry look and she grinned back. He just hoped Kath didn't wind up the entire team before they found the boy.

CHAPTER 4

Only a couple of weeks to go. Not that PC Mark Robertson was counting. Much. "Twelve days, five hours and thirty minutes," he muttered to himself as he strode along Banner Street to the next house, trying to put his imminent retirement to the back of his mind. He'd been knocking on doors since first light and some of the responses hadn't been too friendly. Once they realised that it was a missing child they were searching for, most residents didn't mind the ungodly hour. None of them could help, though. Jayden New had vanished off the face of the Earth, it seemed.

He paused and squinted down the street. A figure hurried through the gloom towards him, a woman in her sixties, perhaps. She had a pale coat on with the hood pulled up, but Mark could see the dyed black hair spilling out from the sides and the pointed glasses. Everything about this woman, from the way she hurried towards him to the expression on her face screamed busybody. Still, that wasn't always a bad thing; busybodies tended to poke their noses where they weren't wanted and that, in turn, was where the best information was. Sometimes.

Mark waited for her to reach him, hands behind his back, rocking slightly on his heels in a stereo-typical 'bobby on the beat' pose. "Can I help you, madam?" he said.

The woman stopped and looked at him, hard. "Are you a real policeman?"

"Yes, madam, a real-life policeman," Mark said, somewhat taken aback.

"It's just your beard, you see. I didn't think you were allowed to have beards..."

"As long as I keep it neat and tidy, madam, then my senior officers don't object," Mark said. "Now what can I..."

"I thought you were one of those other ones, like a traffic warden type thing, you know..."

"I'm not a PCSO if that's what you mean but they do a very valuable job and I'm sure they could help you just as much as..."

"And you're quite old to be a..."

"Is there something you wanted to talk to me about?"

"I know what happened to the boy, Jayden. I saw it."

"Saw what, madam?" Mark said, pulling out his notebook.

"I saw him grab the boy!"

Mark took a breath and steadied his nerves.

"Right, can I take your name, madam and we can start at the beginning."

"I'm Eileen Rapino but it's not me you want to talk to, it's him…"

"Who, Eileen?"

"Father Lanigan. He knows where the boy is."

***

Jayden New pressed himself against the curved tunnel wall and bit into his knuckle until he tasted blood. He mustn't scream. If he screamed, then the man in the wall might come and find him. God knows what he'd do to Jayden if he caught him. He looked horrible, with deep-sunk eyes and a big toothy grin. Like a skeleton man in a dark suit. Jayden's mates at school had told him all about a man who was tall, skinny like a skeleton and wore a black suit. He dragged kids underground. Maybe that's what happened to him and now the Skeleton Man was hunting him. When Jayden had seen the Skeleton Man, he'd run and run, splashing through the tunnels until he didn't know which way he'd come.

He was long overdue his injection, he knew that, and he'd eaten all the butties that Mam had put in his bag. Tears scalded his face as he thought about Mam and Dad. They'd be worried sick about him. He'd never see them again. All he wanted to do was go home and crawl into Mam's arms. She'd wrap him up in her soapy perfume smell and he could close his eyes. His eyelids drooped for a second but he snapped them open. He mustn't sleep here. The Skeleton Man might come. Every plop of water that echoed around the passages, every bump or clank in the dark made Jayden think of the Skeleton Man, with his grinning face and his long, bony fingers fumbling through the dark.

***

It was cold up on Bidston Hill and over a year since Blake had last been up here. He'd gone along with Martin's plan to review cold cases and even made contact with the Serious Case Review team. There were procedures and documents to be read and Blake had quickly become restless, glancing out into the office and wondering about the missing boy. In the end, he had decided to go and see how things were going with the search on the ground. All in his mentoring role, of course. He wasn't trying to catch her out or anything. And so here he was, up on Bidston Hill, breathing in the cold, autumn air. Stuffing his hands deep in the pockets of his waterproof jacket, he followed the track up through the woods towards the windmill. At least it wasn't raining, and the wind hadn't stripped the leaves from the branches yet. For a second, he stared up at the golds, yellows and reds that fluttered above him. Blake shook his head. When was the last time he'd paused to look around? He knew what was happening. Work was devouring him again. When his daughter had died all those years ago and his wife had left him, he fell headlong into the job, letting it blot out any pain. He became a machine, ignoring anyone's feelings. The job was everything. That kind of focus was worth its weight in gold, especially in cases like this but it had an emotional price, too.

He'd sworn to himself that he'd never be that person again but since Laura Vexley, his girlfriend had left him for her ex, he felt like he was drowning. Every now and then he'd break the surface and take a gulp of air before sinking down into a sea of gloom again. He shook himself. Sod Martin and his desk job, when Jayden was safe, he'd take a real break. He was owed holidays, but he never took them unless he was forced to. Maybe he'd go up to Scotland and call in on his sister, spend some time in the hills and sort his head out. Make a decision about the job, his life, everything.

When Jayden was safe and Kath had her promotion well and truly nailed down.

Two old men stood under the windmill, their hands stuffed in their pockets. Blake was surprised they hadn't been cleared off but reasoned that if the team were searching from the other end of the hill, maybe they hadn't seen them. Both must have been in their seventies. One looked stocky and ruddy-faced, a woolly hat pulled over his grey curls. The other looked like he'd been carved out of stone, his flat cap pulled down over his flinty eyes, and a roll-up cigarette poking out of the corner of his mouth. He wore an old donkey jacket with the collar turned up, skinny black jeans and Doc Marten boots. Neither had dogs which seemed odd to Blake. There wasn't a law that said you could only go walking in the morning if you had a dog, but something about the way they stood, staring at each other, struck him as unusual.

He nodded to them as he approached. "Morning, gents," he said. They returned his nod but said nothing. Blake flashed his warrant card. "I wonder if you've seen a young lad around these parts? He went missing yesterday and we're searching the area. He's quite vulnerable."

"Sorry mate. We haven't seen anyone," the round-faced man said, with half a smile and a shrug. "Wish we could help." The other man stayed silent and glared at Blake, giving the impression that he really didn't want to help at all.

"If you see anything, do let us know. Here's a picture of the boy. His name is Jayden New," Blake said, showing them the photo.

The colour drained from the big man's face. "Dave New's grandson?"

"Do you know him?"

The curly-haired man glanced at his granite-faced companion. "Dave was an old mate. Used to be, anyway. He passed away not long ago." His face reddened and he gabbled on. "Hadn't spoken to Dave in ages before he died, really. We lost touch. I don't really know the boy. Hope you find him, like. Probably just run off. Kids these days, eh?"

"So you've no idea of any hiding places he might frequent or anything like that?"

"They wouldn't be very good hiding places if *we* knew about them, would they?" the flinty man said.

Blake turned to look at him, keeping a steady gaze until the man looked away. "We're looking for a ten-year-old boy with a chronic health condition, sir. It's a race against time. Can you tell me the purpose of your visit to this hill?"

"Just walkin' that's all. A bit of exercise. No law against that, is there?" the man said, meeting Blake's searching gaze with a steely glare of his own.

"No, sir, there isn't. If that's all you're doing. I suggest you vacate the hill while the search goes on. Or you could volunteer if you felt moved to do so." Blake walked on but he could feel their stares fixed on him. When he was just out of earshot, he looked back to see the grim-looking man throwing his arms up in the air. Whatever he said made the other man flinch away. Blake was just about to go back to them, when they split and hurried off in separate directions. "Now what were you two up to?" he muttered as they vanished into the woods.

***

Someone was taking the piss. Sammy knew that. Teasing and tormenting him. It couldn't be Jensen. He was such a divvy and could barely write his own name. Besides, it wouldn't make sense for Jensen to the rock the boat. In fact it would be absolute madness. Jensen shit himself when Sammy threatened him. Sammy allowed himself a cold grin.

He hadn't expected the hill to be crawling with police, though. That copper who spoke to them looked kind of familiar. Maybe he'd seen him in the paper or something. Blake, he said his name was. Sammy decided he'd keep a note of that. The new letter was in his pocket, he could feel the thick paper between his fingertips. This one had a sticker of a bee on it and some weird foil flowers. It was like a toddler had been asked to decorate it. Sammy gave a humourless smile and wondered if there'd be glitter on the next one. It just had one word written on it:

Confess!

It sounded kind of religious. Dave New had been a churchgoer. He'd tried to get Sammy to own up to what they'd done like it would make any difference. Sammy had told Dave to do one. Maybe that's why this letter disturbed him so much. It reminded him of Dave.

CHAPTER 5

Josh Gambles was a changed man, there was no doubt about it. It had been a while since Jeff Blake had visited the serial killer in prison and he could see a marked deterioration. Gambles had been obsessed with Jeff's detective brother since he was a teenager and had tried to relaunch Will's fame by committing a series of gruesome murders. In the end, Blake had given the dubious honour of arresting Gambles to a humble PCSO which had infuriated the killer.

In an attempt to secure immortality and to intrude into Will's life as much as he could, Gambles had engaged Jeff Blake as an official biographer. Jeff was a struggling author whose early success had tailed off leaving him in financial limbo. When Gambles approached him about the book from his prison cell, Jeff had agreed to take the commission much to his brother's disgust which is just what Gambles had hoped for. Will and Jeff's relationship was rocky to begin with for a whole host of reasons, but this pushed it to breaking point.

Jeff wasn't oblivious to the serial killer's scheming nature; he knew what Gambles was up to, but he had to confess, he'd been seduced by the man's charisma. Over the months visiting Gambles in remand, Jeff had watched him twist and turn, playing with the legal system, switching barristers and making claims of insanity only to change his mind and say he was as sane as the judge who would eventually sentence him. Finally, he made a guilty plea.

With a ring-side seat to these antics and access to the serial killer, Jeff had also witnessed his decline. The first time Josh Gambles sat in front of him, Jeff encountered an animal energy, an air of threat and danger but also a lot of self-regard. Gambles could verge on the melodramatic when he put on his 'genius psychopath' persona. It was a badly acted cross between Bond villain and Hannibal Lecter. Sometimes, he tipped over into an impression of Mr Burns from the Simpsons cartoon programme, steepling his fingers and smiling tightly at some hidden secret. If Jeff was being honest, he started out afraid of Gambles but, as he became more familiar, there were moments when Jeff had to bite his lip and remind himself what a monster Gambles was to keep from laughing out loud. Now, Jeff was beginning to actually pity him.

In the small, private meeting room that Jeff had managed to negotiate, Gambles sat hunched and trembling slightly. Dark rings circled his eyes. Gambles was always gaunt, but he looked as though he hadn't eaten for days. His hair, usually combed back, hung in lank tendrils down his face. Livid nail scratches scored down his cheek and neck. His knuckles were purple and bruised. He chewed at the edge of his thumb and Jeff noticed that his nails were bitten to the quick. Some were bleeding.

"Are you okay, Josh?"

Gambles looked up, startled and blinking as though Jeff had just shouted at him. "Am I okay?" he muttered, pondering the question. He locked eyes with Jeff. "Do you believe in God, Jeffrey?"

"God?" Jeff muttered, frowning. "I don't know. I suppose I think there's something that connects us all. Some kind of energy... I..."

"Not that kind of wishy-washy, New Age bollocks, Jeffrey!" Gambles hissed through clenched teeth. "I mean God, hellfire, brimstone and judgement. That kind of God. An entity that sees you and finds you wanting."

"No," Jeff said. "No, I don't. I think if there is a God, then he's gone, or is working on another project somewhere and has forgotten us..."

"You're just mocking me, now," Gambles said, tangling his fingers together. He leaned forward. "Seriously, what if there is a God?"

Jeff wondered if he preferred the cock-sure, arrogant psychopath to this trembling heap of self-pity. "If there is a God, then how could he allow you to do what you did?"

"We all have freewill, Jeffrey. I chose to take those lives and imprison Ellen Kevney…"

"But why didn't He protect your victims? Once you'd chosen your course of action, he could have struck you down, couldn't he? Why wait until you'd taken their lives?"

Gambles glanced around the room for a few seconds, thinking. "Proof," he said at last. "He wanted proof of my intentions. I had to commit the crimes… the sins…"

"What's brought this on, Josh? Why the sudden concern about God? I thought you were the master of your own destiny."

Gambles let his head fall to his chest. "I've failed, haven't I?"

"Failed? How? I thought this is what you wanted. Infamy, letters from adoring, twisted fans. My brother's name in the papers again."

"Someone tried to put glass in my food the other day. For each adoring fan, there are at least ten thousand people who would laugh and ten thousand more who wouldn't even blink if I died tomorrow."

"That's true of everyone. Perhaps not the laughter but that's infamy. People are going to hate you."

"But I'm not everyone," Gambles snapped. His

eyes glistened with tears. "It was respect, or at least fear I wanted not hatred. People only fear you when you are free and that isn't going to happen ever."

"So where does God fit into this?"

Gambles looked haunted. "It's horrible here. I spend twenty-three hours pacing my cell. When they let me out, people try to hurt me. They spit at me, shout my name and what they're going to do to me. The prison officers do nothing. There's no respect. It's endless. Have you ever read James Joyce's A portrait of the Artist as a Young Man?"

"A long time ago, yes, why?"

"Do you remember the description of Hell in it? I read it recently: 'In earthly prisons the poor captive has at least some liberty of movement, were it only within the four walls of his cell or in the gloomy yard of his prison. Not so in hell.' Imagine a prison where you can't move, you're trapped in one place being tortured with flames and spikes, your mouth and nose stuffed full of rotting flesh!"

Jeff said nothing. Gambles wasn't fooling around.

"He describes the stench, the fires, the demons, the torment I would endure forever. It makes sense. If there is a God, wouldn't he want to punish me for all the evil I have committed?"

"But can't you repent? Show Him you're sorry?"

"But how? How do I 'truly repent?' What does that even mean? But I think you hit the nail on the head, Jeffrey. God wants proof. Proof that I'm sorry."

"And are you sorry? Do you really regret what you did or are you just scared? How is that the same as being truly repentant?" Jeff said and wished he'd kept his thoughts to himself as he saw Gambles' face drop.

"I don't know. The prison chaplain is useless. She's full of meaningless platitudes." He looked up at Jeff, desperation in his eye. "We can't publish the book, Jeffrey. We can't justify what I've done."

Jeff felt his stomach lurch. "The book? But I've spent the last year writing it. I have interest from at least two major publishers based on the outline alone. One of them is about to make an offer to my agent soon, both might. I can't pull out now."

"It's not up to you, Jeffrey. The book is about me," Gambles said, a little of his old poise returning.

Jeff shook his head. "No, Josh, it isn't. I told you when we first met that the book is as much about me as you. I made a decision at the very start of all this that I wouldn't be dancing to your tune. The book is about how our lives collided. It's about our different paths, the choices we made and those that were made for us."

An angry fire flickered in Gambles' eyes. "But I read it... it was all about me..."

"You read the parts I gave you. It's quite a tome. It spans the decades of our lives, pop culture, politics and even TV of the time but it's very literary, too. My agent calls it 'genre-busting.' She has high hopes it'll scoop a few prizes."

"You can't do this..."

"It's happening, Josh. I couldn't just write another true crime book; that would have been dull. I've put too much time and effort into this to abandon it."

Gambles licked his lips. "Then you can write a chapter warning people. Yes, that's it. We can warn the readers not to be like me."

"The nature of repentance?" Jeff mused. "Perhaps, but it's not a moral tale..."

"It has to be!"

Jeff shrugged. "So the moral of the story is you can carve total strangers up, leave them to rot so that other total strangers find their decomposed corpses and then say, 'sorry,' and God will forgive you? Seems wrong to me, Josh." He suddenly felt powerful as though he was on a seesaw, and he was rising. No, he was at the bottom, holding Gambles in the air like a helpless toddler. It felt good.

"Bastard!" Suddenly, Gambles' hands were around Jeff's throat. The grip was weak and Jeff swatted the clammy fingers away but he'd fallen from his chair and Gambles had managed to sit on his chest. A bony fist smacked into his cheek but then Gambles' weight vanished as two burly guards dragged him away.

"I won't let you get away with this, Jeffrey! You're just like your brother; a twister, a fucking back-stabber. I'll make you pay."

The door slammed and Gambles' muffled curses faded into the distance beyond. Trembling, Jeff clambered to his feet and took a long breath. Then he allowed himself a brief smile. What just happened was a whole new chapter in itself.

CHAPTER 6

If it wasn't for such a grim purpose the line of coppers all grovelling across the overgrown heath as though they'd lost their contact lenses would be quite comical. But Blake had a bad feeling about this case; it wasn't going to end well, he could feel it. He just prayed he was wrong and Kath found the lad safe.

Although it was dry, it was a grey and hazy day. This part of the hill was fringed by trees, blocking any possible views of the Welsh hills to the west or Liverpool to the east. DC Alex Manikas stood behind the line of searchers, listening to an old woman wrapped in a long duster-style coat. Her white hair was cut into a bob and, as Blake drew nearer, he could see her weathered, nut-brown skin. It would be hard to age her; she could be sixty or ninety. What Blake could tell was that she was an outdoor person. She reminded him of one of the old trees that covered the plateau, scoured and hardened to iron by wind, frost and rain. Impervious to all of them.

"Sir," Manikas said, failing to suppress the relief in his voice. "This lady is an expert on the hill. Knows it inside out." He turned to the woman. "This is Detective Chief Inspector Blake…"

The woman extended her hand and held Blake's in an iron grip. "Pippa Fearon," she said, briskly. "I was just telling this young man about the history of the surrounding area. It may be pertinent to the whereabouts of the boy you've lost."

"We haven't lost him, Mrs Fearon…"

"Miss. I never married. I have an ongoing love affair with this hill and all its secrets. Not that I haven't had offers. I went out with Lewis Collins, you know." She tossed her head and beamed at Blake. Her green eyes reminded Blake of Laura. They had the same sparkle and sharp intelligence.

"Really?" Blake said, slightly perplexed by her flirtatious smile. "I'd forgotten he was from round here."

"A lot of people do, Inspector but he was born and raised in Bidston. I've advised DC Manikas of the likely places to find the boy."

"Miss Fearon has been very thorough, sir," Alex said, giving Blake a look that told him how thorough.

"Excellent, Alex," Blake said. He turned to Miss Fearon. "And thank you. We couldn't do our job without a helpful public."

"Not a problem. If you need any more help you can find me at The Skerries, it's the big old house on Eleanor Road at the windmill end of the hill.

Good day." She strode off at a startling pace.

"I thought she'd never go, sir," Manikas said, watching the woman disappear across the heathland. "Who's Colin Lewis, anyway?"

"Lewis Collins, Alex! He was an actor who had some success with a TV series called The Professionals back in the late seventies, early eighties. Apparently, he was quite a heart throb. But he was a bit of a local celeb way before then. It was said he turned down the chance to audition for the Beatles when they sacked Pete Best…"

"Who?"

"Never mind, Alex. You're obviously too young," Blake murmured. "Let's just focus on this search, shall we?"

***

One hour of daylight left. The boy had been missing for more than twenty-four hours and things didn't look good. PC Mark Robertson cradled the paper cup full of coffee in his hands and let the warmth spread through his fingers. He'd been here all day. The team had scoured the hill and knocked on every surrounding door with no result. His feet ached and the idea of his armchair and something mindless on the TV seemed really appealing right now. But he couldn't clock off; not if there was still a chance to find Jayden New safe and well.

The lights of the housing estates had flickered on, making it seem later than it was and, in the distance, traffic rumbled on the M53 as the rush hour got underway. The hilltop seemed bleak and the birch trees that fringed the heath almost threatening. Fireworks popped in the night some distant, some close by. Mark wondered to himself when it was that Bonfire Night became a month long extravaganza.

DC Alex Manikas hurried over the heath to Mark, like a hopeful puppy. "Anything, Mark?"

"Sorry, mate," Mark said. "I wish I could say we'd found something but there's no sign of him."

"Crap," Alex muttered, looking crestfallen. Mark knew that Alex had been in some trouble over a previous case and had come back after a suspension. He'd obviously be keen to prove himself and what better way to do that than to rescue a young lad in distress? Mark wished he could help him and he was sure that Alex's prime motivation was the safety of the lad.

"We could do another sweep of friends' houses," Mark suggested. "You never know. Did you get any leads from the school?"

Alex shook his head. "Nah. Jayden has a few problems there, but nobody has seen him or knows anything."

"Shame. Still, maybe he's just lying low. I mean,

kids are unpredictable, aren't they? He might be worried about being in trouble..." he stopped, peering at Alex who wasn't paying attention. Mark followed his line of sight.

A young boy dressed in a red track suit that almost matched his red, puffing face came sprinting up the rough track towards them. His ginger hair was cut into a short crop and, despite his chubby appearance, he was moving fast. Another lad was close behind him. He was dressed in a black tracksuit top and faded grey sweatpants. He was holding a baseball cap onto his head as he ran and yelling something at the boy in front. "Liam! Don't! We'll get done!"

"Ello, ello, ello," Mark said, raising one eyebrow. "What's all this then?"

Alex gave him an appalled look. "Really?"

"I've always wanted to say that," Mark said, with a grin just as Liam skidded to a halt in front of them.

"It's the lad you were lookin' for," Liam panted. "We've found him..." Liam's sentence was cut dead as the other boy crashed into him.

"Liam, shurrup!"

"Gerroff, Zach, you blurt!" Liam yelled, trying to roll away from Zach's grasp. "We gotta tell 'em. He's got die beeties, hasn't he?"

"I don't care if he's got fuckin' ebola, I'm not get-

42

ting done!" Zach snarled and raised a fist at Liam. Mark stepped in and grasped Zach's wrist before he could swing the punch.

"Come on, Zach, nobody's in trouble, *yet*," Mark said.

"You can't touch me, gerroff," Zach snapped.

"If I think you're going to hurt young Liam, here, I can put you in handcuffs and take you down the local nick. Is that what you want?"

The fight flowed out of Zach and he slumped on the floor. Liam staggered to his feet and dusted himself down.

"Now what were you trying to tell us, Liam?"

Liam skipped from foot to foot and glanced at Zach. He couldn't be more than nine maybe ten. "That lad you were looking for, Jayden New, we think we found him."

"Show me," Alex snapped. Liam nodded and set off back down the track. Mark hauled Zach to his feet and pushed the lad in the direction the other two had gone.

The lads took Mark and Alex down the hill. They plunged down the track and then off into the undergrowth. Brambles tugged at Mark's trousers and branches whipped his face. "This better not be a wind-up Zach," he growled. "Or you will be in trouble."

Finally, they came to a mound surrounded by

shattered chunks of concrete. Mark frowned as he neared what looked like some kind of half-buried structure. A slab of cracked concrete formed a flat roof and a few courses of bricks poked out of the leaf mould and briars. One of the cracks in the roof had been worked at and widened to reveal a darkness that spoke of a cavernous space inside.

Liam leaned over the gap. "Jayden? Mate! Are you there? We got the bizzies for you!"

Mark eased the lad aside gently and shone a torch into the hole. The first section of a brick-lined shaft appeared in the light and a rusty ladder descended into the darkness. "Jayden? This is PC Mark Robertson. Can you hear me? Make a noise if you can, so we know you're okay."

The sound that drifted up from the shadows was one that would haunt Mark to the end of his days. It was a tormented wail of fear. A cry for help. Mark took his hat off and started unbuttoning his jacket as he eyed up the gap, wondering if he could squeeze through and if his knees would stand up to any climbing.

"Mark, what are you doing?" Alex said.

"You heard that. The boy's in trouble. We can't just leave him."

"It's not safe. What if you injure yourself? We can't just go diving in..."

Mark smiled. "I'm not diving anywhere, I'll be careful. Look, I know you've had your arse kicked for freestyling, but I can't stand here, waiting for backup."

Alex ran his fingers through his hair. "Look, let me go. No offence but I'm a bit younger and lighter than you," he looked at the hole in the concrete, "and I'm not certain you'll squeeze through. Call for backup and I'll climb down to the lad."

"Aren't we in trouble then?" Zach said, glancing from Mark to Alex. "We didn't go down there, honest."

"Course you aren't in trouble. What's down there, lads?" Mark said.

"It's an old air raid shelter from the war," Liam said, wiping his nose on the back of his hand. "It's massive, loads of tunnels and stuff. My dad said he used to go down there all the time but then they blocked it up. Someone told us the concrete had been smashed open and we came to have a look. We heard someone crying down there. Recognised his voice. He's in our class at school."

"Listen, lads, you've done the right thing. Just stick around until the cavalry arrives so we can take a statement. You might be in the papers, lads, local heroes."

Zach looked at Liam and then back at Mark. "Will we get a reward?"

CHAPTER 7

The church was a nineteen fifties building made of brick. It reminded Kath Cryer of the Lego buildings she used to make as a child, all blocks and squares. The roof was green and steel grilles covered the windows. Next to the church was a small bungalow, from the size of it, she could tell it would be one bedroom, one living room and a kitchen. Clearly, the priest was expected to live frugally. She and DS Vikki Chinn walked up the mossy paving to the blue front door and Vikki knocked.

Father Lanigan didn't look surprised to see them. He held the door wide and beckoned them in, silently, before they could introduce themselves. Without looking at them, he led them into the tiny living room.

"I'm DS Vikki Chinn, this is Acting DCI Kath Cryer. We'd like to ask you a few questions, Father Lanigan, if that's all right?"

Kath watched the man. He was young, tall and skinny, with soft brown eyes that gave him a hurt look. His brown hair was cut neatly in a short back and sides. The black suit and white dog collar aged him somehow, but Kath would have guessed him to be in his early thirties.

"If I can help you, I will," Lanigan said, his voice quiet.

Vikki produced a photograph of Jayden. "Have you seen this boy recently?"

"It's Jayden New," Father Lanigan said. "He was a regular to my church until fairly recently..."

"Was?" Kath murmured, glancing round the room. The place looked like a museum reconstruction of a fifties living room; tiled fireplace, three ducks on the wall, the furniture was angular and modernist in style. Kath thought about her grandfather's house. The # accommodation must have come furnished and it hadn't been changed for a very long time, if ever.

A cloud crossed Father Lanigan's long face. "His grandfather was very devout. He used to bring Jayden along. It was a miracle in itself that the boy sat still through so many masses. Some might thank God's love for that, but I think Jayden's love for his grandfather had more to do with it."

"So why did he stop coming?"

"His grandfather died," Lanigan said, simply.

Vikki pulled out her phone and looked at some notes. "A witness said they saw you remonstrating with Jayden out on the street. They say you grabbed hold of him."

Lanigan paled. "That'd be Eileen Rapino, no

doubt," he said, with a faint smile. Then he fell silent.

"Were you talking with Jayden yesterday morning?"

"Yes," Lanigan said. "Jayden was having trouble at school, I believe. He passed my house on several occasions when I know for a fact that he should have been on the school bus."

"Do you make a habit of keeping track of school bus times, Father Lanigan?" Kath said, looking quizzically at the priest.

"No! It passes my window every morning as I'm having breakfast. Jayden used to wave to me when he was younger. That's the only reason I know. Why do you lot always have to twist things?"

"We're not twisting anything, sir," Vikki said. "Why did you accost Jayden New?"

"I went out to reason with him. To tell him to get to school and warn him that I'd be informing his parents."

"How did he react to that?" Kath said.

Lanigan flushed red. "He wasn't very happy. Gave me a mouthful of abuse and turned to run. Look, I'm not proud of myself but I admit, I grabbed him. I don't know what I was thinking but I knew he was vulnerable out on his own. I thought I could help him. Anyway, he wriggled out of my grasp and ran towards the hill."

"And you just left it there?" Vikki said, looking puzzled.

"When I realised I'd grabbed him, I panicked. You aren't even meant to look at kids the wrong way these days, are you? I was going to ring and leave a message with the headteacher, but I hadn't got round to it, I'm ashamed to say."

"Have you been here long, Father Lanigan?" Kath said.

"Four years," Lanigan replied. "It's a small congregation but I'm doing my best to grow it."

"And you've no idea where Jayden went after you spoke to him?" Vikki said.

"Absolutely none. With hindsight, if I'd known he was going to go missing, I'd have followed him but after that mouthful he gave me, and my reaction, I didn't dare."

"So you just let him go," Kath said, looking hard at Lanigan. "A vulnerable young boy with a chronic condition."

"If I chased after all the truants in my parish, I'd have a fulltime job, Inspector. There's only so much I can do." Lanigan kept his eyes down and clasped his hands together. "I have my mission here to think of too. My duty to God. I'm not just a social worker in a black suit, you know."

Vikki handed him a card and he showed them

out. Kath looked back at the bungalow from the pavement. "he's a bit shifty. What do you think, Vikki?"

"There's something he's not telling us, Ma'am, but I don't know what."

***

DC Alex Manikas steadied his breath as he squeezed through the hole, feeling his shirt snag on the sides and rip slightly. Part of him wished he'd let PC Robertson wriggle down into the abyss, but he couldn't stand by and watch the old man struggle. The guy was close to retirement. Look well if he tumbled to his death just before he was going to get his big clock. The air was cold and smelt earthy. Far below him, he could hear Jayden whimpering. At least, he hoped it was Jayden. The torchlight swung around wildly as he got himself onto the first ladder. It wobbled a little and creaked ominously but held his weight.

"Jayden? My name is Alex, I'm coming down to help you. Are you okay?" Each rung of the ladder groaned as Alex inched his way down. Soon he found himself standing on a metal platform. It swayed a little as he steadied himself.

"I-I think so," Jayden said, faintly. "I don't feel very well. Feel sleepy..."

"Keep talking Jayden," Alex called. A second ladder led down to the next platform and he lowered himself onto it. Flakes of rust coated his hand and a sewer water smell drifted up from below him. "How did you get down here?"

"I-I don't know," Jayden called back. "I just woke up here."

"Okay, don't worry," Alex said.

"I'm scared," Jayden said in a small voice. "I think the Skeleton Man is here..."

"There's just you and me, Jayden," Alex said.

"No," Jayden said, his voice rising in panic. "I thought I'd run away from him but I've gone in a circle. I'm back where I started. He's here. He's here..."

"Keep calm, Jayden, I'll be with you in a..." The next rung snapped under Alex's foot and for a moment, his stomach lurched as he slipped. Pain seared through his arm from his fingers to his shoulder as he grabbed the next rung and dangled. The ladder shuddered and he thought the whole lot was going to come down on top of him. For a couple of seconds, he hung there by one arm, gritting his teeth. Then he tested the next rung with his foot. It held and he continued down.

"Are you okay?" Jayden said, his voice trembling.

"Yeah. I'm fine. Just slipped. I'll be more careful." The next platform was welcome, even though it could easily collapse under Alex's weight. He shone the torch down and saw Jayden's pinched, pale face staring up at him. The boy was grimy, tear-stained and covered in scratches. "Hiya, Jayden."

As soon as Alex's feet slid into the cold water, the boy slammed against him, hugging onto him like he was some long-lost relative. "Take me away, take me away, take me away," the boy gabbled. "The Skeleton Man is here, he's here…"

"Easy, son," Alex said, wrapping an arm around the lad's shoulder and shining a torch down the tunnel. "You're safe now." But even so, Alex shone his torch down the tunnel, making the shadows dance. "It's just us…" The beam scanned across the brick-lined walls and rested on a scene that froze the rest of the sentence in his throat.

CHAPTER 8

The clank of the mop and bucket cut through Blake's head as he scrubbed at the hall floor and wall. Charlie, the Jack Russell thought it was a great game and kept snapping at the mop as it swished back and forth.

"Don't Charlie, it's bleached," Blake snapped. The bleach wasn't making any difference to the smell; it just seemed to mingle with Serafina's own unique, arse-crafted stench and amplify it. Not that she hung around to garner plaudits. As soon as Blake had opened the front door to let some air flow through the house, the cat had escaped into the garden.

"Hello?" Ian Youde called as he came in through the still open front door. He wrinkled his nose. Charlie gave a cheerful yap and bounded up to Ian who squatted to scratch his ear.

"I know," Blake said. "It's the bloody cat. I'm meant to be in work in half an hour. I hope the traffic's okay, that's all."

"Have you worked out what's got into her, yet?"

"Half the Toms in the district by the sounds of it last night. I don't know what the hell is going on with her but I'm going to have to brace myself and get her to the vet. I can't go on like this."

"Weird though, isn't it? I mean, if your mother didn't have her spayed, how come she's suddenly on the prowl every night? You'd expect more of this in the past. Not to mention a few kittens!"

"I know, Ian. Unless something weird has happened to her hormones. I'll be honest, I'm out of my depth. I thought I'd keep her in last night and lock the cat flap…"

Youde grinned. "It didn't work, eh?"

"I had a chorus of Toms outside and her inside, which sparked Charlie off to join in. And she spent the night redecorating the hall. Nightmare, mate."

Somewhere in the kitchen, Blake's phone rang and he hurried in to find it. "Vikki? What's up?"

***

This had to be one of the strangest locations to find a body Blake could remember. The undergrowth around the vent had been cleared and the area secured. Now a couple of generators chugged noisily in the deep shadow behind the arc lights that created a circle of brilliant light around the old brick structure.

The discomfort of wearing a white coverall had been enhanced by the necessity of a harness and ropes wrapped tightly around his torso. A team had lowered ladders and lights into the tunnels and Blake wondered what he'd encounter as he clambered down into the depths. Vikki had said that a body had been found and it was in an advanced state of decay but she hadn't been any more specific. For a moment, he wondered if she shouldn't have called Kath but then he set that worry aside for later.

He squeezed past the rusted remains of what he assumed was some kind of ventilation equipment and found himself in a long tunnel, ankle-deep in water and strewn with rubbish. The lights blazed, emphasising the squalor and decay of the place, something usually cloaked in pitch darkness. Graffiti coated the sandstone walls, the names of past explorers, leaving their mark. Here and there, brickwork lined the sides, supporting the chiselled roof. Several officers, both police and crime scene, beavered about, mapping out various objects or photographing items of possible interest.

It amazed Blake that he hadn't heard about this place before. A hurried Google search had told him that it was what remained of a Second World War air raid shelter, built to protect key workers from German bombs. It stretched deep under the hill but never ended up being used. It had fallen into disrepair and been sealed up in the eighties. As he shuffled through the detritus, he saw tunnels to his left and right leading off into utter blackness. It echoed with the voices and footsteps of the officers now, but Blake could imagine it in total silence and darkness. He shivered.

Malachy O'Hare, the Crime Scene Manager peered hard into a hole in the wall. He turned as he heard Blake approach.

"You look like shit," the sombre Irishman said. "I mean I can only see your forehead and your eyes cos of the mask and overalls but you still look like shit, Will."

"Thanks, Malachy, I appreciate your candour. If you must know, it's my cat. She keeps shagging on my front lawn and it's bloody noisy. I haven't had a good night's sleep in weeks."

"Bucket of cold water will sort out those she-nanigans," Malachy said, wiggling his bushy, white eyebrows. "Anyway, didn't you have her done when she was a kitten? You know, spayed."

"I thought my mum had her sorted, to be honest. It hasn't been an issue in the past. I'll have to talk to a vet. Anyway, what have we got?"

"Skeletonised body, fully dressed in what could be a man's suit. Hard to tell. He, or she, still looks better than you do, Will."

"Thanks again. Jeez, and the poor kid found him?" He looked at the grinning cadaver that leaned out of the cavity in the wall as though it was drunk. The arms and legs were stiff but slightly bent. The suit hung from the shoulders the fabric blackened with mould. Blake could make out a collar and tie.

"Yep, your DC Manikas met him, too."

"At least it wasn't a dog walker discovering the body, for once, not down here."

Malachy grinned, under his mask, his eyes crinkling. "True. Nobody comes down here except the odd urban explorer when the concrete seals are smashed. It's a wonder the body wasn't found earlier. We'll do a few more tests, of course but it looks like these bricks have come down recently, exposing the body…"

"He was bricked up?"

"Seems like it. There's quite a network of tunnels but it was never used apparently other than as a playground for local kids over the years. I find it hard to believe that the body would lay undisturbed unless it was concealed. These bricks look freshly collapsed. Some are still hanging from the wall there."

"Jeez," Blake muttered. "It's suspicious at the very least. I mean, you can't brick yourself up, can you?"

Malachy shrugged again, sparking a flicker of irritation in Blake. He hated the uncertainty of shrugs. "There's more, watch this," Malachy said. Although the tunnel was illuminated by arc lights, Malachy shone a pen light onto the back of the skull. The light shone in through the back and out through the eye. "That's kind of a neat trick but you need a hole in the back of your head to do it. Whether it was inflicted before death or after is for minds greater than mine to establish."

"So, the body could have been down here any time since 1945?" Blake looked at the skeleton. "The lapels look very narrow on that suit," he said. "Sixties?"

"The tie is very narrow, too," Malachy added. "Could be. Or Eighties. Maybe Seventies…"

"I get it," Blake muttered. "Wait for Kenning to give us the lowdown."

"He's the pathologist, Will. There is a ring on the skeleton's finger, though. Could be useful, assuming it's distinctive in some way. Plus we don't know what might be in the pockets."

"Let's hope there's something we can use to identify him. And see what the boy remembers of his ordeal."

Back on the surface, Blake sucked in a huge breath of cold air. The atmosphere down there was dank and stagnant. As he signed out of the crime scene, Kath Cryer came striding across the clearing, wrapped in a thick coat. "I didn't expect to see you up here," she said, leaving the 'sir' hanging.

"Sorry, Kath," Blake said, slightly nettled by her

abrupt approach. "I just got the call and came up…"

"Who from?" Kath said, she was breathless from hurrying to catch him, and her face was tinged red.

"It doesn't matter who from, Kath," Blake said, keeping his voice low.

"But I thought I was heading up this case," Kath said.

"Yes," Blake said, "you are, Kath. Look, I'm sorry. I just acted on instinct and came down. You go and see for yourself. Mallachy's still down there…"

"Seems like a waste of resources, don't you think?" Kath said, raising her eyebrows. "Two of us going down there…"

"If it's any consolation, Kath, the body's been down there a while. Looks like it could be a cold case," Blake said, not even convincing himself. "I dare say it would have come my way."

"I dare say," Kath said, smiling tightly. "Right, I'd better go and talk to Jayden. He's in hospital right now. I want to make sure all this was just a kid bunking off."

"Okay, Kath," Blake said, watching her as she headed back to her car. He heaved a sigh. Maybe he should have just gone straight to the office and told Vikki to phone Kath. He'd undermined her by coming down here and she was right to be angry.

CHAPTER 9

Jayden New sat up in his hospital bed, blinking and staring at the adults who filled the room. He looked just like his photograph, an explosion of tatty brown hair and a slightly startled expression. His face looked a little lopsided somehow, too. DCI Kath Cryer wasn't sure if it was the curve of his pointed chin or his forehead that did it.

Everyone looked tired and wrung out. It had been a long night. Once Kath knew that Jayden was safe, she'd breathed a sigh of relief but the real work of establishing what had happened began now. If Jayden had been abducted or attacked, then it needed investigating. The truth had to be established. The boy seemed to be the only one who looked rested. Between mulling over the case and finding Blake sticking his oar in, Kath was exhausted already. She was angry with Blake, and she knew it was probably Vikki Chinn who had called him. But she was angry with herself for how she reacted. She'd come over as petulant, spitting her dummy out because she wanted her moment at the crime scene but it wasn't like that. It was more a question of establishing herself as being in charge. Blake had taken that away from her. She shook herself and looked around.

A woman sat next to the bed, clutching Jayden's hand in hers. She was late thirties with the same colour hair but controlled by straighteners and clips. She had a kind, round face and wore a flowery blouse.

A big man with a close-cropped head and sleeve tattoos, leaned against the far wall, arms folded and his foot twitching. He wore grey work trousers and a blue polo shirt that proclaimed the name of a tile shop. There was also a nurse, a doctor and Tasha Cook, the Family Liaison Officer.

Kath stepped into the room and Tasha approached her. "Jayden's okay. He was lucky not to go into a hypo, given his low food intake and lack of meds. But he can't really remember what happened to him. Mum and dad want answers, obviously."

"He's lucky to be alive," Kath murmured. "That air raid shelter he stumbled into is a maze of tunnels and pitch black. If those boys hadn't heard him calling for help…"

The big man at the window had stepped forward and Kath introduced herself. "Terry New," he said. "Jayden's dad. This is my wife, Sarah." The woman gave Kath a smile and a nod.

"He hasn't said any more, then?" Kath asked.

Terry New shook his head and then looked darkly at her. "We all know, though, don't we?"

Sarah New stiffened in her chair. "Terry, don't..."

Kath frowned. "I'm sorry? Know what?"

"Who put him there. That priest. Father Lanigan."

"We don't know that, Terry," Sarah said, glancing at Jayden.

"What makes you think that Father Lanigan had anything to do with this?" Kath said, frowning. "Jayden could have just fallen into the shelter."

"Yeah, right," Terry New snorted. "Lanigan grabs him in the morning. He knew that Jayden was vulnerable and played on that."

"You have any evidence of this?"

"Yeah, that Rapino woman saw him, Eileen..."

"She's a gossip, Terry," Sarah New said. "She exaggerates..."

"She saw him," Terry said.

"But Father Lanigan was so good when your father passed away..."

"Oh, sure. Hanging around like a vulture, hoping for a donation to the church to keep him in communion wine. I tell you, if I find out he's been messing with my lad..."

"Terry, that's a horrible thing to say," his wife gasped. "Y-you know your dad was troubled towards the end. Father Lanigan brought him peace of mind."

Kath raised a hand. "I really don't think we should be having this conversation in front of your son, Mr New. Unless Jayden has some clear memory of what happened, we can't just assume Father Lanigan has any kind of involvement with this."

Terry looked over to his son. "Well, what can you remember, son?"

Jayden blushed and shrugged. "Not much. Getting up in the morning. Missing the bus. Then I was in that place." He lowered his head and began to cry. "With the Skeleton Man."

"Don't worry, Jayden" Kath said, quietly. "You're safe with mum and dad, now."

Terry New rolled his eyes. "Come on son, man up. You're okay now."

Jayden's shoulders shook and his mum wrapped her arms around him. "Leave him alone Terry. He's had a bad time…"

"Yeah and we all know why," Terry said.

"Terry, he is *here* you know…" his wife said, nodding at the boy.

Kath cleared her throat. "When Jayden is recovered enough, he can talk to DC Cook," she said, pointing to Tasha, "our Family Liaison Officer and we can get to the bottom of what happened."

"He's had a tough time, Inspector," Sarah New said, quietly, her face paling. "You'll be kind to him, won't you?"

"Of course we will, Mrs New," Tasha said, stepping forward and smiling. "We'll work out what happened together and you'll be involved every step of the way."

"I know what happened already," Terry New muttered, glancing at his wife, "and who's to blame."

"As I say," Kath muttered, "talk like that isn't helpful, Mr New. Do let me know if Jayden mentions anything and when the doctors think he's ready, we'll have a chat with him." Kath smiled at the boy hiding in his mother's bosom. "You've been a brave lad, Jayden. I wouldn't like to be stuck down in that shelter on my own." She thought it best not to mention the skeleton. "You kept it all together. Well done."

Jayden New stopped sniffing and blinked at Kath. His mum gave a grateful smile. As she left she gave Terry New a nod that indicated she wanted a word outside.

"I just wanted to make it clear that I expect you to stay away from Father Lanigan," Kath said once they were in the corridor. "We have no evidence that he had anything to do with Jayden's disappearance."

"But…"

"If I hear of you going anywhere near him or contacting him in any way, I'll throw the book at you, understand? I get that you've had a fright. Any father would feel helpless and angry if their child vanished like that but lashing out at the first person you suspect isn't going to help. If you have real evidence that Father Lanigan is somehow involved, then let me know, otherwise, stay away from him. Clear?"

Terry New clenched his teeth, making the muscles in his neck pulse. "Okay."

"Good," Kath said. "Let me know when Jayden feels well enough to chat again." She turned and walked towards the exit but she could feel Terry New watching her as she left.

***

The more she thought about it, the more a quick visit to Father Lanigan seemed to be in order. He was only a ten-minute drive away and Kath was worried that Terry New might visit the priest on the bounce. It was only fair to warn him. Something else about Lanigan nagged at her, though, she wasn't sure what, but she wasn't happy when she'd left Lanigan yesterday. An unexpected drop-in might take the priest by surprise and that could often yield results.

The drive back to Lanigan's house took Kath through various housing estates, some originally council-owned and others more modern, comprising of large, mock-Tudor semi-detached houses. This part of Wirral was largely grass verges and well-kept front gardens until the tangle of Bidston Hill drew nearer. It gave Kath a chance to think.

Jayden's adventure seemed little more than an accident to her. The boy was unharmed, she was sure, unless the medical examination at hospital revealed any sign of abuse. If Jayden had been put down there deliberately, then why not tie him up? It was possible that an attacker might have panicked and pushed Jayden down there in the hope of making his death look like an accident. That seemed unlikely to Kath, though. What she hadn't missed was the look Terry New gave his wife as they talked about Father Lanigan. There was bad blood between Terry and the priest, even before this incident, of that, Kath was sure.

As for the body the poor lad stumbled upon, Blake was welcome to it. She thought the world of the man but wondered if he would be able not to backseat drive her every move. Maybe a historic case might keep him busy. Kath would much rather be working in the land of the living.

There was no answer at Father Lanigan's house, so Kath decided to try the church that stood next to it. The door creaked open as she pushed it, the noise echoing in the large hall. Kath wasn't a great churchgoer, but she marvelled at how light and airy most Catholic churches were inside. Compared to the dark, Victorian Gothic Anglican places she went to as a child or for weddings, the few catholic buildings she had entered seemed bright and cheerful places. St Patricks was no exception. Light streamed in through clear glass windows, no stained glass to darken things. The whitewashed walls bounced the light around the hall and made the pictures that marked the stations of the cross stand out. Even the pews were made of pine and not some dull, red mahogany, polished black over the centuries.

Father Lanigan knelt at the altar and turned at the sound of the door swinging open. He rose to his feet and met Kath halfway down the central aisle. "Inspector Cryer," he said, hesitantly, fishing the name from his memory. "I believe the boy is safe and well."

"Jayden is unharmed," Kath said, "as far as we can ascertain up to now, anyway."

"Thank the Lord," Lanigan muttered and crossed himself. "Where was he?"

"I'm not at liberty to discuss any details right now in case it becomes a criminal case, Father Lanigan. I'm sorry."

"It's enough to know he's safe and sound, that's all. Something to give thanks for."

"Terry New mentioned your name in connection with Jayden's disappearance. Can you account for that?"

Lanigan blushed. "Maybe he's heard about my encounter with him yesterday morning. I mean, it doesn't look good, does it? But Jayden will clear it all up. He'll confirm that I didn't pursue him."

"Jayden can't really remember much of what happened after leaving home for school that morning, Father. Terry New doesn't seem to have a very high opinion of you, though. Can you explain that?"

"He never liked his father's return to faith, Inspector," Lanigan said, sinking onto the nearest pew for support. "Terry seemed to resent the fellowship his father found here. And the peace of mind."

"Peace of mind from what?"

Lanigan gave a brittle smile. "I'm afraid I'm not at liberty to discuss what goes on between me and my flock, Inspector, you must know that."

"Fair enough, Father, I understand. It's just that he seemed very keen to mention your name and appeared quite hostile to the idea that you helped his father in any way."

"Who knows what goes on in people's minds? They say God moves in mysterious ways, but I'd argue much of mankind does the same. The actions of some of my parishioners perplex and try me daily, Inspector."

"Amen to that," Kath said, with a brief smile. "Just be aware of Terry New. He was angry when he spoke to me. Frustrated that he hadn't been there for his son. I suspect he might be thinking of taking it out on you. I've warned him off but keep the security chain on your door. Have your mobile handy and call us if you have the slightest worry."

Lanigan glanced up the church to the cross over the altar. "I have all the security I need right there, Inspector. Don't you worry about me."

CHAPTER 10

Another night of broken sleep left Blake feeling like something the cat had dragged out, through a bush backwards and then kicked around the garden. He'd considered sleeping in his car and the idea didn't seem so fanciful in the glare of morning. Nor did the prospect of stumbling straight into a post-mortem with everybody's least favourite pathologist, Jack Kenning. The man had seen too many TV crime dramas and decided to take his cue from them. Underneath the colourful bowties, the terrible humour and, frankly bizarre theatrics that Kenning often employed, was a dull man desperate to be considered interesting.

Blake had promised himself that he'd leave this to Kath, after their tense encounter on the hill but Martin had called him, late, asking if he would go. He wondered if Kath had said something to Martin or if the Superintendent had another motive. Either way, Blake was happy to go but he still felt as though he was pushing in again.

This post-mortem was a little different, Blake had to admit. Normally, he and a colleague would be up in the gallery watching Jack Kenning performing in what for him was certainly more a dramatic theatre than an operating theatre. Today, though, the skeletonised body was laid out like a museum exhibit on one table. A parchment of blackened skin and tissue covered the dark bones. The clothes and a pair of boots lay on another. Blake, encased in the usual protective clothing and facemasks, stood alongside Kenning.

The pathologist had done something weird to his grey moustache, waxing it so that it stuck out at either side like radio antennae. Of course, the effect was totally lost once he donned his surgical mask.

"Well," Kenning said as he approached the body as if for the first time, "this one's late to the party, eh, Blake?"

"How late?" Blake asked, trying to play Kenning's game as little as possible.

"We'll come to that in good time, my man," Kenning said, wagging a finger. "Subject is male, late teens or early twenties. Height six foot on the dot. Teeth and bones indicate a good state of health although there is sign of an old break in the left leg, probably a childhood injury. It was poorly set and might have left him with a slight limp or an odd gait."

"There's hair on the skull," Blake said, glancing at the exposed bones. "Was it always black?"

"Indeed it was," Kenning said. "I'd hazard a guess and say that our stranger would be the tall, dark and handsome type."

"So what happened to him?"

"Smashed in the back of the head with a lump hammer," Kenning said. "Although there were other extensive injuries around the rest of the body, cracked ribs, left eye socket and jaw, and broken fingers. All very suggestive of a good roughing up before he was finished off with the hammer."

"How do you know it was a lump hammer?"

"It was in the wall cavity with him. It looks like whoever killed him hid him there deliberately. The brickwork was rough and ready, but it stood the test of time. Kept him dry, too. The cool breeze through that place must have slowed down the decomposition."

"Jeez," Blake muttered, staring down at the cadaver. "Any ID?"

"Nothing official, no bus passes or driving licence. Mind you, everything was made of card or paper back then. I'm not sure how any documents would have fared down there."

"Back when?" Blake muttered.

"*That* brings us onto your first question, DCI Blake," Kenning said, airily and swept over to the other table where a jacket and pair of trousers lay alongside a belt, a ragged shirt, a tie and a pair of boots. "The suit is Mohair and you can just make out the Beno Dorn label in the lining…"

"Beno Dorn? Wasn't he a tailor in Birkenhead? Brian Epstein first took the Beatles to him when he wanted to smarten them up. Winkle-picker boots, narrow tie," Blake added. "So would you say we're looking at the nineteen sixties?"

Even though he wore a mask, Blake could tell Kenning was annoyed at having his thunder stolen. "Early sixties, I would say. Of course, clothes maketh not the man, if you see what I mean; but it's a good working hypothesis. He's well preserved considering he's been dead for almost sixty years, though. If he'd been in the ground or insects had had a chance to get at him, there'd be very little left."

Blake looked back at the body. "So, who is he?"

"That's for me not to know and you to find out," Kenning laughed.

"There was a ring on the body, wasn't there?" Blake said, remembering O'Hare mentioning it.

"Yes, that might be your way in," Kenning said, pointing to the table where a small plastic bag held the metal object.

"Can I have a closer look?" Blake said.

"Be my guest," Kenning said, with a flamboyant gesture.

Blake picked up the bag and held it up to the light. "It looks quite cheap, copper maybe?" he said. "Is that a crown etched on it?"

Kenning produced some close-up photographs and once again, Blake couldn't help thinking he could have done that sooner rather than later. "It's a crown, I'm pretty certain of that. It has what looks like an 'A' and a 'G' carved inside the crown, too. Initials, perhaps?"

"Possibly," Blake muttered. He turned back to the skeleton. "A good-looking young man goes missing all those years ago. Someone must have reported it. He must have had friends, associates, people who would miss him."

"He'd need a job to afford a suit like that," Kenning said. "Or someone who cared enough to buy it for him."

"Either way, there's a chance that someone may well have raised a concern about him," Blake murmured. "I'll get a check done on any cold cases." He waved the photos. "Thanks Jack."

Jack rubbed his eyes. "My pleasure," he said, airily. "I was up half the night working on this. Fascinating. There'll be more information once the lab work comes back. I suspect that a lot of what was trawled up there is junk, but you never know."

Blake stared at the unknown corpse. "You never know, Jack, you never know."

***

Questions swirled round in Blake's head on the journey back to HQ. Apart from trying to digest everything he'd learnt at the post-mortem, he couldn't help wondering why Superintendent Martin had asked him to actually attend in the first place. The text from Martin asking him to drop in when he got back, didn't settle his nerves, either.

Martin looked over the top of his reading glasses as Blake entered the room and gestured for him to sit down. "How was the post-mortem, Will?" he said once Blake was settled.

"As good as these things can be, sir," Blake said, trying not to eye the senior officer with suspicion.

"Jack Kenning on top form?" Martin said, smirking.

"You know Jack, sir," Blake said, raising an eyebrow. "All the world's a stage…"

"Indeed," Martin said. "And this body… I heard late last night that it was quite… old…"

Blake tried not to give a knowing smile as all the pieces fell into place. It was an old case so it was probably a cold case. Martin could stick him onto trying to find out who it was and forget about him. "Yes, sir, Kenning reckons the body was probably bricked up down there in the early sixties. No obvious ID but we do know the victim was young and walked with a limp. They were also wearing a distinctive ring, so plenty to go on..."

Martin gave an approving look and nodded. "More than a few fragments of bone, teeth and wisps of hair. We should count ourselves lucky."

"So..." Blake started.

"So, you take Alex Manikas and work on identifying the poor chap and finding out what happened to him. Kath Cryer can wrap up the young lad's case and move onto something else. Don't worry too much about supervision, Matty Cavanagh is keen."

"He always is, sir," Blake said. DCI Cavanagh was a young and thrusting DCI, who always looked slick and well-groomed, but Blake suspected cut corners whenever he could. Cavanagh's trusty sidekick DS Bobby Dirkin often saved the man's bacon and it rankled with Blake. "Can I ask why this change of plan?"

"Just seems to make sense, Will," Martin said. "Between you and me, Kath was a bit arsy about you being called to the crime scene yesterday instead of her. But this seems a great solution."

"I see, sir," Blake said, hiding the irritation in his voice. He knew Kath was annoyed by that and he had apologised. There was no need to go crying to Martin about it. "Well, I'll get on and find out who this young man is, then."

"Great," Martin said. "It's a challenge, Will, I'm not denying it. Many of the witnesses will be senior citizens, some may no longer be with us. I'm not expecting miracles. Just take your time. I don't think even with your celebrity background, you could make headlines with this one."

"I'll do my best, Sir?" Blake couldn't resist putting a slight barb in his voice.

CHAPTER 11

It had been a couple of days since Jeff Blake had been attacked by Josh Gambles in the prison meeting room. It had unnerved him, he couldn't deny it but at the same time, a certain spite had galvanised him into wrapping up the book and sending the modified manuscript off to his agent. He'd been nothing but straight with Gambles; he'd told him from the outset that he wasn't writing a dull biography for true crime anoraks to pore over for gruesome titbits.

Jeff was a serious writer, a literary novelist. In his short time back on the Wirral, he'd encountered far more characters and inspiration than he had when he swam in London publishing circles. The difference was, here he was in the thick of things, meeting real live crime lords. Harry Thorpe had been very interested in the idea of Jeff writing about him. Sadly, Thorpe had been buried up to his neck in sand with a fast-approaching tide to drown his screams. Jeff had met him, though, been kidnapped by him, in fact, the whole bag over the head deal. Experiences like that were worth their weight in literary gold. Jeff could return to the capital with a sack full of anecdotes and insights into the 'real world.'

He was pleased when during a recent phone call, his agent had remarked on how Jeff's 'Scouse' accent had become more pronounced. Jeff wasn't going to point out that, in the eyes of most of Liverpool's citizens, he was what they called a 'Wool.' He just knew his audience would lap up the 'authentic' voice.

Jeff had already decided that somehow, he was going to give a share of the profits from the book to the families of Gambles' victims. If they'd accept it. He could still be accused of profiting from someone else's misery and suffering but he hoped that his book would shed light rather than cast shadow. And wasn't he a victim as much as anyone else? He just needed to establish how much of a share. He had to live after all and he'd poured his heart and soul into this book.

Looking out of the window into the street, he half expected to see a dark figure lurking behind the trees that lined the roadside. Gambles bragged about a few ardent fans who might take it upon themselves to do his bidding. There was nothing, though. Gambles was a spent force; he was more concerned about the afterlife and his immortal soul. Surely taking revenge on Jeff would just add to his guilt. But Gambles' moods could turn with a change in the wind, Jeff knew that. Maybe he should phone Will, just to let him know. He picked up his phone and then put it down again.

What would Will be able to do? He could imagine his brother's voice dripping with sarcasm, "Okay, Jeff, I'll have a twenty-four-hour guard placed on your house. Helicopters, the works…" Jeff laughed at himself. Fancy being so nervous. Gambles was locked in prison. What harm could he do now?

Jeff's phone buzzed and he picked it up, frowning at the unknown number. His first instinct was to shut the call off, thinking it was a scammer or cold caller. But he stood on the cusp of a book deal. This was when publicists and editors might ring you for a cosy chat and he wouldn't always recognise the number. So his curiosity got the better of him and he answered it. "Hello?"

It wasn't totally silent at the other end of the line. Jeff could hear distant, echoing voices, some angry, some plaintive but all incoherent. The line crackled and somebody breathed out.

"Jeffrey. How are you?"

Jeff's stomach lurched at the sound of Josh Gambles, and he swallowed hard. "Josh," he said, trying to keep his voice steady. "What do you want?"

"I was bored. I just wanted to check you were all right, that's all. We are co-authors after all…"

"No, Josh, I am the sole author. You signed papers to that effect. You are partly the subject of the book, that's all. Nothing more."

"You know, I've been thinking. It's just about all you can do in this place. I've decided to forgive you, Jeffrey."

"What for? I haven't done anything wrong."

"Search your conscience, Jeffrey. You duped me. I thought you were writing a book about me and me alone, but you weren't. You lied to me. But I will forgive you. All you have to do is repent."

"What?" Jeff squeaked. He cleared his throat. "I see. So you're God now, are you? Dispensing forgiveness from on high."

"That's blasphemy, Jeffrey. You shouldn't talk like that. Just say you're sorry and that you will change the book and I'll forgive you."

"I don't need your forgiveness, Gambles. You put yourself outside the sphere of human decency when you killed those people and left them to rot. If I want to write about you through the prism of my own life, then I'll do that."

"I'm warning you, Jeffrey. Stop now or I won't be responsible for the consequences. You'll bring retribution on yourself."

Jeff's heart thumped against his ribs. It felt as though Gambles was in the room with him. The old menace had returned to his voice. "Just leave me alone. How did you get hold of a mobile phone anyway? I thought they weren't allowed."

"Oh, I may be despised by most, but I still have

friends on the inside *and* on the outside too. Friends who can make things happen for me. I only have to give the word."

"A-are you threatening me?"

"Yes, Jeffrey I am. Repent and desist with this foolish book."

Panic and fear made Jeff spiteful. "What happened to your new-found faith, Josh? I thought you were seeking some kind of salvation. That didn't last long."

"*You* are provoking *me*. It is you who are bringing this down on yourself. You're creating your own Hell. We all have free will, Jeffrey, I'm giving you the chance to turn back."

"I'm ending this call and blocking this number, Gambles. Just leave me alone." Jeff stabbed the screen with his finger and blocked the call. For a second, he stared at the phone then threw it onto the sofa. "Creepy, bloody bastard!"

He sat down, heavily, and rubbed his face. There was nothing to fear. Gambles often talked about his 'little army of acolytes' on the outside but Jeff was pretty sure it was all bravado. At first, Gambles had been something of a celebrity. More recently only a small number of people wrote to him each week. He had shared some of the letters with Jeff. Some of them were from women who wanted to marry and change him, believing in some twisted way that all he needed was a little

Christian love. Perhaps they'd had some degree of success, given that Gambles was talking about God, now. Or maybe they'd just fed his twisted view of the world. There were one or two that expressed a veiled admiration for his planning. Jeff had often wondered if the prison officers held back more salacious or congratulatory letters. Either way, Jeff had never seen any evidence of people swearing undying fealty to Gambles. It only took one, though.

Pouring himself a whiskey with trembling hands, Jeff flicked on the TV to distract his thoughts and almost dropped his glass.

Flanked by a sweaty-looking local councillor with a bad comb-over, Kyle Quinlan grinned out of the screen at him, his perfect teeth gleaming in his tanned face and not a hair out of place. They stood on what looked to be New Brighton promenade, with the lighthouse behind them. The big cranes of Liverpool stood red and blurred in the background.

"Councillor Greaves and I have been finalising a deal to explore the rebuilding of the New Brighton Tower Complex. It's a great investment opportunity that would bring construction jobs and, ultimately tourists flocking back to the Wirral. This peninsula could be the Las Vegas of the North…"

The words washed over Jeff, who sat, rerunning

some of Gambles' reminiscences in his mind; the ones about his early prison days when he was befriended by a young man called Kyle Quinlan, how they became a feared duo on the inside, and how they were inseparable friends who would do anything for each other. Anything.

CHAPTER 12

It was an awkward conversation, of that there was no doubt. Blake had dreaded it but decided he had to bite the bullet. Shutting himself in his tiny office, he lifted the receiver, almost curling up with embarrassment in his chair as he spoke to the vet.

"Yeah it's my cat, Serafina."

There was a moment's silence as the vet processed the news. She'd experienced Serafina's wild cruelty before and it was clear from her tone that she remembered. "Ah, yes, how is she? I think it was a badly infected tooth last time, as I recall. Quite nasty." Blake wasn't sure whether the 'nasty' referred to the infection or the fact that the cat had chased her around the surgery until she'd taken refuge on top of a filing cabinet.

"Yes, this is something a little more delicate. She's just very... well I can't think of a better word than randy."

"Randy?"

"Making a lot of noise, spraying all over the house attracting Tom cats and generally very, very affectionate. It's not right."

"Has she been spayed, Mr Blake?"

"I don't know. I inherited her from my mother and thought she'd got her done but I don't have any records. The one thing I would say is that she hasn't been like this before not as long as I've known her and that's years."

"Yes, I see what you mean. If she hadn't been spayed then, you'd expect this kind of thing on a regular basis. That is a strange one."

"I can bring her in if you like…"

"No!" the vet almost screamed. "No. Not for now. No need to upset her for no reason. The main thing will be to establish whether or not the behaviour is psychological or hormonal."

"You think the cat might be going mad?"

There was a pregnant pause that suggested the vet thought Serafina was psychotic anyway. "Let me do a little research and I'll get back to you."

"Thank you," Blake said. "I wouldn't trouble you but it's the noise and the smell I can't cope with. I never realised female cats were so…" Before he had chance to finish his sentence, DC Alex Manikas knocked on his door and came in just as Blake was finishing the sentence. "So noisy when they had sex. On the front lawn too, I'm worried the neighbours will complain." Manikas bit down on a smirk as Blake realised he was there. "Look, I'll have to go, but thank you…"

"Sorry, sir," Manikas said, "I should have waited

outside. I didn't realise you were making a delicate phone call..."

Blake grinned, feeling himself reddening. "It's my bloody cat, Alex. Bang at it every night. I need to get it sorted..."

"Right, sir," Alex said, not quite sure where to look. "Anyway, I've trawled through the mispers who might fit the bill for our young man from the sixties and narrowed it down to three possibles. There's a Sidney Elston, went missing on his way home from the bank in 1961, and Earnest Hughes, a young man who vanished after a night out in 1964 and a Robert Pearce who never returned from a Liverpool away match in 1966. All fit the bill, but Pearce is an outside bet as he may well have never got back on the coach in Leeds."

Blake sat back at his desk and looked at the photograph of the ring found on the corpse. "Anyone with the initials AG, Alex?"

"None, sir, I did use that for my first check. There was an Alison Griffiths who ran away from home in 1970 but she was fourteen and five foot, one. The only other thing I thought was that AG is the symbol for silver on the periodic table, sir, but..."

"But the ring is obviously made of copper. A joke? I wonder if the owner was a Chemistry student. Seems a bit out there, but you never know."

"No, sir, I was more thinking it would be a small 'g' in the AG"

"Ah, right. Oh well, maybe not. Great work, Alex, start with the first two and see what background you can get on them. As you say, Pearce is an outsider for now."

"Yes, sir," Alex said. He hung back instead of rushing off to carry on the search.

Blake looked up at him. "Are you okay, Alex?"

"Yes, sir," he said, reddening. "Can I ask, have we been… side-lined or something? I mean, it seems odd, just you and me stuck here sifting through old misper files…"

"I can see that it might seem like that, Alex," Blake sighed, almost trying to convince himself, "it's just a sensible division of labour, that's all. Nothing more. I wouldn't read anything into it. The way you saved that young lad the other day shows your commitment. We'll get this case sorted and it'll be business as usual, trust me."

Manikas gave a brief smile and nodded. "Thanks, sir. I'll crack on then."

Blake stared after him. "Yeah," he muttered. "Get this one sorted and that'll be it. I really hope so, Alex."

***

Alex Manikas sat poring through the files, trying not to wonder if he'd been stuck on this case with Blake as some kind of warning or punishment. It was a forlorn hope, trying to identify someone who vanished sixty years ago. Who the hell would be around who remembered anything about them in any useful detail? But Blake was right; all they could do was work as hard as they could on the case and hope they got a breakthrough. He opened the file on the first missing person and pulled up a few photographs on Google from the year Sidney Elston went missing. It seemed like another world, Liverpool and the Wirral in 1961. People huddled in big overcoats, wearing hats and the cars looked strangely bulbous, and rounded.

There were very few notes on Elston; a few references to him being quiet, 'bookish' and 'not really into sport' but very little of value such as what his mood was like on the day he went missing, whether he seemed depressed. Manikas frowned at the photograph of the lad, flat and clean, preserved in a folder that hadn't been opened in decades. It was a portrait photograph, clearly taken for a proud parent. He was a good-looking lad, not ruggedly handsome but he had a certain fine beauty about him. His black wavy hair framed a pointed face and a soft smile. Manikas had a sudden, jarring memory of the photo of the corpse that lay in the crime scene report and he shook himself.

Obviously, any violent death was horrible and

unacceptable, but, for Manikas, there was something even more disturbing about one that had never been solved. It reminded him of the gulf between the idealistic, almost naïve view he had of the police as a youngster and the actual reality. However hard Manikas worked, some people would get away with the most heinous crimes and the bodies of the innocent would quietly decay in the darkness forever.

There was no phone number but there was a family address in Wallasey, 9 Curzon Park Road. "Not much point calling there," Manikas muttered to himself. The mother, Violet Elston's date of birth was listed as 1920 meaning she would be over a hundred if she was still alive.

Elston had set off for a day at work in a bank in Birkenhead one Tuesday morning in March 1961 and never came back. He'd done a full day's work, seemed his normal, quiet self, said goodbye to his colleagues and walked into oblivion. There were a lot of notes about his mother, Violet, who it seemed made herself a thorn in the side of the local police. To be fair to the coppers of the time, there was no evidence that Sidney Elston hadn't just taken off for a new life. There was certainly no evidence that he had been killed. He hadn't taken any of his clothes from home or packed a case of any kind, which suggested to his mother that he had no intention of leaving. Mrs Elston continued to pressure the police and there would be sporadic activity, a lead that would then prove to be a dead end.

A bloodstained suit jacket was found on wasteland in Birkenhead and Mrs Elston identified it as Sidney's but, as the police pointed out, it was so stained and messed up, even the tailor who made it didn't recognise it. There was also doubt that it was Sidney's because it had quite a broad chest and Sidney was a slighter build. Manikas paused. If it was Sidney's, then he had to consider the fact that the body in the air raid shelter was wearing a full suit. Was it likely that he would be set upon, dressed in a mohair suit and hidden? Not impossible, of course but improbable. On the other hand, there seemed to be a lot of scepticism around the jacket and without the advantage of DNA testing, officers then would have to rely on their instincts and testimony of other experts.

Over on the other side of the office, Kath Cryer and the others were deep in discussion about something. He sent something to print and watched them as he waited for it to come out. The final sheet flopped onto the tray and Alex glanced down at the list of Elstons resident in Merseyside. His eyes widened. One address sprang out at him, 9 Curzon Park Road, Wallasey. There was still a family member at the address.

***

Sleep never came easily to Gary Jensen these

days. When he was a young man, he could nod off anywhere. "You could sleep on a clothesline," his old mum used to say, bless her. That was in the old days, though, before everything went wrong. Nowadays, between having to get up for a pee every ten minutes and Gary's racing mind, sleep was a rare commodity. He'd be awake half the night and then doze off in his chair in front of the TV during the day. He'd used sleeping tablets for a while, but they gave him bad dreams and made his thoughts muddy. His wife said he was like a zombie when he was on those pills, so he'd kicked them.

In the last two days, he hadn't slept at all, not even in his armchair, and the world seemed hazy and slightly distorted. The bang on the door startled him out of a daydream that could possibly have been the gateway to a deeper sleep, but he'd never know. He blinked, wondering where he was for a moment. Another bang on the door forced him, grunting, to his feet. Maybe she was back and had forgotten her keys.

"All right, I'm coming, stop your banging," Gary growled. "What do you think you're playing at?" He stopped dead, staring at the stony-faced man glowering at him from the doorstep.

"Sammy, what the fuck are you doing here? I thought you said…"

"Never mind what I said. Have you heard the

news? They've pulled a body out of the shelters. An *old* body, Gary. You know what that means?"

Gary nodded. "Yeah, but…"

"But nothing, Gary," Sammy said. "I saw you when that copper spoke to us on the hill. You looked like you were going to wet your pants. Just remember, you don't know nothing, and you don't say nothing, okay?"

"Okay," Gary said. "It's just that I don't understand how…"

Sammy lurched forward and grabbed Gary by the front of his dressing gown. "Look, just pretend you're a doddery old fool. It shouldn't be hard for a dickhead like you. If I have to come back here, you won't like it, got that?"

Sammy turned and stalked off without giving Gary time to respond.

CHAPTER 13

The houses in Curzon Park Road were large semi-detached. DC Alex Manikas wasn't really a good judge of age, but he reckoned by the red brick, slate roofs and pointed gables that they were old. Blakey would have regaled him with an account of rich managers, possibly working at the ship-yard or in the banks over in Liverpool. He didn't need Blake's history lessons to realise they were desirable residences today and would have been sixty years ago. Sidney Elston came from a well-to-do family. There was little mention in the files about his father other than he was something high up in one of the shipping offices over the water.

Many of the front gardens of these properties had been turned into carports but some retained their front walls and gardens. Manikas could imagine bowler-hatted executives striding down the road past neatly clipped privet hedges. Maybe Sidney accompanied his father to the train station, wishing each other a good day before parting company at the platform. For some reason, Alex imagined it would be a stiff, uncomfortable farewell.

Number nine Curzon Park Road wasn't as well-kept as some of the other properties adjoining and opposite. Many of the neighbours had replaced the sash windows with double glazing, their front doors were UPVC replacements and some had clad or pebbledashed their walls. This house hid behind an unkempt hedge of privet and rambling rose. The wooden gate looked original and ready to tumble from its hinges. Manikas inched it open and walked up the cracked tiled pathway to the peeling front door. If someone had told him that Sidney's hundred-year-old mother still lived here, he would have believed them.

The front garden had a few severely pruned roses and a shaggy lawn. Heavy net curtains shrouded the front windows. The whole house looked as though it could do with a little TLC, Manikas thought. Not that he was particularly great at home maintenance. He knocked on the door and stepped back a little. His neck prickled as the nets swished for a second and a pale face peered out, then vanished.

The door chain rattled, and an old woman pulled the door open a crack. "Yes?" she said, her voice crackling. "Can I help you?"

Alex flashed his warrant card. "DC Alex Manikas, Merseyside Police, madam. Can I ask, is your surname Elston?"

"It is." The door didn't open any wider and Manikas was conscious of the dark, glittering eyes on him.

"I'm sorry to disturb you but are you related to the Sidney Elston who used to live here?"

The old woman paused, her dark eyes blinking. "Yes, I'm Sidney's sister."

"I see. We're currently looking into a number of missing persons cases, following the discovery of remains over in Bidston. You might have heard about it on the news."

"I never watch the news," the old woman said. "It makes the world such a scary place."

"Would it be possible to come in and have a quick chat with you about Sidney?"

The door opened a little wider and Alex got a closer look at her. The family resemblance was there, he thought. When she was younger, she would have had the same slight build and fine cheek bones. But the years had made her heavier and she was slightly stooped as she held the door. The hallway behind her looked clean and tidy. "I don't think I can help you. It's been sixty years since Sidney disappeared. He's dead and gone…"

"Sorry, Ms Elston. I know it won't be easy but we're keen to identify this body and if there was the slightest chance that it was Sidney, surely you'd want to know."

"Sidney went down south. He's not around

here," Ms Elston said. "My mother thought he would come back but she never saw him again. Whoever that poor soul you found is, it isn't my brother. Now, if you don't mind, I have a lot to do." The door shut in Alex's face.

As he walked back to his car, Alex cursed himself. He was too direct. He should have been a bit more circumspect and got a bit more information from her before she slammed the door. Maybe he should have been a little less formal. A rapid knocking on glass broke his thoughts and he looked around.

In the window of a house on the other side of the road, another elderly woman was waving wildly to him, whilst using the curtain to shield herself from the view of number nine. She looked older than Ms Elston, her hair frizzed from her pink scalp like white candyfloss. Alex pointed to himself, and she nodded, beckoning for him to come to her front door. She pointed to the other side of the house where Alex could see a side gate.

With a shrug, Alex hurried across the road. The first thing he realised was that the side gate was out of view of number nine, shielded by the shaggy bushes. After a moment's pause, a bolt on the gate rattled and it swung open. The old lady stood there, wide eyed and breathless. She had a brown cardigan wrapped around herself. "Are you a policeman? You look like a policeman."

"Yes, Madam," Manikas said, pulling out his warrant card again. "DC Alex…"

"Oh, thank goodness for that. Is it about the murder? It's about time. I knew she couldn't get away with it forever. Come in, DC Alex and I'll make a statement."

***

It always amazed Blake just how many people went missing every day. Of course, most of them resurfaced days, weeks or months later. Some returned after years of wandering. Others never did. His mother had been one of those people. She'd walked out of the house one dark night and for two years, Blake didn't have a clue where she was. She'd had the misfortune to meet Josh Gambles, although he always maintained that he never killed her, only tried to help her. He didn't bring her home, though. But now wasn't the time to dwell on his own past; the history of the man in the shelter was far more important if they were going to identify him.

Looking out from his room into the main office, he saw Kath at her desk. As though sensing his stare, she stopped typing and glanced round at him. Blake beckoned and she got up.

"You okay?" she said, still not confident enough to call him by his Christian name but omitting the 'sir.'

Blake rubbed his forehead. "Yeah, if ploughing

through old case files is your idea of fun, Kath. Listen, I'm sorry for barging in on your crime scene, yesterday, it was wrong of me. I should have called you."

"Not a problem," Kath said, simply.

"I just wish you'd felt able to have a word with me instead of going straight to Martin, that's all. I mean, we've been through a lot. I thought…"

"I never said anything to Martin," Kath said, looking puzzled. Maybe he saw I was in a shitty mood but he never spoke to me."

"He said you weren't happy about it. 'Arsey' was the word he used. I thought you'd spoken to him."

Kath shook her head. "Nope. I'll admit I wasn't happy. It probably hasn't happened to you, but I've been dogged by men trying to micro-manage me every time I go for promotion. 'Give her a chance to show us how good she is,' they say and then watch every little move, question each decision so that it looks like I didn't know what I'm doing. You didn't give me a moment's thought when Vikki Chinn called you. You just rocked up…"

"I know and I've apologised. I didn't know what the situation was, Kath. You could have been ill or something…"

"Have you known me to take a day off sick?

All it would have taken was a quick phone call to check. You'd have shown Matty Cavanagh that courtesy. How can I demonstrate I have the capability if nobody gives me the space to make my own decisions? Yes, and my own mistakes?" She looked at her watch. "I've got to go. But I didn't say anything to Martin, trust me."

She bustled back into the office, snagging a few glances from other desks as she went. Blake groaned and buried his face in the nearest file, not even bothering to take in the words.

CHAPTER 14

There was a pile of paperwork back at the office and the plate of biscuits in front of him, made Alex Manikas feel a little guilty. Blake had been left to sift through files while Alex was munching Jammy Dodgers. The old lady, whose name was Gloria Parsons, had bundled Alex into her kitchen and plonked him down on a chair. Alex found himself wondering if she did this to a lot of passers-by because the plate of biscuits was ready and waiting on the table and the kettle had just boiled. The kitchen looked clean, which was one blessing. Often he found himself in places where you wouldn't even sit down, let alone accept a brew.

The woman shuffled round the kitchen making tea, her frizzy white head bobbing up and down and her big brown cardigan still wrapped round her. "I've lived here for more than sixty years," she said, plonking a mug of tea in front of Alex. "Is that how you like it?"

"Yes, thanks, that's perfect," Alex said. "So you lived in this road when Sidney Elston went missing?"

She settled in the chair next to him and leaned forward. "I did. Poor lad. So delicate."

"Delicate?"

"Yeah. He looked like a puff of wind would blow him away. He never enjoyed good health but then I don't think he had the chance."

"Why not?"

"It was his mother and father wasn't it? His dad was a bigwig at the shipping offices over the water, a very bluff man. He'd been an army captain or something during the war. He wanted his son to be a man's man, you know, rugger, pipe smoking and beer. But Violet, his mother mollycoddled him. The first sign of a sniffle and he'd be off school, all wrapped up."

"Did the parents argue about him?"

"All the time," Gloria said. "I felt sorry for the poor lad. He did some acting in school, even a bit of ballroom dancing. His father put a stop to all that. Army Cadets, bracing walks at the weekend. He looked proper miserable."

"So do you think he ran away in 1961?"

"I do. Poor Violet was never the same. She couldn't accept that he'd left. His father never mentioned his name again and left the room if anyone started talking about him. 'He's dead to me,' he'd say and that was that."

Alex sipped his tea for a moment. "You asked me if I was here about the murder. If Sidney ran away, then there was no murder…"

"Not him," Gloria said, rolling her eyes, as though Alex should know exactly what she was on about, "her. Violet. She was murdered. By that woman... Suzi or whatever she calls herself."

Alex suppressed the urge to groan and started to figure out a way to extricate himself from the interview. Clearly, Gloria was just a lonely old woman with a vivid imagination. "Right, Gloria, I really need to get going and..."

"I understand, so I'll be brief. I get it. Are you going to take notes?"

Alex froze, his notebook halfway into his jacket pocket. "I thought I'd just listen. You know, get the headlines..."

"Okay then. She turns up sometime in 1978, I think it was October time because Mr Elston, the father, he didn't die until April of that year... or was it May?"

"So dad dies and Suzi... the woman at number 9 turns up," Alex said, trying to keep up and speed Gloria along so he could escape.

"Correct. You've got a good head for facts, haven't you? No wonder you're a policeman."

"Suzi turns up," Alex prompted again.

"Yes. Just out of the blue. Violet hadn't been well for a while, not sure what it was. Elsie at Number 5 said it was her water works but I thought it might have been a cancer scare. She lived a good few years after that so maybe not." She paused and stared at Alex who nodded encouragingly.

"Go on."

"Anyway, that's it. She moves in with Violet. Says she's going to look after her and we said to Violet, 'you don't know where she's come from, you don't know what she's got planned.' Violet wouldn't have it though. 'She's my daughter,' she said. Called her an angel and a godsend."

"But why do you think she murdered Violet?"

"Well, it's obvious isn't it? Violet dies ten years ago and she's still there, living in the house, like she owned it."

"That doesn't mean she murdered her. Maybe she inherited it. She is Violet's daughter after all."

Gloria shook her head in frustration. "That's what I'm trying to tell you. Violet *never had* a daughter!"

***

Kath Cryer ground her teeth as she drove through the tunnel to Birkenhead. Martin had called her 'Arsey?' Normally, she'd have a thicker skin when it came to the language used by her colleagues but right now, she felt strangely vulnerable. This was a big step up and she wasn't even sure she wanted it. Martin had sprung it upon her. Over the last few months, she'd been considering alternative careers, ones that didn't involve being shot at or spat at. It felt as though she'd been thrown onto a conveyer belt and was speeding along without time to think. So why was she so touchy about Blake seemingly undermining her? She shook her head. Maybe she was in a bad mood because she didn't actually want to do any of this. Right now, all she wanted to do was get to the bottom of what made Jayden run and wrap up the case.

Eileen Rapino lived in a mid-terrace in Bidston. Kath got the impression that this had been the family home for some time. There were decorations and furniture from another generation mixed in with new acquisitions and more modern wallpaper and carpets. Eileen Rapino's hair spilt over the shoulders of her turquoise cardigan, the dyed black making her look pale and sickly. She wore thick-framed glasses and a necklace of wooden beads that kind of went with her cardigan, Kath thought.

"Is it about Father Lanigan?" Eileen asked, sitting on her armchair with one leg under her bottom. It looked quite uncomfortable. "Have you arrested him?"

"I just wanted to go through your statement again, Eileen," Kath said, opening her notebook. "So you say that on Monday, at around 8:45am you saw Father Lanigan and Jayden New together."

"Yes," Eileen said, toying with the chunky beads round her neck. "They were shouting at each other. Jayden's language was blue!"

"And what was Father Lanigan saying?"

Eileen blinked at Kath. "Well I couldn't hear him, could I?"

"But you could hear Jayden?"

"Just a few choice words," Eileen Rapino said, her foot began to twitch and she shifted position in her seat. "You know, the effing and blinding."

"So what happened next?"

Eileen's eyes widened. "Well, Lanigan grabbed Jayden by the shoulders, like this," she said and held her arms out in front of her. "He yelled in his face. I mean it's not nice, is it? He's a man of God. Anyway, Jayden broke free and ran off up the street."

"And what did Father Lanigan do?"

"He just stood there, didn't he? Watched him run off," Eileen said, matter-of-factly.

"But when you approached PC Robertson..."

"Was he the one with the beard? I didn't know you were allowed beards in the police," Eileen said, leaning forward in her armchair. "He was quite old, too."

"Why did you tell PC Robertson that Lanigan would know where Jayden was?"

Eileen Rapino licked her lips. "He'd watched him run off, hadn't he? He'd seen where he went..."

"Nothing else?"

"Nah. I was just doing my duty. Reporting what I saw, wasn't I? Dunno why I'm being made to feel like a criminal..." she looked up at the ceiling and then her head snapped back to Kath. "That body they found in the shelters. Do you know who it is?"

"I'm afraid I'm not working on that case, Eileen," Kath muttered. "Is there anything else you want to add to your statement?"

But Eileen was staring off over Kath's head. "They're saying it's been down there a long time. The past is a terrible place, you know. When I think of our Peter and what they did to him..."

"I'm sorry," Kath said. "You've lost me..."

"No I haven't," Eileen replied, pointing at her. "You're right there. What are you on about?"

"I mean, I didn't understand what you meant... about the past and Peter."

But Eileen had snapped back into the present. "Never you mind about Peter. He's nothing to do with any of this. You can't hurt him anymore."

"Right," Kath said, standing up. "I'm sorry to have disturbed you, Eileen and thank you for your time."

CHAPTER 15

Partly out of frustration and partly to spite Martin, Blake had finished work early. His intention had been to go home and walk the dog along the front at Rock Park, maybe stray a little further and wander into Port Sunlight. Instead, he found himself strolling along Bidston Hill with Charlie pulling at the lead. The cold, grey weather had kept most people indoors, but the threat of rain also made the view of Liverpool sharp and clear.

Across a clearing, he saw Pippa Fearon striding off into the woods, deep in thought. For a second, he thought to pursue her but then reminded himself that he was meant to be having some downtime. However, she spotted him and gave him an enthusiastic wave.

"Inspector Blake, we must stop meeting like this," she said, laughing, breathlessly. "People will talk!"

"Do you spend all of your time up here, Miss Fearon?"

"Call me Pippa, please. And yes, I virtually live up here. It's all I've known since I was a young girl. The Wirral has been through so many changes but this place stays the same. I wouldn't be anywhere else."

"But you have the Welsh hills just over the way," Blake said, pointing off into the distance.

"True and some days you can see them so clearly, you could touch them," Pippa said, her face darkened and she looked troubled. "I heard the news. You found a body down in the shelters."

"We're trying to identify him," Blake said. "He was a tall, dark and handsome young man with a limp. We think the body has been down there since the sixties."

Pippa looked troubled. "I'm sorry, Inspector. That doesn't ring any bells. Besides, my father wouldn't let me mix with what he thought were the riff-raff that lived around here."

"I can't imagine anyone cooping you up when you were younger," Blake said, giving her a conspiratorial smile. "You seem far too adventurous."

Pippa waggled her eyebrows. "You're a good judge of character, Inspector. My father was a terrible snob. He sent me to Birkenhead High School for Girls and hoped I'd marry well, if you know what I mean?"

"And he tried to keep you away from the local boys," Blake said.

"Which made them all the more alluring! Oh, the trouble I caused him, sneaking out at night, going to dances without telling him. I didn't roam the streets of this part of town, Inspector but I knew all the handsome lads, not your young man with a limp, though."

"What did your father make of Lewis Collins? You said you went out with him, last time we met."

"Not much. Lewis's dad was a jazz band leader. My father liked his music but I was destined to be a bank manager's wife or better!"

"Would any of your friends be able to help us identify this body?"

"I'm sure they would, Inspector, if they were still alive. Sadly, they've all passed on. I'm the last of them. The hill has repaid my love with good health."

"I see," Blake said, crestfallen. "And you used to sneak out to the dances around here…"

"Around here and all over, Inspector, St Patricks Church Hall, Wallasey, New Brighton. The furthest we went was Eastborough Hall in Eastham. I think it burnt down in the end. They were such great times. There were so many bands playing in the halls, Inspector, you really were spoilt for choice every weekend."

"I'm just wondering how someone might get a body down into the shelters, without being spotted."

"They were quite accessible in those days, Inspector. People dumped their rubbish in them all the time. The kids played in them. People got up to all sorts of mischief down there. I can't imagine the sight of someone heaving a heavy load, such as a body, into the shelter would raise any eyebrows."

"But the way I accessed the shelters was through a steep vent..."

"That's the emergency exit. There was a street level entrance on Brow Road."

"Thank you. If you fancy a little sleuthing or anyone mentions anything, just let me know," Blake said, handing her a card. Charlie sniffed at her walking boots.

"This chap seems a little too cute to be a police dog, Inspector," Pippa said, stooping and scratching Charlie's ear.

"Charlie's too ill-disciplined to be in the ranks," Blake said.

"Jack Russells are the bandits of the dog world, Inspector. Too independent-minded for their own good! Now, judging by your casual clothes and the little dog, I'm guessing that this is actually your day off, Inspector. I'll leave you to enjoy the rest of it without questioning me."

Blake watched her march off across the clearing again, then he looked down at Charlie. "You're a bandit, mate. Did you know that?"

**

We all have regrets in our lives, Jeff Blake mused but one of his biggies, he decided, would be ever letting a psychopathic serial killer have his mobile number. Somehow, Gambles had managed to get through so many times, that Jeff wondered if the man had a suitcase full of mobiles under his bed. Jeff had considered changing his number or just switching his phone off for a while but his agent might be calling about the book deal any time and he couldn't miss that. There was nothing for it but to phone Will for advice.

Jeff paused and composed himself before making the call; a kind of cold truce had fallen between them since Will had used Jeff's back garden to engineer a meeting with Laura Vexley. It had all gone horribly wrong and she'd sent her boyfriend Kyle Quinlan in her place. Jeff's heart sank at the implication that Quinlan knew where he lived.

Obviously, Jeff hadn't been best pleased about being drawn into Will's cunning plan to entrap Laura but he hadn't really been given any choice. In turn, Will was still furious that Jeff was writing a book about Josh Gambles. Having taken a breath, Jeff made the call.

A muffled curse answered followed by a loud purring. "Hello? Will?"

"Bloody cat," Will muttered. "Hi Jeff, sorry. Serafina is being …" the purring came back, obscuring Will's voice, "… affectionate… can't… arse in my face…"

"What?"

There was a thud followed by, "Oh Lord, that stinks," and footsteps. Clearly Will was outside now. "Sorry, Jeff. I'm having a spot of bother with Serafina. What was it you wanted?"

Jeff's mouth went dry. "Look I'm sorry to ring so late but I think I'm in trouble, Will. It's Gambles."

A loud snort of disgust made Jeff pull his head back from the phone. "Well you made that particular bed, Jeff, I guess you're going to have to lie in it."

"He keeps phoning me up…"

"I thought they were only allowed one phone call a week," Blake said.

"From a mobile. He keeps threatening me."

"How the hell did he get your number anyway? Jeez. This is what happens when you work with psychopaths, Jeff. You should have left well alone. I did warn you…"

"Okay, okay. As a matter of fact, the reason he's threatening me is because the book isn't exclusively about him. It's more about me."

"It's usually *all* about you, Jeff. No wonder he's

pissed off, he's found someone with a bigger ego than himself. Just phone the prison and tell them he's got a stash of mobiles. They'll raid his cell and confiscate them. It's not rocket science."

"I'm worried, Will. He was talking about friends on the outside..."

"The only friend he has on the outside is you and that's your fault," Blake snapped. "If you hadn't decided to write his stupid book..."

"There's Kyle Quinlan," Jeff interrupted. "What if Gambles asks him for a favour, eh? I won't stand a chance."

Will was silent for a moment. "Look, the last thing Quinlan wants is to get tangled up with Gambles again. Haven't you seen him on the TV? He's trying to disguise himself as a respectable businessman. Any association with a psycho serial killer is going to torpedo all his grand schemes. Thinking about it, maybe someone should leak that little bit of info to the media."

"Maybe I should talk to Quinlan then? He could persuade Gambles to leave me alone..."

"Do you remember the old saying, Jeff? Never wrestle with a pig, you get dirty and the pig likes it. If you go talking to Quinlan, you'll probably land yourself in deeper shit than you're in now, and Gambles will just love that. Trust me, Quinlan has no interest in you or Gambles. Just lie low and stay away from Quinlan or you'll regret it.

***

A sense of unease washed over Sammy. Things were unravelling. They'd discovered a body. How the fuck could that happen? He tried to reassure himself. Maybe it wasn't him. Maybe it was some old down-and-out who'd been trapped in there years ago. Somehow, Sammy knew he was wrong, though.

He swigged the coffee from his mug, and grimaced. It was cold; how long had he been sitting there just turning the same thoughts, the same memories over and over in his head? How could he make sense of how his world had shifted on its axis? For years, he'd carried on, ignoring the truth of what had happened, of what he was and now, it looked like everything was about to come tumbling down.

One thing was certain, Jensen would be wetting his pants over this, and a calm head was required. The last thing they needed was someone running to the police and blabbing. He might shutting up, if push came to shove.

But it all happened a long time ago. A very long time ago. Memories were distant and indistinct. Some witnesses had passed away in years gone by. The decades between him and what happened were his friend and he'd use them if he had to. But someone remembered. Sammy looked at the new letter:

I seen you that night. Murder!

The same paper, a big smiling frog in the bottom corner of the paper this time. Whoever sent these was deranged. Possibly dangerous, too. What did they want? The frustrating thing was he couldn't answer back. Were they just sending them to disturb him? The last letter had told him to confess. In a way, he kind of wished they'd wanted money. Not that he had any.

Sammy clenched his fist. He'd keep watching, looking out. Once he knew who was doing this. He'd bloody well show them.

CHAPTER 16

If Blake had been concentrating, he would have noticed the small pack of journalists camped outside HQ but his mind was on other things. Jeff's phone call had disturbed him for a start. The case had woken up memories of his mother and Jeff working with Gambles just made him see red again. That Jeff would have the nerve to phone him and ask for help was beyond belief. Maybe it was lack of sleep that was making him so touchy, but he was annoyed with Martin too. What was all that about, when he said that Kath had complained about Blake? It had just been a pretext to side-line him on this dead-end case.

"Detective Chief Inspector Blake, is it true that you've uncovered a body from the sixties over in Birkenhead?" A voice called.

Blake looked round and noticed the journalists for the first time. "What?" he muttered.

"Have you managed to identify the body yet?" Someone else said. Cameras and Dictaphones were being shoved towards him.

"Is it male or female?"

"Do you suspect foul play?"

"How long has it been down there?"

Blake held up his hands. "We've found the remains of a young man in his twenties. The body has been down there since the early nineteen sixties, we suspect. We believe that the young man walked with a limp due to a leg injury acquired some years before his death. He also wore a distinctive copper ring with the initials AG on it. It was a long time ago but if this jogs anyone's memory, please do get in touch via the usual channels. Thanks." He turned and entered the building without looking back. No doubt Martin would have something to say about impromptu news conferences but what was done was done.

***

Superintendent Martin didn't look at all amused as he sat back in his chair. Hannah Williams, the media consultant sat to one side of the Superintendent's desk, her face poker straight. "You didn't clear things with me or Hannah," Martin snapped, pointing a biro at Blake as though it was a dagger. "Just grandstanding in front of the press as usual…"

"With respect, sir, I didn't summon the journalists and they took me by surprise. I did the best I could under the circumstances."

"You could have kept silent and entered the building without comment. This was meant to be a low-key investigation but, no, once again, you have to turn it into a media circus. You've invited the public to contact us. Now we'll be swamped with calls from every seventy-year-old in Merseyside reliving their memories of the Swinging Sixties." Martin threw his pen down on the desk in disgust. "We just don't have the resource."

"There's no way we can identify this body without the help of the public, sir," Blake said. "Not within a respectable timeframe, anyway."

Martin opened his mouth to reply but Hannah cut in. "If I might make a suggestion, Superintendent," she said. "I think there's a way we can turn this to our advantage. If we play our cards right, it could be something of a PR coup."

"A PR coup, eh?" Martin said, the angry red fading from his cheeks. "Go on, weave this sow's ear into a silk purse for me, Hannah!"

Hannah flashed him a brief grin. "As you know, Sarah New has expressed a desire to personally thank Alex Manikas for saving her son. Jayden and his parents are coming over here this afternoon. What if we combine the two? Link the saving of the young lad with trying to establish the identity of the poor young man whose body was discovered."

Martin chewed the idea over. "It'd make them both seem like a victory before we start," he said at last. "I like it. It's going have a resource cost, though…"

"Well, it was always going to, really," Hannah said, looking apologetic. "Journalists love a mystery body. And a mystery body from the sixties, the heyday of the Beatles and the Cavern Club was always going to be like catnip to the press. Whether you announced it or not, one way or another, they would have been all over it."

"So you're saying we should harness that enthusiasm," Blake said.

"You're loving this, aren't you, Will?" Martin said. "Another chance to get in front of the camera…"

"To be fair," Hannah said, "Will seems to have quite an aversion to appearing in the media from what I've seen." She flashed him a huge grin. "No offence."

Blake couldn't help smirking. "None taken. I'm just glad someone has noticed at last."

"Which is why he's probably the best person to front this media offensive, with me co-ordinating, of course…"

"Me?" Blake said, glancing from Martin to Hannah.

Hannah raised her eyebrows. "You have media experience, Will. If we're to put out a request for help to the public, I can't think of anyone better suited. Can you?"

Blake winced a little. "I suppose not," he said,

reluctantly. "It might help us establish who this man is and how he ended up down there," Blake added. Although he didn't really understand why Hannah was supporting him so enthusiastically. Their last encounter had resulted in Blake being told to apologise to her. For all that Martin saw him as an attention-seeking lime-light addict, he detested being in front of the camera.

Martin rubbed his chin, slowly. "Okay," he said. "Let's go with it. Hannah can you schedule a conference? Liaise with Will and we'll get the details out to the press. Will, take Manikas and Kinnear to help you to begin with. And please, don't make me regret this."

As they walked out, Blake glanced over at Hannah. "Thanks," he said. "I think. Do you want me to send you the details of the case over when I get back to my desk?"

Hannah narrowed her eyes. "You could do or, how about we discuss them over a coffee after work?"

***

Josh Gambles sat in his cell, staring at the wall. Shouts echoed into his room from some distant altercation. Probably an argument over cigarettes or Spice. Who cared? They were lost souls, beasts fighting over scraps of illusory comfort. Imagine the sound truly tormented souls made, screaming for forgiveness that would never come. This place was an introduction to Hell, a warm-up act for the main event. This was nothing. Things could only get worse. He looked at the notepad covered in scribbled notes that lay beside him on the bed. "If I'm sorry, then I have to prove it, don't I? Deeds not words are what count," he muttered, scribbling in the pad. He would forgive Jeffrey anyway. Absolve him of all sin. Wasn't that what God wanted? Even those who had fallen furthest could be redeemed if they followed His example. Wasn't that right? Wasn't that what the letters he received told him? He could be redeemed. Gambles smiled and felt wrapped in a blanket of peace.

"Jeffrey Blake, I forgi..."

A prison guard rapping on the metal door interrupted Josh. "Stand away from the door," the gruff voice commanded.

Panic filled Josh as he stared down at the mobile on his bed. Before he could do anything, the door crashed open and a phalanx of officers burst in. The wave of bodies crushed Gambles to the hard floor and he could only lie there and watch the men pull his room apart, overturning his bed, rifling through his books and clothing.

One of them swept a clutch of phones from under his mattress. "I don't know how they got there," Josh said, feebly. "Somebody must have planted them..."

The men left as quickly as they had arrived, leaving Josh to piece his cell back together. Any feelings of peace had long gone, swept away by the tide of officers violating his room. His sadness and shock slowly sparked into anger and then fury as he slammed his mattress back on his bed and his books back on their shelf. Somebody hadn't planted them.

"But somebody ratted on me," he muttered at the sealed door, "and I know who that someone is. I was going to forgive you Jeffrey but I see that it's too late for that." Didn't God also say an eye for an eye?

***

A meeting room had been booked for Jayden and his parents to meet Alex Manikas. Clearly, they had expected maybe one or two people and a photographer rather than the audience of journalists and photographers that squashed into the small space. Jayden looked wide-eyed at the assembly and swallowed hard. He looked an incongruous figure in his Tranmere Rovers strip and black trainers. His father, stocky and dressed in sweatpants and hoodie, seemed equally taken aback. Sarah New flicked a strand of hair out of her red face. "If we'd known there was going to be so many people, we'd have got dressed up, Hannah," she whispered.

"I'm really sorry," Hannah said, smiling. "There

was a last-minute change and we need to make an important announcement. If it's any consolation, I think DC Manikas looks as nervous as you."

Alex adjusted his tie and collar as he stared at the pack watching them. "Do we need all these people here, sir?" he whispered to Blake.

"Don't worry, Alex, just smile and be nice to the lad. You don't have to make a speech or anything."

Hannah gave Blake a nod and he stepped forward. "Thank you everyone for coming to today's press conference. I promised that we'd give you more information on the body found in the Bidston shelter but we also felt it was important to use this moment to acknowledge the bravery of one of our fellow officers involved in the current investigation. I know Mrs New wishes to say a few words first..."

Sarah New stepped forward and gave Blake a strained smile. "I-I just wanted to say thank you to Alex... DC Manikas... for saving our son. He told us that you nearly fell when a ladder broke but you climbed down to help him and for that, we'll always be grateful." She turned and nodded to Jayden. "Come and say thank you, son."

Jayden edged forward and extended his hand. "Thank you, Mr Manikas."

Alex smiled and took his hand. Then he froze,

gripping the boy's hand and staring down in amazement at his fingers. Or rather at the copper ring on them. A ring bearing the initials AG.

CHAPTER 17

Blake assumed the press conference had gone well enough, once he'd managed to prise Jayden's hand out of Manikas' grip and sit him down. They'd been bombarded with questions. As Hannah had predicted, the press fell on the mystery of the unknown young man like flies on a cadaver.

"Inspector Blake, have you any theories about where the young man came from? Is he local?"

Blake could almost see the stories writing themselves as the questions were asked.

"You say he was fashionably dressed for the time, do you think he may have frequented nightspots such as the Cavern Club all those years ago?"

"Is the ring the symbol of some kind of secret society?"

By the end of the conference, Blake's head buzzed. He couldn't help noticing Jayden looking down, fixated on the ring on his finger and his father's face darkening with each question. As quickly as he could, he ushered Mr and Mrs New, and Jayden into a side room. Alex followed them in.

"What was all that about?" Terry New said before they had even sat down at a desk. He seemed troubled by something, but Blake couldn't work out what.

"The ring that we found on the body, Mr New," Blake said, glancing over to Jayden. "It's identical to the one your son is wearing."

Alex squatted by Jayden and lifted his hand. "It's a cool ring, Jayden," he said. "Where did you get it?"

"It's just a toy," Terry New said. "He probably found it somewhere…"

Jayden looked puzzled. "No I never, Dad," he said. "It was Grandads', wasn't it? That's why I wore it today, to help me be brave."

"I think we've had enough excitement for one day," Terry said, standing up again. "Come on, we're going home."

Sarah New bit her lip and clasped Jayden's hand. "Where did your grandad get the ring from, Jayden?" Alex said, keeping his voice low and calm.

Jayden smiled at him. "He was in a band. Like a rock band. Called…" Jayden frowned as he struggled to get the name right. "Arthur and the Galahads. Yeah… that's right…that's what the AG stands for."

"Right we're finished here," Terry said.

"I can't detain you, Mr New but it's pretty clear

that there's some connection, however tenuous between the body we found and your father or his band. We're going to have to look into that."

"It's just a coincidence, that's all," Terry said.

"Terry…" Sarah New began.

"DC Manikas, thank you for saving my son. I'm grateful," Terry said, speaking over his wife. "We're going now."

Blake watched as they walked off. Sarah New gave him one backward glance before the door shut. He turned to Alex Manikas. "Arthur and the Galahads."

"Arthur and the Galahads," Manikas replied.

***

CHAPTER 18

Quite how Blake found himself in the Jacaranda Club on Slater Street, he wasn't sure. It had been late, and Hannah Williams had appeared at his desk, reminding him about coffee. After a fruitless search on the internet for Arthur and the Galahads, and any possible variations, Blake had sent a dispirited Alex home. Blake wasn't quite as downhearted; there was still the fact that Terry New held some information. And surely a request for information about the band might flush out more facts, maybe even a couple of members if they were lucky. Tomorrow, Kinnear joined them and the phone lines would be jangling.

Blake had already decided to make an excuse and duck out of his meeting with Hannah, but when she appeared at his desk, the prospect of going home to the stench and racket of Serafina suddenly didn't appeal. It was almost eight and they quickly realised that many of the nearby coffee shops would be shut. Undeterred, Hannah had led him through Liverpool One and down Seel Street to the Jacaranda.

The street level of the club was a bar where Hannah settled quickly in a window seat. She gave a nod to a woman behind the bar who gave her a wave. "You come here often then?" Blake said, then felt himself blush. "Sorry, that sounded terrible, I..."

"Yeah, I'm a regular," Hannah said, grinning. "Some great bands play here and upstairs, you can buy records, even listen to them while you have a drink. I love it."

"So it wasn't the sixties connections, the Beatles playing their first gigs here, the fact that their first manager used to own it," Blake said, raising one eyebrow.

Hannah gave a smirk. "Maybe. What do you want to drink?"

"Just a flat white for me, please," Blake said; he never really got his head around the bewildering array of choice when it came to coffee.

"Okay," Hannah said, jumping up and going over to the bar.

Blake scanned the room. It was bright and airy, part pub, part café. In the hiatus between people going home from work and others turning up for a Friday night out, there weren't too many people in yet. A few students sat around laughing and chatting, maybe getting used to life away from home for the first time. Blake felt a protective warmth towards them and then a sting of sadness as he thought about the young man lying cold in the shelter for sixty years.

He would have been around the same age as these kids when he had his life so brutally stolen from him. The intervening years between his death and discovery only underlined the lost possibilities. Had he lived, he could have had grandchildren this age, possibly attending university in the city now.

Hannah returned, shaking him from his thoughts. "Listen," Blake said, clearing his throat and casting his eyes around the room. "I want to apologise before we start this…"

"Right," Hannah said, that playful smirk returning. "What for?"

"Well, I haven't always been as cooperative as I could be in the past…"

"You've been a pain in the arse," Hannah said, but her voice was light. "But no worse than many of the officers, better in lots of ways. You wouldn't believe some of the things I have to put up with on a daily basis. Anyway, I kind of get it with you."

"You do?"

"You've got Searchlight hanging like a millstone round your neck. Martin's always going on about your 'celebrity' status like you're courting publicity…"

"Believe me, I'm not."

"I know that, and Martin knows it, too, really.

It's as though people feel they have to follow the same old trains of thought, run along the same old furrows. So, yeah, I can imagine you get hung up about media engagement."

Blake paused as the coffees were brought over to the table. "It's a machine that gobbles you up and spits you out. I mean, we're using it for good but at the same time, it can do so much damage if you don't know what you're doing…"

"I like to think I know how to handle it," Hannah said. "Without being complacent. It can be a powerful tool for public involvement."

"I can't argue with that," Blake said. He looked at Hannah. "Look, why did you invite me here? I can't be your idea of good company. Are we celebrating a successful press conference?"

Hannah shrugged. "I dunno," she said. "Maybe I wanted to see what you were like out of your natural environment."

"What? You mean work?"

"Yeah," Hannah said. "You intrigue me. You've had an interesting life, there must be more to you than DCI Blake, policeman, though. I wondered what you did to relax."

Blake snorted. "Relaxation? Most of my time is spent trying to stop my cat from destroying reality. Or clearing up after my dog."

"So you have pets," Hannah said. "Already

you're more human."

"Jeez, thanks," Blake said, laughing. "They're more acquired pets. I'm not sure I'm an animal person. How about you? What do you do for kicks?"

"Music, reading, theatre," Hannah said. "The city is my playground."

"You sound like Batman," Blake said, finishing his coffee.

Hannah laughed. "And I never had you down as a joker."

"Look, I've got to go," Blake said, rising from his seat. "My cat is going through some kind of mid-life crisis and I should get back to her." He paused and flashed her a brief smile. "Thanks for the coffee. It was nice to get away from the office."

Hannah nodded, not showing any intention of moving on. "Any time, Will, any time."

***

Whether it was the coffee or the curious conversation with Hannah, Blake wasn't sure but his head whirled as he drove home. His mind drifted back to Laura. Their relationship had put him back on his feet after spending so many years like a crime-solving automaton. It was a tribute to how much she had built him up that he didn't quite come crashing down so hard when she left him. He could never forgive what he saw as her betrayal of him by returning to her abusive ex-husband Kyle Quinlan. It wasn't as though she was intimidated back into his arms; she made a rational choice to return to him, thinking she could never fit in with Blake's life. Maybe she was right. Even so, Laura still lurked in the back of his mind, making him suspicious of people's motives.

Hannah had said she was just trying to get to know him but what if she was playing some kind of office politics? Blake doubted that, really. He never indulged in backstabbing or undermining colleagues and he didn't imagine Hannah did either. She seemed to know how to enjoy herself at least. For a second, he wondered if she was single and then shut down that line of thought. It was just coffee, and she was curious about him. Nothing wrong with that; a good way to build team relations and get to know colleagues. He couldn't help hoping she'd suggest another drink some time, though. Maybe he'd do the suggesting.

The house was quiet but smelt like a dozen Tom cats had popped round and done their business in every corner. Serafina met Blake on the doorstep, twisting herself around his ankles and meowing incessantly. A note in the kitchen from Ian, his neighbour, told him that Charlie had been out for three walks that day as, when he came in, the place had been overrun with cats and it had driven him demented. In the end, Ian had put Serafina out and locked the flap.

Charlie was pleased to see Blake and scampered from his basket, tail wagging. Serafina rubbed up against Charlie, too. "What has got into you, girl?" Blake muttered, putting some food down for her. Serafina ignored the bowl but continued to wind herself between Charlie and Blake's legs until he was in danger of falling flat on his face. "There's something wrong, Charlie," Blake muttered. "Constantly meowing, always amorous, spraying everywhere, not very hungry. I think it may be the vets for her…"

Charlie wasn't listening, though. He was too busy enjoying the novelty of having access to Serafina's food bowl without the associated feline punishment.

CHAPTER 19

DC Andrew Kinnear was considering the best way to exact his revenge on Alex Manikas and Blake. He'd been answering the phone all morning and seemed to be the only one who had come in. Quite apart from Kath Cryer looking like she was sucking a wasp when she heard that Blake had snaffled him away from her, he'd promised his husband, Chris that he'd be home this weekend to spend some time with their daughter Niamh. Judging by the number of calls, he could sit here all day and people would ring to tell him all about their heady youth when Liverpool was the capital of rock n roll. Any other time, he would have found it fascinating. There seemed to be no end of people who wanted to reminisce about their days and nights dancing to live music. All of them were of the opinion that the body was of someone coming home from a night out.

Kinnear heard about bands he never knew existed, like The Remo Four, The Beatnicks, Kingsize Taylor, Rory Storm and the Hurricanes. He Googled Rory Storm and fell in love with the Greek god in the photograph. Andrew loved listening to people's life stories but right now, he had more pressing matters. Of course, there were a few jokers, too. One character called himself Ivor Biggun and Kinnear just hung up.

Kinnear didn't necessarily subscribe to the idea that the man was returning home from a night on the town. He may have been wearing a suit for work or for attending a funeral or a wedding. He could have been in court that day or had an interview or been out for a family meal. Or maybe he'd just proposed. But the tide of public opinion placed the victim at a dance or club on the night of his demise.

Some calls were informative but not particularly relevant to the actual identifying of the body. The phone rang again. "Merseyside Police, thanks for calling the information line. Can I take your name please?"

"I'd rather not give my name, if it's all the same to you," said a gruff voice. "I just wanted to say, it wasn't all like Austin Powers, groovy man, kind of stuff going on back then."

"I'm sorry, sir, you've lost me."

"Liverpool and Birkenhead back in the sixties were bloody rough. There were fights and all kinds of trouble between gangs. People got hurt on a regular basis."

"Right. Do you have specific information relating to the body found on Bidston Hill, sir?"

"I'm telling you, aren't I? The dance halls could

be terrible. Some of the guys in the bands were tough cookies, too, they had to be to fight off the jealous boyfriends or defend their instruments. Often the drummers were the really hard ones, they were fit, like."

"Drummers, right. Thank you, sir. That's been very helpful."

"Honestly, Liverpool back then was a dark, smoky city full of dockers and sailors and all kinds of reprobates. It was a dangerous place. If your dead man was all dressed up in a mohair suit, chances are he was coming back from the clubs over there and got rolled or something. I'm just saying, don't go thinking that it was all beer and skittles back in the day. Even the Beatles got into punch-ups and fights."

The next call chilled Kinnear to the bone.

At first, he thought it was a heavy breather. There was a moment of silence and a deep breath. "Hello? Merseyside Police, can I help you?"

The caller gasped as though they'd been holding their breath. "We didn't do it on purpose..." the voice stammered. Kinnear thought it sounded like an older man but it was muffled, as though he was covering the phone with something or holding it away from his face.

"I'm sorry, do you have some information about the body found on Bidston Hill?"

"It wasn't our fault," the voice said and then Kinnear heard sobs of grief before the line went dead.

***

There should have been someone on duty. That was Blake's initial thought as he arrived at the entrance to the shelter. He'd parked in the road at the north end of the hill and picked his way along the path through the trees until he came to the vent. Blue and white tape fluttered pointlessly in the cold November breeze but there was nobody standing guard. The vent lay open and gaping. Either there should be a body there to stop people going down or it should be filled in.

It was still early and he'd only seen a couple of dog walkers but it was only a matter of time before someone more adventurous risked their life exploring. He had been heading to the office but had decided to have one last look at the crime scene before it was sealed up again. With nobody at the top to summon for help, Blake wondered at the wisdom of going down. He was eager to get this case moving and hoped that giving the place where the body lay one last look would help. He glanced around to see if anyone was nearby. "Oh, what the hell," he muttered. He had dressed in his crime scene scruff anyway.

Last time he came down the vent, he'd been lowered on ropes but now he had to clamber on rusted iron ladders that creaked under his weight. He was a big man and the noises the old scaffold of iron was making worried him. With a sigh of relief, he planted his boots onto the wet ground below. For a moment he stood still, listening to the drip of water and letting his eyes grow accustomed to the dark a little. The light from above barely penetrated beyond the shaft and a wall of blackness waited for him just down the tunnel.

Pulling out his torch, he clicked it on, taking in the graffitied brickwork and slimy, littered floor. His boots sloshed through the water on the ground, the noise echoing around the tunnel. Last time he'd been here, other officers surrounded him. Now he was alone. Jayden must have stumbled and thrashed around in this place for hours. In the pitch black, it would be so easy to get lost, even now, Blake was keeping an eye on the shaft of light behind him. Luckily, the body had been close to the vent which would make sense, Blake thought if you were accessing the shelter from the street at the other side. This would be as deep as you could venture into the tunnels from the front.

The hole where the body had been for sixty years gaped at him as if inviting him to fill the vacancy. Blake shivered and tried to apply his mind to less fanciful thoughts. The tunnels were wide, which would make it easy to transport a body, maybe in a barrow or truck. Kenning had suggested that the victim was beaten up first, so it was possible that he was still semi-conscious before he died. Maybe he staggered up the tunnels, supported by the killer who brought him to this spot.

Blake shone his torch on the ragged line of bricks. It was a lot of effort to go to, sealing someone up like that. You'd have to want to hide them very well and you'd have to have been prepared beforehand. Cement, a trowel, the bricks themselves. He almost admired the lengths the killer had taken. It beat a shallow grave in the woods by a country mile.

A noise made Blake freeze. It was a scraping of a foot on stone and a slight splash. He wasn't alone. Spinning round, he flashed his torch down the passage in time to glimpse a dark shape vanish into one of the side tunnels.

"Hello?" he called. "I'm DCI Blake, Merseyside Police. You shouldn't be in here. This is a crime scene. Come out now."

Silence. Whoever it was had slipped up one of the tunnels. Blake pursed his lips. This is what happened when you leave a place unguarded. Anyone could slip in. and he did tell himself it could be anyone. Kids, or someone who was just curious about the shelter. Blake couldn't escape the feeling that he was being watched, though.

How would that be possible in the dark? Blake shivered again. He shuffled forward, keeping his torch beam steady. "You need to leave this place immediately," he called. In the distance, he thought he heard the splashing of feet in water as though someone was running back into the complex of tunnels.

"Jeez!" He muttered. This was insane. They could become totally lost or fall and hurt themselves badly. Blake didn't want to be responsible for another Jayden New. He couldn't leave them. Striding forward, he tracked his torch down each side tunnel. The trouble was, he couldn't see what lay ahead of him and had to keep swinging the light back to his front. His torch, although strong, only illuminated a third of the tunnel, if that and whoever was hiding was out of range.

It was pointless. He could play chase with whoever it was all day long and never catch them. The best bet was to head back to the entrance and summon help. There was only one way out, after all. All he had to do was wait until they came out. He turned and something swished through the air in front of him, a stick or cane, maybe. A burning pain spread from his wrist up to his arm and he watched in horror as his torch went spinning into the shadows, its light vanishing the moment it hit the hard ground. Blake was plunged into a smothering blackness.

Sensing that his attacker was nearby, he flailed

around, blindly, with his fists, hoping to keep them at bay. Splashing feet danced around him and he spun to try and face them. Then the steps hurried away, leaving Blake panting for breath and cradling his wrist. It was then that he realised he wasn't sure which direction the exit shaft lay.

***

When Sammy was a kid, he used to love going to the matinee performances of Westerns at the cinema. There were so many of them, all gone now, turned into bingo halls, then supermarkets, then pulled down for housing. He used to love trying to bunk in for free, sneaking past the usherettes and concierge and hiding in the dark. The thrill of nearly being caught was almost more entertaining than the films. He always remembered those movies in which the cowboys had formed a circle with their wagon trains and the Indians were circling them. At some point the Indians would withdraw and someone would declare that it was 'quiet... too quiet.' This foreshadowed a cataclysmic attack that the heroes only manged to fend off at great cost.

That phrase stuck in his mind now. Initially he'd seen policemen knocking on doors, combing the area and talking in groups around the hill. It was strangely reassuring for him because he could see that they didn't have a clue what they were looking for. He felt safe.

Now, though, he couldn't see a copper anywhere and all he had heard was the request for information on the local radio. Somewhere out of sight, the investigation was happening. People he didn't know about might be phoning in, giving tenuous but useful leads, a forensics team would be analysing the body they found. Inch by inch, they'd be working their way towards him.

He hadn't had another letter, either which made him more uneasy than if he'd had a whole sack of them. What was the writer up to? Maybe they'd just decided to go to the police. Somehow, he thought not. Whoever sent those letters wasn't following normal patterns of logical thought. Somehow, they wanted to be part of the story, an instrument of his... his what? Salvation? Perhaps. Maybe he was reading too much into the letter that told him to confess. On the other hand, surely if the writer had gone to the police, they'd be banging on his door by now.

If the letter-writer had seen what he'd done, they'd be a valuable witness to the police. On the other hand, they wrote letters with bee stickers on them, so maybe not. Plus it was a long time ago and the decades were his friend...

Sammy smiled. Maybe he didn't need to circle the wagons just yet.

CHAPTER 20

The phone rang but Kinnear pointedly ignored it. Alex Manikas, just about to leave, looked at it. "Andrew," he muttered.

Kinnear folded his arms. "What? Running off already? You've only just got here. D'you know the grief I'm getting from Chris for being here today? You answer it."

"I've got to go and have another crack at Suzi Elston, see if her brother had a limp and was in a band..."

"That call could be important," Kinnear said, with raised eyebrows and arms still tightly crossed.

Rolling his eyes, Manikas reached for the phone. "Okay, okay, I'm sorry. No need to be so... hello? Merseyside P..."

"Wayne Prosser," said a creaky voice.

"I'm sorry, sir? Can you say that again?"

"Wayne Prosser, that's who you should be looking for. He liked pretty boys, he did, and he wasn't always too gentle with them."

Manikas scribbled the name down. "And can I take your name, sir?"

The line went dead and Manikas threw the pen on the pad. "What is the point of that? Just say a name and then hang up?"

"Welcome to my world," Kinnear said, narrowing his eyes. "You better bring back two packets of Jammy Dodgers and some good intel, Alex or you're toast."

Manikas grinned, crumpled up the note and threw it at Manikas. "How about you check this name out, instead of twiddling your thumbs here?"

"Cheeky," Kinnear muttered as he unfolded the paper to look at the name. He considered rolling it into a ball again and throwing it back at Manikas' retreating back but instead he typed the name into Google. There were a number of references to a Liverpool music manager in the sixties before it degenerated into Linked-in pages for Australian businessmen or builders in Bristol with the name Wayne or Prosser but not both. Kinnear clicked on the first link which brought him to the Mersey Sound Madness website. It looked to be an online archive of interviews with notable and less well-known people who were active in the music scene during the sixties. Obviously, there were plenty of links to the Beatles, Gerry and the Pacemakers, and Cilla Black but Kinnear noticed a few names he'd heard mentioned in calls yesterday. The first was an interview with someone called Oliver Kline who had been in a band called Olly and the Twisters.

'Wayne Prosser offered us a residency in Hamburg and we were made up but when we looked into it, we got a bit worried. Prosser had a bit of a 'reputation' shall we say? And people warned us not to go with him. I don't want to speak ill of the dead, but we all knew he had underworld connections. The way he died wasn't exactly peaceful. Anyway, some other band went instead of us, I forget who but they didn't do very well and came back pretty quickly. I wish I could remember their name. They weren't very good, but they all had these posh mohair suits and wore identical rings."

Kinnear held his breath and bookmarked the page, searching further for any mention of Wayne Prosser or the band.

"Anyone who went with Wayne Prosser expected a certain amount of harassment from him, especially if they were young and good looking. It was common knowledge that 'Wayne liked the pretty boys.' Times were different then and it was never talked about. People were embarrassed to admit that Wayne had come on to them. Of course, some guys gave him a black eye for it, but he never held a grudge."

"And some probably reciprocated," Kinnear muttered under his breath. He knew how hard his adolescence had been as he grew to understand himself and even in these more enlightened times, he encountered prejudice and bigotry. What must it have been like when homosexuality was illegal? From the sound of it, Prosser was predatory, but the attitudes of the day enabled that, clamping a wall of silence around the whole thing. Prosser would have been in deep trouble if someone had gone to the police but in all likelihood, they'd bring trouble on themselves too. So it all stayed hush-hush.

There was another reference to Prosser in a blog published by a man called Brian Wise. From what Kinnear could glean, Wise had worked on his PhD in Popular Culture at Liverpool John Moore's University, focusing on the Sixties Merseybeat Phenomenon and its Contribution to a New Northernism Movement. Kinnear wasn't really sure what that meant but Wise had published his thesis online and there was a paragraph about Prosser.

'Some of the self-styled managers of these Merseybeat bands met with great to moderate success, securing their bands a range of opportunities from residencies at holiday camps to recording deals. Others were less effective. Wayne Prosser had a constantly changing roster of groups, some quite good and others who looked good but could barely play. Prosser, a gay man in a tough, Northern city, lived outside of the standard norms of the time. Pushed into a hinterland of criminality, he is said to have

done business with the Kray twins and was certainly involved in illicit activity around Liverpool...' Kinnear skimmed through the listings of Prosser's crimes until he came to another section. 'In 1975, Prosser was found stabbed to death in an alleyway down the side of a nightclub. Police arrested a rent boy for the murder but there was some suspicion that his death had been arranged by a rival local gang, unhappy with Prosser dealing drugs in their territory.' As he read on, his eyes widened.

***

The house in Curzon Park Road, didn't look any more inviting to DC Alex Manikas than it had the first time he visited. He'd driven into the road from the opposite end and parked some distance away so as to avoid the watchful eye of Mrs Gloria Parsons. Now he stood at the front door again and knocked. Suzi Elston looked about as pleased to see Alex as he'd expected.

"Look, I'm sure this is harassment of some kind. I've told you I have no information, why can't you just leave me alone?"

"I'm sorry, Ms Elston, I was all prepared to strike you off our list but my boss told me to have one more go. Just give me something to write up in my report and I promise I'll never bother you again." He gave her the little boy lost look he used to use on his mother when he knew he was pushing it.

She paused, weighing Alex up. "Come in then, but I'm telling you I don't know a thing and my memory is terrible."

The house was neat and tidy inside, if dated. Like the homes of many long-term residents, the older features remained but had modern fittings superimposed on them. A stairlift marred the old, rather grand banister and stairs and they went into a room with a two-bar electric fire stuffed in the fireplace. Suzi settled in an old flowery armchair and pointed at a matching sofa for Alex to sit on. The curtains were thick and old ornaments cluttered the shelves. There was one picture of a woman who Alex took to be Suzi's mother, Violet. There were no pictures of Sidney Elston at all. "What do I call you? Detective? Inspector?"

"I'm just a lowly constable," Alex said, blushing a little, more at his attempt at false modesty than anything else. "You can call me Alex, if you want. Or detective Constable if you don't."

"Alex. That's a good name." Suzi gave him a brief smile, those dark eyes glittering at him. "Did she tell you tales of murder, Alex?"

"I'm sorry?"

"I saw Gloria enticing you into her house. Did she tell you I'd poisoned my mother?"

Alex smiled. No point lying. "She did ask me in for tea and biscuits. She didn't actually say you poisoned your mother." He shifted on the sofa. "She did say something about Violet Elston not having a daughter…"

Suzi rolled her eyes. "My mother always had a daughter. Gloria Parsons doesn't know everything. She only moved into this street in the mid-fifties. I wasn't here then."

Alex nodded. "I see," he said, not really seeing at all but conscious that he was treading on thin ice by probing into this woman's past. "You lived somewhere else, then?"

"I don't think I really started living until I came back here to look after my mum," Suzi Elston sighed. "I had a difficult childhood and I don't really like talking about it. Take it from me, Alex, Gloria Parsons has it all wrong. Once I was able to, I came home. Mum wasn't well and Dad had passed away, so I did what any loving daughter would."

"I'm sorry," Alex said, giving her a sheepish grin. "I shouldn't pry. I'm here to talk about Sidney. Gloria did say that he didn't get on with his father."

Suzi paled a little at the mention of her father. "Father was a tyrant with a hatred of women, Alex. He kept my mother firmly in her place and me? Well, I wasn't allowed to exist, hived off and put out of mind. My brother missed me terribly, I know that, but father wouldn't have me in the house."

"That must have been very painful for you all."

"He tried to make my brother, Sidney into what he thought was a 'real man.' Cold showers, morning runs, camping, long walks in the hills..." Suzi drifted off for a moment. "He quite liked the walks in the countryside," she said, quietly. "He could walk ahead of his father, leave him behind until the old man would catch-up, red-faced and panting. Sidney half hoped he'd die of a heart attack but he never did."

"It's a wonder he didn't run away sooner."

"Sidney loved his mother, though, you see? He worried about what father might do to her if he wasn't around. That's what held him here."

"Your father was violent? Was that what made Sidney finally run away?"

Suzi looked troubled as she stared into the past, her old, wrinkled face twitching. "Maybe he thought if he was away from home, then the arguments about him might stop. His father did beat him, I know that much."

"Can I ask, did Sidney have any serious injuries as a result of these attacks or any other trauma? Broken limbs or anything like that?"

Suzi paused to think, then shook her head. "No.

Nothing like that."

"Only, the body we found had an old injury that would have left him with a permanent limp," Alex added.

"No, my brother never had any kind of injury like that, Alex. That wasn't to say the beatings weren't bad. I think he ran away to find me, too."

"So, you saw Sidney after he was declared missing?"

"Yes," Suzi said. "Down in London. I'd see him a lot down there. We shared a flat. But we drifted apart and I saw less and less of him. He's gone now, I'm sure of it."

Alex thought for a moment. He didn't need to go on; if Sidney Elston never had a broken leg, then it wasn't his body they'd found in the shelter. But he felt as though he should listen to Sidney's story rather than cut things short. "Why didn't you tell your mother? She was beside herself, convinced that Sidney had been murdered. It must have been torment for her."

"It might have been Alex, and I know Sidney felt that, too, but he could never go back and if he'd told her he was alive, then she would have spent all her time searching for him." Suzi looked deep into Alex's eyes. "But my mother is dead now and I know Sidney is at peace, too. Is someone still a missing person if nobody misses them anymore, Alex?"

CHAPTER 21

For a few moments, Blake stood still, collecting his thoughts and letting the pain in his arm subside. The darkness was total, it pressed against his eyes until he felt he had to close them. He could still hear footsteps receding into the distance. His attacker had duped him into spinning round until he wasn't sure which way he was originally facing. If he wandered off in the wrong direction now, he could spend hours trying to get back to the exit.

He pulled out his phone. The lantern on it wasn't brilliant but it reflected nicely off the ground water and soon he recovered his torch. It was broken but Blake realised that he had walked forward along the main corridor that led to the vent before he was attacked. He was pretty sure he had turned right round when the stick hit his wrist, so the torch had spun off back towards the vent and the exit.

Slowly, he inched his way along the tunnel. He tried walking a little faster but stumbled over stray bricks and old cans. The last thing he wanted was to fall flat on his face here and knock himself out. Eventually, he could see the light filtering down the shaft in the distance. Something moved up there. An indistinct figure climbed up-wards.

Blake tried to hurry towards it, the water swirl-ing around his feet, old carrier bags snagging him and making him stumble. He got to the foot of the ladder in time to look up into the dazzling light that shone down from the exit. His attacker had escaped.

***

By the time Blake had waited for back-up, re-ported what had happened, got to HQ and cleaned himself up, Manikas was back from Suzi Elston's. He decided not to mention the assault to Kinnear and Manikas, he didn't want to cloud their thinking. His attacker could have been any random stranger caught trespassing in the shel-ter. Besides, although it was bruised, his wrist had almost stopped aching. Unaware of Blake's adventures in the shelter, DC Andrew Kinnear had collated as much visual and written in-formation as he could about the sad history of Wayne Prosser. Alongside the picture of the corpse in the shelter, he'd placed a grainy photo-graph of a handsome young man with black, wavy hair and dressed in a dark suit. The ring on his finger was just visible but no detail was obvious.

When Blake walked into the room, he stopped dead and stared at the display. "Jeez, Andrew, you have been busy."

Kinnear smiled. "It was a tip-off on the phone, sir. Might have wrapped up the case."

"He's been cutting and pasting like he was making a Christmas card for his mum, sir," Manikas said, giving Kinnear a sly grin.

Kinnear stood by the board and pointed at a photograph of a skinny man in his sixties, leering at the camera, dressed in a fur coat, his fingers dripping with gold. "Meet Wayne Prosser, crook, swindler, friend of the Kray twins and self-styled music empresario."

"Empresario," Alex said, raising his eyebrows. "You swallowed a dictionary, mate?"

"Had Alphabetti Spaghetti for dinner, Alex," Kinnear said, bowing slightly but not letting him put him off his stride. "There are lots of stories about Prosser, suffice to say he had a reputation as someone you wouldn't do business with unless you were desperate. He came up from London around 1962 when the whole Merseybeat phenomenon was at its height..."

"Merseybeat?" Manikas said. "Is that like the Beatles and that?"

Blake nodded. "The Beatles were part of it but there were hundreds of bands active in and around Liverpool..."

"Between 350 to 500 bands, sir," Andrew said,

with a grin at being able to give Blake a fac-toid for once. "Believe me, all these phone calls today have been an education. Bands routinely split and merged into new ones but those that stood out were snapped up by local managers. Of course, once the sharks down in London smelt blood, or hard cash, they came up here looking for young people to exploit."

"So, Prosser was a known criminal by the time he came up to Liverpool, Andrew?" Blake said.

"Yes, sir, as I say, he had a loose association with the Firm. He was gay and had convictions for cottaging. He dabbled in drugs, too. Ended up getting stabbed to death. Later, rumours sur-faced about his connection with the disappear-ance of Ernie Hughes, AKA Arthur King, lead singer of..."

"Arthur and the Galahads," Blake guessed, star-ing in wonder at the picture Kinnear had found. "So our dead man could well be Ernie Hughes. He was one of the mispers you pulled from the files, Alex, well done."

"He was next on the list, sir," Alex said.

"What were the rumours about Prosser and Ernie Hughes, Andrew?"

"Arthur and the Galahads were managed by Prosser. He was a sucker for a pretty face, the story goes that he made a pass at Ernie Hughes and Hughes threatened to go to the police."

"So the stakes were high for Prosser," Blake said. "If the police had listened to Ernie Hughes, then Prosser could have been jailed."

Kinnear nodded. "The rumour has it that he did away with Ernie and hushed it up."

"And that's it?" Manikas said, sounding a little too hopeful. "Case closed?"

"We need more evidence than this," Blake said. "The ring on the body suggests that it was a member of the Galahads or someone associated with them. But there's no proof of that or that it's Hughes. We need to establish the identity of the body beyond reasonable doubt. Alex, what's the verdict on the other missing person?"

"Sidney Elston, sir? His sister says she met up with him down in London a few times, but they lost touch. So in terms of him being missing, she's next of kin now that her mother is dead. She didn't really consider him missing. Plus, Elston never had a serious leg injury of any kind, so no limp. Case closed; I suppose."

"You don't sound all that convinced Alex," Blake said.

"I dunno, sir, I feel like I'm missing something, but I don't know what it is. The neighbour was going on about how Sidney Elston didn't have a sister, but she clearly exists and the mother acknowledged her before she died. I can see a family resemblance..."

"It sounds like we can shelve that for now, as intriguing as it sounds. We're going to be stretched enough looking into the Galahads. You had a third person missing..."

"Robert Pearce, sir, never came back from a Liverpool/Leeds match in 1966," Alex said. "Looking through his file, it says he was under sixteen cross-country champion for his school, so I don't think he fits the bill in terms of leg injuries."

"Let's focus on Ernie Hughes, lead singer of Arthur and the Galahads, then. Terry New seemed very keen to shut down any discussion about his father but, if Jayden is telling the truth, we do know he was a member of the band. This is great work, though, Andrew, well done. A real breakthrough."

"Thanks, sir. It took some digging but Brian Wise's blog was buried quite deep. Plus it was a tip-off on the phone that gave me the name. I'd say someone who was around at the time, from the sound of their voice."

"We're going to need more people to cover all these people ," Blake muttered. "Or at least some input from Kath and Vikki. I'll talk to them and Martin in the morning."

Kinnear looked sheepish. "No disrespect, sir, but Kath wasn't best pleased when I came over onto this case..."

"We'll cross that bridge when we come to it, Andrew," Blake said. "Let's regroup on Monday and see what we've got, shall we?"

CHAPTER 22

It was a rare moment of peace; coffee, a Sunday newspaper, voices on the radio quietly mumbling away, without demanding any of Blake's attention. There was even a break in the clouds and he found himself sitting in the front room armchair, bathed in a pool of morning sunlight that shone through the window. Warmed by the sun and deprived of sleep after Serafina's nightly antics, Blake had begun to doze. When the phone startled him to wakefulness, he reflected ruefully that he should have known it wouldn't last.

To his surprise, it was the vet. "I'm sorry to ring you today but Serafina's condition has been puzzling me all weekend and I think I may have an answer. So, I considered the possibility that the operation to spay her hadn't been totally successful Sometimes ovarian tissue is accidentally left behind and so the cat continues to come into season and attract mates."

"But if that was the case, Serafina coming into season would have been a regular thing, right? And in the years that I've known her, I've seen nothing like this."

"Exactly, which would suggest that it's not a botched spaying. If it was psychological, then I'm not sure she'd be attracting Toms in the way she is. Put simply, tell me, has she had any kind of exposure to hormones?"

"How do you mean?"

"Like hormone creams or powders of any kind? If she'd ingested anything like that, it might provoke a response like the one you're observing."

"I don't know."

"You aren't using oestrogen at all are you?"

"What? Me? No!" Blake flushed red on the phone. He remembered the vet from their last encounter and how he had almost thought she was a sixth former she looked so young.

"Your partner?"

"I don't have a partner," Blake said.

"Does Serafina have access to anyone's house who might be using oestrogen creams or gels? Menopausal women or maybe someone transitioning genders?"

"Honestly I don't know. She wanders off during the day sometimes. I don't know where she goes."

"It's worth checking that first."

"Listen, are you certain about this?" Blake said, wondering if it was some kind of wind-up. "There isn't *some* kind of physical explanation for the change?"

"I've thought long and hard, Mr Blake and spoken to colleagues," the vet said, sounding slightly defensive. "I mean, I *can* book Serafina in for a physical examination if you want, but it's quite intrusive and if we suspect she might be partially spayed, we'll have to operate again just to find out. I think that would be a pointless exercise and not in her best interests when the cause is likely to be something else entirely."

"I understand," Blake said, his stomach sinking. "I suppose I was just hoping for a simpler explanation. I mean, how on earth am I going to find out who in his neighbourhood is using oestrogen cream? What do I do? Send out a questionnaire? Knock on doors?"

"It's a tricky one, Mr Blake, I'll grant you that," the vet said. "Am I right in thinking that you're a policeman?"

"Yes," Blake muttered, wondering where this was going.

"Well then, you'll have the requisite skills to solve this mystery more than most, won't you? Let me know how you get on."

Blake hung up and stared out of the window. "Jeez." He contemplated trying to settle back in his chair, but the call had presented him with a new problem to consider. A flash of movement in the front garden caught his eye. Serafina had just scurried under the bushes. "Now where are you off to?"

The words of the vet echoing in his mind, Blake sidled out of his front door and squatted on the step. He wanted to see Serafina but not get so close that she'd be distracted by him. The tip of her tail slid into the bushes and Blake crept after her as she padded up the road. It felt strangely exciting, stalking a natural-born hunter like Serafina and Blake was amazed that she hadn't spotted him. She seemed focused on her journey, walking with purpose along the walls that shielded the big houses from clear view.

Suddenly, she sprang up onto one of the walls and Blake's heart sank. She was going to disappear into a front garden and he'd lose her. Instead, though, she bounded along the top of the wall. Blake envied her grace and agility and then cursed as she vanished over the other side.

Blake was a tall man, but he wondered if he'd manage to pull himself up, so that he could see where she had gone. Grunting he heaved himself onto the top of the wall and looked down into a well-kept garden. Serafina had scurried across the lawn and he just saw her disappear into the house through an open window.

A scream startled Blake and he glanced down to see a woman staring back at him in horror. She wore leggings and a sports bra and was kneeling on a yoga mat in the garden just beneath him.

"I'm sorry, I..." Blake stammered, putting out a hand to reassure her, overbalancing and falling headlong into a bush beneath the wall. He gasped for breath as he hit the ground, the foliage only partly breaking his fall. Sharp twigs scratched his face and snagged his hair and clothes.

The woman jumped up and ran for the house. "Steve! Steve!"

Bleeding and covered in dirt from the border, Blake staggered after her. "Please, madam, I'm sorry, I just wanted to..."

The front door slammed and Blake was left panting on the gravel driveway in front of the house. "Shit," he muttered.

The door swung open and a man with short, greying hair and horn-rimmed glasses stood on the step. He held a cricket bat. "My wife is calling the police. You'd better clear off now. Or I'll... I'll..."

"Woah, look I'm sorry," Blake said, trying to recover his senses. The scratches on his face stung and he was distracted by the sight of Serafina sitting on the windowsill inside the house staring out at him. He knew it was his imagination, but her eyes seemed to be laughing at him. "It's my cat," Blake stammered, pointing at the window. But Serafina had vanished. "I was looking for my cat..."

"And you just happened to follow her over the

very tall wall into the garden where my wife was practising her yoga wearing next to nothing," the man said, wryly. "Sure…"

"It's sounds crazy but it's true," Blake said, wiping blood from his face. "If you go inside, you'll find my cat…"

"I'm staying right here, pal, until the police arrive. So you'd better push off."

"Okay, okay, I'm going but can I ask… does your wife use oestrogen cream?" Blake felt himself shrivelling inside. If there was ever a time to ask such a question, this was not it. Plus it made him sound deranged.

"What?" the man hissed, raising the bat.

"Or gel," Blake stammered. "I think you can get it in gel form too…"

"That does it," the man lunged forward, and the bat hummed over Blake's head. Blake staggered backwards, raising his arm to defend himself. It clipped his already aching wrist, sending a lightning bolt of pain up to his shoulder.

"Okay, okay, I'm going," Blake snapped. "I'm sorry, just have a look around your house for my cat. You'll see I'm telling the truth."

"You can see if *they* believe your story," the man hissed through gritted teeth, nodding towards the front gate. Two uniformed officers hurried along the drive towards Blake. Just beyond them,

Serafina sat on the top of the wall, licking her paw and watching the fun.

***

One of Pippa Fearon's greatest delights in life was to eavesdrop and watch people without their knowledge. Through her love of Bidston Hill she knew exactly where to hide when she was spying on people. There were all kinds of thick bushes or rocky outcrops one could stand behind and just listen. Unlike many her age, her hearing was sharp. She'd seen them all in her time, lovers having a tiff, lovers making up, youngsters buying and selling drugs, husbands confessing to wives, even the most mundane conversations could prove fascinating. If she was of a criminal turn of mind, she probably could have hacked any number of online bank accounts just by noting down passwords and the answers to security questions that people bawled down their phones in public. It was quite amazing just how much people did give away about themselves when they thought nobody was listening.

Two people she kept a close eye on were Gary Jensen and Sammy Treadwell. She hadn't seen them together for a very long time but recently they'd taken to meeting under the sails of the windmill. It was a clever place to talk if you didn't want to be overheard because the land around the mill was clear and open. No bushes to hide behind. That would have made it difficult for most people to spy on them, but Pippa was no ordinary person. Her status and intimate relationship with this small outcrop had earned her a place on the Bidston Hill Preservation Society's board until she tired of their endless meetings and minutes and procedure. Her split with them, as with so many in her life had not been amicable but she took a secret, perverse pleasure in knowing that, despite their insistence on policies and rules, none of them remembered that she held a spare set of keys for the windmill. So it was a piece of cake to let herself into the windmill, sit up in the eaves of the mill and let their darkest secrets drift up to her.

Her father had told her to steer clear of Sammy Treadwell many, many years ago, when she was a teenager. Treadwell was a thug, her dad had told her. Gary Jensen was just a fool. If she saw them, she always liked to listen-in on what they were talking about. It was most illuminating.

Despite all the excitement on the hill, she noticed Jensen huffing and puffing his way up the slope towards the windmill. He didn't give her a second glance, so she hurried ahead of him and got into position in the mill just in time. Meeting on a Sunday morning was odd because there were more people up on the hill then. This must be important. Their voices were muffled but Pippa could make out most of what they said. Jensen was almost shouting at the top of his reedy voice.

"It's on the bloody radio and telly, Sammy! Someone will say something!"

"I told you, just act stupid, that should come natural to you," Sammy said, his gruff voice an octave or two lower. "You've nothing to worry about."

"But what we did…"

"We did *nothing*, Gary. *Nothing*. Christ, you can't even remember what you had for breakfast, let alone anything that might have happened sixty years ago. Get a grip."

"I can't sleep. I keep thinking about it…"

"Look, Prosser is dead. Nobody can point the finger at anyone it was so long ago. It's all sorted. Now go home and have a snooze on that bloody recliner of yours. Take a couple of pills. And don't bring me up here again until this has all blown over, got it?"

Up in the darkness of the mill, Pippa Fearon smiled quietly to herself. Perhaps she should make the authorities aware of this development. After all, as a good citizen, it was her duty. Or perhaps she should keep it to herself for now. See what happened next. She hadn't known so much excitement on the hill in a long time.

CHAPTER 23

PC Mark Robertson poured hot water into three mugs and savoured the smell of coffee that drifted up with the steam. He'd recognised Will straight away of course and knew that nothing untoward was going on. The man with the cricket bat had taken some reassuring that Blake wasn't some kind of pervert.

"To be honest, sir, I was one step away from arresting him for assault," Mark said, handing Blake the hot drink. They had retired to Blake's kitchen once they'd calmed the irate couple down.

Blake took the mug and flexed his other arm, wincing slightly. "Nah," he said. "Couldn't blame him, really, a big ugly fella like me leaping over his garden wall while his wife was in the garden. They're pretty new to the area so didn't recognise me."

"So, run it by me one more time, sir, about the cat," said PC Julie Irwin, the other officer who had come to Blake's rescue.

"The vet is convinced that Serafina has access to some kind of oestrogen cream. It's pretty potent stuff for her, apparently, given her body weight. Long story short, it's making her randy as hell and bringing all the Toms to our yard."

"Not conducive to a good night's rest, I'll bet, sir" Irwin said and sipped her coffee and hiding a smirk.

Robertson leaned forward in his chair. "Could you keep the cat in quarantine for a few days, sir? See if the stuff wears off. If she's regularly topping up the supply from somewhere, that might break the link."

"Maybe," Blake said. "Serafina is a bit of a force of nature. I'd feel a bit cruel locking her up like that and I wonder if it would stop the cats' chorus outside from rocking up each night."

"Worth a try, though, eh, sir?" Irwin added.

"Absolutely," Blake said. "But I worry what'll happen when I release her. Will she just go back to the source and the whole thing starts again?"

"What about a leafleting campaign, sir?" Irwin said. "Asking people to make sure their medications are locked away. You could knock up a flyer on the computer and get some printed. I think you can even pay for them to be distributed."

"That would beat lurking in people's shrubbery hands down," Blake said, with a grin. "Although I'd have to think about the wording carefully."

***

Clearly Will's idea of phoning the prison and telling them that Gambles had been calling him on

172

a mobile device had worked because there hadn't been a squeak from the serial killer again. But Jeff Blake couldn't relax. Gambles had got inside his head, somehow.

The manuscript of the book was with his agent and he knew that if he started faffing around with it or changing anything while she was looking at it, she'd go mad. The trouble was, Jeff was a tinkerer. In the past, he'd mess about with chapters and rearrange things while he waited, so that what he'd sent the agent bore no resemblance to his most recent draft. "What's the point in me suggesting edits if you're looking at a different manuscript, Jeff?" And Jeff had to admit that she did have a point. Plus, this draft would have gone off to editors, so he had to be strong.

Unfortunately, the act of deliberately not looking at the book, put him on edge and made him fidgety. In his mind, he ran over the sections with Gambles in them, rewrote them, changed things until all he had was Gambles' voice bouncing around his skull. On top of that, for some reason he couldn't explain, he hadn't deleted the threats left by Gambles on his voicemail. Instead, he listened to them over and over until each word was imprinted on his mind.

He'd taken himself for a walk, wandering around Port Sunlight, even past Will's house and along the shore. He nearly called in but thought on balance that all he'd get was a lecture about the wisdom of working with Gambles. In all like-lihood, Will would be at work anyway; he never seemed to be anywhere else. Of course, the house was just as much his as Will's. It had belonged to their mother, Will just occupied it. At one point, Will had looked like he was going to sell-up. Jeff would have welcomed the money; the rent from his flat in London covered his costs here but he wasn't exactly living it up. He made a mental note to tackle Will about either selling the house or buying Jeff and their sister out. It wasn't like Will was short of cash, he worked all the time and rarely went out. He must be loaded. He should be paying them some kind of rent.

It was late now, Jeff was weaving his way home from the Rose and Crown, having decided to sink a few pints and a tot of whiskey to help him sleep. A light drizzle had settled over the Wirral and the pavements glistened in the street-lights. Jeff shivered and pulled his jacket tight as he walked. To his left, Mayer Park sat, shrouded in darkness. Only a few weeks ago, it had been crowded with families watching the Bonfire Night firework display. Now it lay cold and silent. Anyone could be stalking along after him, their feet making no sound on the soft grass. Tracking him.

Jeff increased his pace which made him feel more nervous. Soon, he'd left the park behind and come to the shops. He distracted himself with memories of this place. When he was a kid and travelling from Eastham to the grammar school just up the road, this used to be a thriving little village with a supermarket, a newsagent, a butchers and a green grocer's store. He remembered a fab cake shop that made all their own stuff. There was a big DIY store on the corner where he remembered his dad randomly buying a wheelbarrow. Now it seemed to be alternating hairdressers and coffee bars with a few estate agents thrown in to break up the pattern. How many nail bars did one town need?

Jeff remembered Saturdays when they would come down to the library here because it was bigger than the one near their home in Eastham. He chose some books, fantasy or science fiction usually and sit and read them. He never really remembered Will coming with them and wondered what he had been up to.

He'd come to the crossroads that led back down to Port Sunlight. Mayer Park stretched behind the buildings and reappeared here. Jeff stared into the darkness, and it seemed to shift. He shook himself and strode on. That was when he heard the footsteps.

Glancing back, he saw a figure in a dark hoodie walking towards him. Well, it could have been towards him or just in the same direction. "Calm down," Jeff muttered to himself. It was probably just a teenager going home after a night's mischief. Nothing to worry about. Even so, Jeff took a right turn and was dismayed to hear the footsteps follow him.

He speeded up, feeling scared and ridiculous at the same time. There was a fifty percent chance that the boy behind him would have turned right too. He was being silly, but he couldn't resist another backward glance.

The boy was hunched up, hands stuffed into his front pocket, his face lost in the darkness of the hood like some evil monk. His shoulders swaggered a little as if he was walking with a purpose, aimed straight at Jeff. Trying to control his breathing, Jeff increased his pace. He wasn't far from his front door at all but the boy was gaining on him.

Jeff risked one more look. The lad was smaller than Jeff. It was possible that Jeff could overpower him or at least get a punch in and run. But what if he had a knife? Kids were always going around 'tooled up,' weren't they? The papers were full of fifty-somethings who had thought they'd be a have-a-go hero, only to end up dead at the hands of some knife-wielding child.

The boy was close. Jeff could hear his breathing now, ragged and heavy. He could smell cheap deodorant and cigarette smoke. There was nothing Jeff could do. He couldn't run now, he was too close. All Jeff could do was turn and face the music but he wouldn't go down without a fight. He spun round. "What do you want? Did Gambles send you?"

The boy's startled face stared out of the hoodie, his mouth open. "I…"

Jeff grabbed his sleeve. "Just leave me alone. It's not worth it he's a psychopath…"

Shock, anger and confusion twisted the young lad's face as he recoiled from Jeff. "Fuck off, what are you on about? *You* leave me alone, you weirdo!"

"You mean you haven't been sent by…" Jeff said in a faint voice, backing off.

The boy jogged past him, giving him a wide berth but watching him closely all the time. "Dickhead," he snarled and ran into the night.

For a moment, Jeff stood watching the boy disappear up the street. Then he began to laugh. A few lights came on in bedrooms and curtains twitched but Jeff didn't care. He chuckled at his own stupidity as he made his way home, shaking his head and thinking what a fool he'd been.

As he approached his house, however, his smile faded. The front door stood ajar, splinters of wood poking from the frame and glass littering the step.

CHAPTER 24

Acting DCI Kath Cryer sat in Blake's office, looking less than happy. Blake had shut the door so that if their conversation got lively, it wouldn't leak out into the main office.

"Look, Kath," Will said. "I'm not doing this on purpose. I genuinely think Terry New is hiding something he knows about the identity of that body in the shelter. Jayden had an identical ring given to him by his grandfather, Dave New who was a member of Arthur and the Galahads. The lead singer of the Galahads, Ernie Hughes was reported missing in 1964. I think Dave New might have told Terry something about Hughes."

Blake could see the battle going on inside Kath. She wanted a case of her own to manage but had realised that in all likelihood, Jayden had taken himself off down the shelters to bunk school. On the other hand, she was a good detective, and he could see her mind working on the facts he'd given her already. She was interested and had theories.

"I've spoken to Martin and he's agreed that you can still act up on this case... you won't lose any money..."

"It's not that, sir," Kath said, the 'sir' slipping

out through habit. "It's being in charge, it's running something and seeing it through…"

"There'll be other chances to do that, I promise. And you call me, Will. Okay?"

Kath bit her lip and then looked at Blake. "Okay. Everything you say fits in with what I've observed anyway. Both Jayden's mum and Father Lanigan implied that Dave New was troubled before his death. I didn't think much of it when I heard it the first time but when Lanigan repeated it, I began to wonder. Of course he wouldn't elaborate. It all kind of suggests that there's a secret being kept there."

"I agree. Terry New was very cagey about the ring. Okay Kath, shall we go out and talk to the team?"

Kath gave a brief smile. "Okay… Will."

***

While Kath and Blake were meeting, Manikas and Kinnear had given DS Vikki Chinn and DC Tasha Cook the highlights of what they had discovered over the weekend. They gathered around the board that Kinnear had assembled. Kath looked at Blake and he nodded for her to take the lead.

"We have a theory that the News have some kind of information about the disappearance of Ernie Hughes. Whether Dave New, Jayden's grandfather was involved in any way, we aren't sure. It's all a working theory. We have to prove that the body in the shelter is Ernie, first of all."

"Does Ernie Hughes have any living relatives, Ma'am?" Vikki said.

"He was next on my list to check, Sarge," Manikas said. "So we don't know."

"I can chase that up," Vikki said.

"Great, thanks, Vikki," Kath said. "What about this Wayne Prosser theory? It sounds plausible. The man had a reputation and underworld links. Could you dig a little deeper into that, Andrew?"

"We need more info on the actual band. The names of other members, whether they're still alive," Blake said. "I'm going to arrange a meeting with Brian Wise, the man who wrote the sixties music blog. He seems to have academic credentials to back up his knowledge. If you're agreeable, Kath?"

"Sounds fine by me," Kath said. "Tasha and I will go and pay Terry New a visit. Maybe we can put some pressure on him."

"There were two callers over the weekend. One who gave us the name of Prosser and another that was just a wee bit creepy and sad. Someone sobbing and saying they didn't mean to do it…"

"Could be a prank," Kath said. "It wouldn't do any harm to put a call out on local media again.

Will, can you talk to Hannah? You seem to be in her good books lately."

Blake felt himself reddening. "Yes," he said, clearing his throat. "That should be fine."

"Oh fuck," Kinnear muttered, looking up from a file he'd picked up from the desk.

"You okay, Andrew?" Blake said.

"Sorry, sir, I just noticed the name of the investigating officer in the Wayne Prosser murder..."

"Let me guess," Blake spat, "DCI Jimmy Leech?"

***

DCI Matty Cavanagh sat in the kitchen and Jeff got the impression that even if he'd made a huge effort, put his best suit on and spruced up, he'd still look shabby in comparison. The young inspector looked like he was about to be best man at a wedding, with his dark suit and waistcoat. Jeff could see his own haggard reflection in Cavanagh's shiny black boots.

A crime scene officer was dusting down the door frame and another was taking photographs in the front room where Jeff normally worked. Jeff had conducted a brief, heart-stopping search of the house when he'd come in. He didn't find anyone, but some items were missing. He'd spent most of the night standing on the pavement waiting for a response and then dozing in the back of a police car while the crime scene officers did their work. The kitchen had been left untouched as far as Jeff could tell, so he'd been allowed into that room.

DCI Cavanagh ran his perfectly manicured fingers through his thick red mane of hair and heaved a sigh. "I believe you've been having a spot of bother with Josh Gambles, too."

"That's what I told the first officer who interviewed me. I had to phone the prison governor to tell him that Gambles was harassing me from his cell."

"And you think this has something to do with him?"

"I don't know, do I? But doesn't it look odd to you? My Mac Book is the only thing that was stolen..."

Cavanagh scanned the kitchen, assessing the dated décor, his look implying that if this was what the rest of the house was like, then maybe that was the only thing worth stealing. "Right," he said, dismissively.

"I'm looking after this house for someone who lives abroad. I don't have much control over the fixtures and fittings but surely if it was some random junkie, they'd take anything they could sell."

"Fair point," Cavanagh said. "So Gambles had your laptop stolen to stop you from publishing the book about him."

"It's a MacBook! Look, I know it sounds ludicrous but you didn't see him when I said that the book was as much about my life as his. He attacked me in the visiting room. The guards there had to restrain him. You can hear the threatening voicemails he left if you want."

"I'd certainly like access to them, Jeff. Anything that keeps that monster behind bars is all right by me." Cavanagh inclined his head. "But…"

"But what? Don't you believe me?"

"It's just that this is all a little bit convenient, isn't it?"

"What d'you mean convenient? Me standing in the cold while strangers ransack my house to find out which other strangers have already ransacked my house is in no way convenient."

"Well, when you put it like that," Cavanagh agreed, "but at the same time, it's great publicity for your book, isn't it? And if you managed to get Gambles' phones confiscated, he'd have a job organising a burglary like this, wouldn't he? And who would do it for him?"

"Oh, come on, Cavanagh," Jeff snapped. "You know as well as I do that Gambles has some pretty heavyweight friends on the outside. One at least, anyway and he knows my address."

"You're saying that Kyle Quinlan arranged this,

now?" Cavanagh said, his smooth brow wrinkling slightly. For a split second, Jeff found himself wondering if he used Botox. "This is like a chapter from a crime novel."

"It would take no effort for Quinlan to send someone to steal my work," Jeff said. "I know you'd never pin it on him but…"

"Your book is all backed up, right? In the cloud or something, yeah?"

"Of course," Jeff said, "I'm not an idiot. Plus my agent already has the first draft. So it isn't lost if that's what you're worried about…"

"I wasn't really worried about that, Jeff. In fact, I was kind of hoping it had been lost. Anything that glorifies what that piece of shit did needs throwing in the bin, if you ask me."

"Spoken like a true protector of democracy and freedom of speech, Cavanagh. For your information, it glorifies nothing. If you were listening, you'd know that Gambles hates it and doesn't want it published."

But Cavanagh's phone had buzzed and he was busy scrolling down the screen. "Look, Jeff, I might send someone to talk to Quinlan about his links with Gambles, but it'll be more to make him uncomfortable than to solve the mystery of your missing laptop…"

"It's a MacBook…"

"In the meantime, get a crime number from the officer and get a new laptop on the insurance. I don't see we can do much more here, to be honest. I only came out because you're Will's brother and there might have been a genuine Gambles link. Pop into the station and hand over your phone during the week, too. I'd love to hear those voicemails." He drained the mug of coffee Jeff had made for him and sauntered out through the hall.

"It's a MacBook! You aren't meant to walk through a crime scene like that are you?" Jeff called after him, then slumped back in his chair. If nobody believed him, then where could he go for help?

CHAPTER 25

Terry New was not pleased to see Kath and Tasha at his door again. Kath wasn't surprised at New's resentment either. He stood at the door of his house in his overalls staring down at them. "I'm just about to get off to another job," he said. "I'm very grateful for all you did finding Jayden and everything but this is getting a bit much now, don't you think?"

"We just want a quick word, that's all, Terry," Kath said

"And what might that be? I feel like a criminal," New said, glowering at her.

Kath held up the picture of the copper ring. "I wondered if you could shed any more light on this?"

New stared at the image. "I told you, Jayden must have found it somewhere. Maybe when he was down in the shelter. I dunno."

"Come on, Terry, Jayden told me he got the ring from his grandfather, your dad. He said Dave was in a band called Arthur and the Galahads. Now, the lead singer of that band went missing in 1964. Sixty years later, we find a body with that ring on. How do you account for that?"

"Nah," Terry said, distantly, his eyes still fixed on the picture of the ring. "You aren't gonna do that."

"Do what?"

"Blame my dad for this singer's death. He might have been in that band but he never hurt anyone in his whole life."

"We aren't trying to pin anything on anyone, Terry," Kath said. "We're just trying to find out the truth of what happened to this young man."

"Okay" New said, "My dad did have an AG ring but he never wore it. Not when I was a kid. Jayden found it when he was rummaging around in my dad's stuff. After he'd died. I didn't know what it was, so I let him keep it. That's all I know." He sounded calmer now but Kath had detected a quaver in his voice that suggested he was still holding something back.

"Your wife said something about Father Lanigan bringing your dad peace of mind before he passed away," Kath said. "Can you tell me what troubled him?"

"How would I know?" New snapped. "Probably the nonsense that stupid priest was feeding him about hellfire and damnation. Dad never really talked to me about stuff like that. Are you finished? Only I have to go to work."

"Of course, Terry," Kath said, "but there's somebody's son lying in our mortuary and he's been under the hill, lost to his family for sixty years. Just think about what you've been through with Jayden this last week. You'd want to bring him home, wouldn't you? If you do know anything about this, please tell us. Think about it."

Terry New hesitated, looking from the picture to Kath and Tasha. "I'm sorry. I can't help you," he said quietly and pushed past them.

**

If he was being completely honest with himself, Blake had agreed to handle the media side of things just so that he had an excuse to talk to Hannah again. The fact that Hannah's interest in him hadn't escaped Kath's notice made him cringe, too. So, as he paused outside her office, he felt a little ridiculous. He could have phoned from his desk but instead, he'd hurried up three flights of stairs with a sheet of paper in his hand like some love-struck teenager. He put his hand on the door then noticed she was on the phone, deep in conversation. This was mad. What was he playing at? Blake pressed his fingertips on his brow until it hurt.

There was a time, back when he was TV eye-candy to millions of housewives on Searchlight, that Blake would have had the self-confidence, the bare-faced cheek, some might say, to walk up to a woman he found attractive and ask them out. The intervening years, with their tragedies and setbacks had kicked the legs from under him and he no longer had that unshakable self-belief. He'd only met Laura by accident at the cattery, when he'd gone there to ask for help with Serafina. It was Laura who took the initiative, almost imposing herself on him.

He hovered by the door. This was ludicrous. Why did he feel so nervous? Because it was obvious why he'd come up to her office in person? What was he expecting, another invitation to coffee? Or did he think he'd have the balls to invite her out? Hissing in frustration at his own stupidity, he turned away, only to hear the door click open.

"Hi, Will, can I help you?"

"Sorry to bother you, Hannah," Blake muttered. "I should have called you..."

"I was on the phone. It would have been engaged," she said, that knowing smirk creeping across her face again. "You could have left an email, I suppose."

Blake's stomach lurched. "Yes! Email. I could've emailed."

Hannah slid the sheet of paper from his grip. "Ah, a request for more assistance. Better come in."

"Okay," Blake said, clearing his throat. "So, we

had a caller who sounded quite upset and we want them to get back in touch. We also think that if we mention some names, that might jog the public's memory. They're open missing person cases, so I think it should be okay. And I really want to focus on the ring, too."

Hannah scribbled down a few notes on the paper she'd taken from Blake. "Right. D'you think you should record a statement we can release to the press or d'you just want it printed?"

"Printed will be fine, I think. Don't want Martin accusing me of seeking the limelight," Blake said, giving a strangled laugh.

Hannah smiled and nodded. "I dunno, Will, you're media savvy, you can still read out a press release and not sound like a robot. Those are skills we should be using. It's a shame Martin seems so set against it."

Blake gave an awkward smile. "Thanks."

"Was there anything else?" Hannah held him in her steady gaze and the time seemed to stretch out in a yawning chasm between them.

"No. That's fine. Thanks," Blake stammered. "I'll get back to it, now. See you later, or whenever. Have a good day..."

He hurried out of her office, grinding his teeth. *Have a good day?* Why didn't he just shake her hand or salute and make himself look a total pillock? Blake took the lift and was glad it was empty; it meant he could bang his head against the wall in total privacy for the few seconds it took to get to his floor.

***

The news that Jimmy Leech had been in charge of the Wayne Prosser investigation filled Blake with a sense of foreboding. As he drove home that night, he wondered what kind of stone they were about to turn over. Leech had been at his height in the seventies and eighties, the worst kind of copper, a corrupt twister who came from a family of criminals but had somehow managed to make it to the top. It amazed Blake that the man was still alive, given his propensity for cigarettes and booze. The fact that someone as wicked as Leech could live so long was a testament to the injustice of the world.

Blake knew Leech of old and had last encountered him a couple of years earlier when he was investigating the murder of a teenager. The old bastard had been grudgingly helpful then but not before he'd managed to antagonise Kinnear so much that the young DC had lunged at him. Leech revelled in conflict and Blake questioned the wisdom of allowing Kinnear to go back and interview him, tomorrow. Hopefully, Manikas would keep Kinnear from strangling the old tosser.

He pulled up outside his house, the lights of Liverpool dancing on the black waters of the Mersey. The house lay in darkness and Blake felt another wave of dread, this time from the thought of Serafina. He'd taken PC Julie Irwin's advice and shut the cat in the spare room with food and water but no way out. Serafina would bear a grudge, he was certain of that, but he hoped it might also allow her time for the hormones to wear off. Again, he puzzled over how she was getting access to them. He couldn't go back to the house he'd seen her enter at the weekend for fear of them making an official complaint about him.

The musky, pissy tang of Serafina's spray hit him as he entered the hallway. He'd put her in the spare room upstairs and he grimaced at the idea of what it might look and smell like now. Cautiously, he crept upstairs and pushed the door open.

If the smell was strong downstairs, it was eye-watering up here. The room looked as though a whirlwind had hit it. The newspapers that Blake had put down had been shredded as had the covers that had been on the single bed. Serafina's food bowl lay upside down but Blake noticed that the food had gone at least. Then, from nowhere, the cat leapt up at him. Blake fell backwards onto the landing, just avoiding falling headlong down the stairs. He held Serafina at arm's length as she pedalled the air with her feet, claws first.

Then she was on the floor and down the stairs in a flash. There was a rattle of the cat flap and then all Blake could hear was Charlie's excited yap from the kitchen. Somehow, Blake knew he was in for a sleepless night.

CHAPTER 26

Not for the first time, the alarm rang too early, and Blake forced his eyes open and stared into the darkness. True to form, Serafina and her mates had been up and active half the night. He'd tried to ignore the noise but worried that neighbours might be hearing it too. What if, in those rare moments of silence, they'd just decamped to a nearby property just to annoy someone else for a change. On one level, Blake didn't mind, he was just glad of the respite, but on another, the idea mortified him.

Blake consoled himself with the thought that he didn't have to get into the office first thing as he had a meeting with Brian Wise. Wise wrote the blog that had given Kinnear the background information on Wayne Prosser. Kinnear had contacted Wise and the man was happy to talk to someone. If Blake was honest, he had been eager to meet the man himself and find out a bit of Merseybeat history in the process of interviewing him. Blake just hoped that Kinnear's own meeting with Leech didn't go awry. Kinnear was older and calmer than when he had last met Leech but the old bastard had a way of getting under your skin.

Wise lived in a large, detached house in Aigburth, just opposite the John Moores University's I.M. Marsh campus. It was rendered white and had a front garden full of shrubs and small trees. As he walked up the short drive to the front door, Blake wondered why he noticed so many details about people's gardens when he had little interest in plants himself. Perhaps he should cultivate an interest, he thought.

Brian Wise was a white-haired man, round and jolly with a goatee beard. He wore a thick cardigan, green cords, and a pair of brown slippers. "Inspector Blake, good to meet you," he said ushering him into a hall decorated with black and white photos of Liverpool in the sixties. There was a lot of framed memorabilia, too, signed ticket stubs and album sleeves, a football shirt and a pair of white gloves with 'John' written on one and 'Lennon' written on the other. Behind the gloves was a picture of Lennon dressed in a top hat and club doorman's uniform. He was standing in front of a public toilet with a sign which read: 'Gentlemen, Members only.'

Wise paused and smiled at the framed gloves. "He wore them in the 'Not Only, But Also,' Christmas Special, 1966. D'you remember it? It was a TV comedy programme with Peter Cook and Dudley Moore?"

"A bit before my time, I'm afraid, sir," Blake said. "But I'm aware of Cook and Moore. Very funny."

"Lennon played a club commissionaire outside a public toilet," Wise said, with a gentle laugh. "I remember it being hilarious at the time. Sometimes humour doesn't age well but I think a lot of that stuff did. I bought those gloves at an auction decades ago. He looks so pleased to be part of it all, doesn't he?"

"I believe he was a great fan of that kind of oddball humour, sir."

"Call me Brian, please. Those gloves are probably worth a fortune now, given their connection to the two comedians, too."

"They're fascinating," Blake said. "A real link to the past."

"I'm glad you like them, come through," Wise said, leading Blake into a large kitchen. It smelt of coffee and cooking and Blake felt at home immediately. He recognised a place where people relaxed and enjoyed good food or settled into one of the armchairs by the fire and read a magazine. For a second, Blake thought back wistfully to Sunday morning and that rare moment of peace he'd experienced before it all went wrong. Wise busied himself with coffee. "Before we talk further, I feel the need to establish my credentials, somewhat. Although I'm old enough to have been there, I never saw the Beatles rocking the Cavern. I caught plenty of other bands there but somehow missed them. I saw them elsewhere, of course, the Liverpool Empire and other theatres but they weren't the only show in town at first. I've studied the whole Merseybeat phenomenon for years and my blog has a vast array of collected information about all those bands…"

"I believe you also did a PhD, Brian," Blake said. "Something to do with Northernism…"

"Yes, for a moment in the sixties, the North was cool. I argued that the growth of Merseybeat and the way Liverpool drew in bands from around the North, presented a new dynamic threat to the music establishment of the South, in particular London. The academic side of the study nearly killed me but it was interesting. I was a mature student, just retired."

"You said in your blog that agents and managers came up from London in search of new acts. Wayne Prosser came along with them…"

"Without harking back to my work too much, Inspector, yes he did but a little later. The agents and managers in London suddenly saw all these groups coming down from Liverpool and taking work from their acts. Some band members told me that many Northern acts were bought up by southern agents, tied up in red tape and left to rot. Or they were given residencies in holiday camps rather than record deals. The 'Tottenham Sound' was promoted but it didn't have the organic roots of Merseybeat. There was a dark underbelly to that whole time and Wayne Prosser personified it."

"Did he exploit his acts?"

"I believe so. Many complained about lots of work, lots of travel, living in slum accommodation and never getting paid. Others made more serious allegations against Prosser; sexual impropriety, assault, bullying, even rape. Suffice to say, he wasn't a nice man."

"And what was his link to Arthur and the Galahads?"

Wise's eyes twinkled. "Now *that* is an intriguing story."

***

The last time Kinnear had seen Jimmy Leech, he'd been enthroned in his armchair in a cloud of cigarette smoke, thumbing through a porn magazine. He looked old and wizened but indestructible, Kinnear had thought, like a stain on a carpet that never comes out, no matter how hard you scrub. So in some ways, he was surprised to find the ex-copper sitting in a hospice with an oxygen mask strapped to his face. In other ways, he wasn't; Jimmy Leech hadn't led what you'd call a healthy or blameless life.

Whereas in the past, Leech had greeted Blake and Kinnear with a malign chirpiness, now, Kinnear was gratified to detect a leaden weariness in his voice. "What the fuck d'you want, Nancy?" he said, his dull eyes scanning the two of them. "Brought your boyfriend?"

"Sad to say, he's straight, Jimmy," Kinnear said, sitting down. He leaned forward and whispered. "Still, at least he's easy on the eye. You, on the other hand look a bit under the weather, if you don't mind me saying so."

"Fuck off," Leech hissed and started coughing into his mask.

"Steady on Jimmy, we need to talk to you before you croak," Kinnear said.

"All right, Andy," Manikas said, "give the man a break, yeah? He won't tell us anything if you wind him up. Or kill him."

Leech nodded and pointed at a glass of water on the bedside. Manikas poured him a drink and Jimmy pulled his mask down, taking a sip. "Tha's better. Your partner's got more manners than you, Kinnear."

"He's never met you before."

"You been promoted yet? Or haven't you found a Chief Superintendent with the same... proclivities?"

"Less of that, old man," Manikas growled.

"Wayne Prosser," Kinnear said, stonily. "What do you know?"

Leech wobbled his head from side to side and took another drink. "That's going back a bit. What are you investigating now, old hate crimes?" he seemed quite pleased with this joke and allowed himself a chuckle which became another phlegmy spluttering fit.

"The case notes say he was stabbed by a rent boy but there were other rumours circulating around Prosser, weren't there?"

"There were, yeah," Leech said, once he got his breath back. "He might have been selling a few drugs on the side and there was…" A malicious grin split Leech's face and for a second, he looked like the wicked scumbag of old. "Wait a minute. Is this about Ernie Hughes?"

Kinnear's face didn't flicker. "And who might Ernie Hughes be?"

"Ooh, you're very good, DC Kinnear. You should try your hand at poker. Ernie Hughes as you may or may not know, was a young man who went missing about ten years before Prosser's death in 1975. He was a singer in a pretty ropey band, so I believe. Handsome devil, by all accounts. I heard a rumour that Prosser had killed Ernie because the lad threatened him with the police. Didn't like Prosser's advances, if you see what I mean. Of course, it was all hearsay, no solid evidence and no corpse, but I always favoured it as a motive for killing Prosser."

Manikas frowned. "A motive? You mean someone taking revenge for the death of Ernie Hughes?"

Leech covered his face with the mask for a while and sucked in the oxygen, then lowered it again. "Yeah, exactly. You see, Prosser was a tight-fisted son of a bitch, by all accounts and he never paid for sex. He was a drug user but had no real history of dealing. So he had no business being in the alley at the back of the club on the night he was murdered."

"This rent boy," Kinnear said. "Did he have a connection to Ernie Hughes?"

"Him?" Leech said, struggling to remember. "He had a funny kind of name. Italian or Spanish or something… Rapino! That was it. Peter Rapino. No, I don't think he had any kind of link."

"Sorry, you've lost me," Manikas said, blinking with incomprehension. "Why would this rent boy want to get revenge on Prosser if he didn't know Ernie Hughes?"

"You fitted him up, didn't you?" Kinnear said in a low voice. "Rapino wasn't anywhere near Prosser that night."

Leech shrugged. "Rapino was there all right. He lured him out into the alley, that's for sure. Prosser was seen leaving the club with him, next thing he was dead. He was obviously up to no good. But I don't think Rapino had the backbone to stand up to Prosser. I always thought it would be someone from his past that killed him, though."

"Who?" Kinnear snapped.

Leech took a long gulp of oxygen. "I don't know, do I? All I do know is that Hughes was in a band, right. Prosser had got them a club residency in Hamburg. You know, it was all the rage back in the day. I blame the Beatles."

"Yeah, yeah," Kinnear said. "The Reeperbahn, The Kaiser Keller, Top Ten, and the Star-Club. I know."

"A sixties buff eh, Kinnear? Anyway, the night they were about to go, Ernie vanished. Never seen again." He took another breath. "Prosser made the rest of the band go on without him and supplied some woman to sing for them once they got there but, by all accounts it was a disaster."

"So the band blamed Prosser," Manikas muttered.

"If one of the band had somehow found out that Prosser had killed Ernie and scuppered their supposed chances of success, well, who knows what they might have done?"

"What? Ten years later? Seems a bit thin, to me, Jimmy," Manikas said. "Why wait all that time? You must have had a stronger reason to think Rapino had an accomplice."

Leech looked downcast. "Seemed to make more sense then." He lay back and went quiet, letting the sound of the hissing oxygen fill the void. Then he sat up. "That was it. One of the band had form. He'd been to prison for GBH for a few years and was a nasty piece of work. Can't remember which one. Maybe that was why I thought it was him. Anyway, Prosser was a big fella, even when he was old, and Rapino was a skinny, little runt. He couldn't have killed Prosser alone."

Kinnear leaned in on Leech. "So who was the band member?"

"I really can't remember. Names come and go."

"And you think it plausible that Prosser killed Ernie Hughes?" Manikas said.

Leech sucked at the oxygen. "Sure, why not. Could have easily slipped him a mickey and dumped him in the river."

"What about Rapino? What happened to him?"

"God. I don't know. He was a druggie, banged up. Probably dead now. Look, I'm running out of breath and I need a kip. I can't help you any more than that."

Kinnear looked at Leech. "Do you have regrets?"

Leech's eyes half closed and he slumped back into the pillows. "What do you think?"

"I dunno. All those people you set up, all the corners you cut. People like Peter Rapino. The justice that people never received because you were too lazy or corrupt…"

"No comment, constable," Leech said, closing his eyes.

"We probably won't see you again, Jimmy and I for one, am glad." Kinnear turned his back on the dying ex-copper. "Come on Alex, we're finished here, I think."

"I see them," Leech said, quietly. "The people I let down or shafted or… worse. Every single one of them comes to visit me in my dreams every single night. Does that make you feel better?"

"I don't know how it makes me feel," Kinnear said and turned his back on Leech.

CHAPTER 27

Following up the leads from the media request for information about the body had brought DS Vikki Chinn to Florence Smith who lived in a nursing home in the North End area of Birkenhead. She had mentioned Ernie Hughes by name in her call but an ember of doubt glowed in the back of Vikki's mind that maybe she was about to encounter an unreliable witness.

Old age troubled Vikki more than she cared to admit. She looked at her parents who had worked so hard all their lives and shivered when they started talking about how she would look after them, one day. They often harked back to a mythical past when older relatives lived with their extended families and didn't have to resort to the kind of accommodation like the one she stood in front of now. They had spent almost their entire adult life running a small business and she couldn't remember them looking after any elderly relatives.

The building was modern and bright and, as a young care assistant led Vikki through the corridors, she heard snatches of conversation, some singing of hymns from a communal room. The whole place smelt clinically clean and reminded

Vikki of a hospital but Florence Smith's actual room felt homely.

Florence was a small, round woman with a frizz of white hair. She sat, almost curled up in her armchair, her back was so bent. She smiled at Vikki through thick glasses, her head shaking a little as she held it up.

"This is Vikki," the carer said in a loud voice. "The policewoman you rang up."

A frown creased Florence's brow, almost undetectable amongst the other wrinkles. "I spoke to a nice young man. Aren't they sending a nice young man?"

"I'm sorry, Mrs Smith, DC Kinnear couldn't make it," Vikki said, showing her warrant card. "I'm Detective Sergeant Vikki Chinn. You'll have to make do with me I'm afraid."

"Call me Florrie, luv. I'm a hundred and two, Vikki. What d'you think of that?"

"Impressive," Vikki said, her heart sinking. She generally tried her hardest to be a 'glass half full' kind of girl but she was worried that this interview was going to lead nowhere. "I believe you said you remembered Ernie Hughes."

"Who?"

"Ernie Hughes, Florrie, the young man who went missing all those years ago. Back in the sixties."

"That's half a lifetime ago, luv," Florrie said, wistfully. "Yeah, I remember him. Lovely young man, he was. Always dressed well. Had his hair long, but I didn't mind that much. He walked with a limp."

"Do you know why that was?" Vikki said, trying to keep the questions simple.

Florrie licked her lips and cast her mind back. "Oh, I remember that. He fell off a horse."

"Was he a good rider?"

"Well obviously not, love or he wouldn't have fallen off, would he?" Florrie chuckled at her joke for what seemed like an eternity. "It wasn't his horse. It belonged to some girl who was chasing him. Handsome devil, he was, even as a young lad."

"Did you live close to them?"

"Ooh, yes, right next door. His mum, Mary and I were good friends. He was a lovely boy, Ernie. He could sing like an angel, too. Used to be in the church choir and everything."

"His mum and dad must have been very proud of him," Vikki said, watching Florrie's reaction.

Florrie's lip curled slightly. "Mary was. Ivan wasn't really around much. He worked in the Merchant Navy so he was at sea a lot. When he did come home, he was in the pub most of the time."

"So what can you remember about the time Ernie went missing?"

"He was in a band at the time. A bit like the Beatles. They were doing very well for themselves according to Mary. Playing in the Cavern and all that. It was never my cup of tea, that kind of music. All those thumping drums gave me a headache. Give me Bing Crosby any day."

"Can you remember the name of the band?"

"Ooh, I don't know, luv. It was so long ago. But I remember Mary being worried sick because he was going to Germany to play with this band."

"Germany?"

"It was a big thing, apparently. They all did it. I wondered what the appeal was, myself. Bloomin' Germans had tried to blow us up only a few years before but there you go," Florrie said and shrugged. She fell silent for a while, staring down at her knees until Vikki wondered if she had fallen asleep.

"Did Ernie go to Germany, then?"

"I don't really know. Mary said that he didn't," Florrie leaned forward, almost folded in half. "Listen," she whispered. "I'm not one to gossip but it was said he was a bit queer, like. What do they call it nowadays? Gay, that's it. Of course, it wasn't okay then, but someone told me that he went to Germany and stayed there to... you know... be gay..."

Vikki looked dubious. "How do you mean?"

"Well, like, they're more accepting of it over there than we are, so he stayed but Mary couldn't bear that idea, so she said he was dead. Somebody told me she got a letter from him some years later, from Germany."

"Did Ernie have any brothers or sisters, Florrie? Anyone who we could talk to today?"

Florrie Smith blinked at Vikki. "Haven't you spoken to Mary's daughter? She should be able to tell you everything."

"Ernie Hughes had a sister?" Vikki said.

"That's what I said, didn't I? I send a Christmas card to her every year. Do you want the address?"

**

Brian Wise sat back in his armchair and sipped his coffee. "You have to understand the culture back when Arthur and the Galahads were strutting their stuff, Inspector Blake. Anyone could have a go. That was its strength and its curse. There were people forming bands when they could barely play. People making their own instruments out of old furniture. Demand was so high across Merseyside, not just in city pubs and clubs but in church and village halls all around the region. And not just in Merseyside. Bands roamed up into Cumbria, Cheshire, Lancashire and North Wales. The demand for dance music was so high."

"A quick look online shows just how many bands there were," Blake said.

"Bands would morph and names would change," Brian said. "And some of the names were hilarious My particular favourite is The Verbs. I never heard them but I can guarantee they were better than the Galahads. Almost everyone was."

"So, the Galahads weren't that good, then?" Blake said with a smile.

"Apparently not. I've done some digging into my archives and there are a few accounts by people who went to dances and a couple of musicians' accounts, too."

"I've read Oliver Kline's interview. He said they looked better than they sounded."

Brian gave a smirk. "Olly and the Twisters weren't exactly setting the world on fire, either but, yes, he was probably right. From what I understand, Ernie Hughes was the front man, he was good-looking, could hold a tune when he wasn't drunk and danced like a demon. The rest of the band were pretty plain-looking, and barely competent musicians"

"From what you've said, that could put them in a higher league than many of the bands out there at the time."

"True, and Ernie Hughes' gammy leg allowed him to do a superb Gene Vincent impression."

"So he did have a limp. That's interesting."

"Yes, so, on paper, they weren't too bad. But the flaws of this band lay in the personalities of the musicians rather than their skill. Ernie liked a drink and, once he was drunk, he forgot words, sang off key. By all accounts, it was pretty terrible. The rest of the band had skin as thin as an eggshell when it came to criticism and would resort to fists."

"I imagine, if Ernie was hitting the pop, and the band laying into anyone who dared criticise them, they would quickly run out of friends."

"Wayne Prosser had been sniffing around the Galahads for quite a while. According to one source, Prosser wanted Ernie Hughes to go solo. He said he could make him the next Billy Fury."

"I bet that pleased the rest of the band."

"I wouldn't imagine they'd be over the moon," Brian agreed. "This was around 1963. The clubs and dance halls were swinging but the Galahads' reputation had gone before them, and they were having to travel further afield to get gigs. Finally, in 1964, Wayne Prosser got his claws into them and found them a residency over in Hamburg."

"That was a big deal, right?"

"It was, Inspector," Brian said. "A lot of the Merseybeat musicians had day jobs and couldn't afford to drop everything to go abroad. It was a gamble for those who did. Hamburg was seen as a dangerous city, the bands worked in clubs in red light districts. It was hard graft, playing all night to drunks and sailors looking for strip clubs."

"But it was the making of the Beatles, I believe," Blake said.

"So they said. Maybe the Galahads hoped it would sharpen them up, too. Whatever the reason, they jumped at the chance." Brian stopped and produced a plastic wallet with some printed sheets in it. "I managed to find an interview with Prosser from an old music magazine in which he talks briefly about the night Ernie disappeared. It's here. They were all going to meet at the Birkenhead Tunnel entrance and Prosser was going to drive them to Felixstowe to catch the ferry. Ernie never appeared and, in the end, they had to go without him or they'd miss their boat."

"Why meet at the tunnel entrance?" Blake said.

"Prosser lived over in Liverpool. He tried not to cross the river if he could help it. I think he preferred the city life. Anyway, he describes how they nearly missed the ferry because he stopped the car at every phone box he saw, trying to get in touch with Ernie."

"Seems strange behaviour for someone who is meant to have murdered him," Blake murmured.

"That was the rumour, but it only surfaced around the time of Prosser's death as far as I know. Prosser went with them to Hamburg, and they ended up backing a drag act called Sasha Schatzi. They managed to last two months before returning. As far as I know, the Galahads never played together again."

"Dave New, the guitarist, died a few months back," Blake said, "but we don't know the identity of the other band members apart from Ernie Hughes."

Brian Wise tapped the folder he'd just handed to Blake. "All in there, Inspector," he said. "Sammy Treadwell and Gary Jensen. Surprisingly for his age, Treadwell, the drummer, was active in a local punk band, The Blood Beggars at least until a couple of years ago. I don't know if he still is. Jensen, who played bass didn't play professionally again as far as I can see. Maybe if you find one you can find the other. I'd counsel caution, though, Inspector."

"Caution? What do you mean?"

Wise gave a pained look. "I'm a huge fan of the Beatles. They changed everything for me when I was younger and made such an impression on music of all genres..."

"But?"

"Imagine being so close to something that globally successful, that transformative. Some people were swept along by the sheer gravity of it, pulled to stardom or good fortune in its wake. Others were left behind, lost in a world of 'could have beens', or 'should have beens'. Have a read up on what happened to people like Tommy Quickly, or even Wayne Fontana. There are so many people who had a fleeting taste of fame, only to have it taken away from them. I've found in my years of interviewing band members that some have an axe to grind. You might find Tread-well and Jensen bitter and resentful about the past. They might not want to revisit it."

CHAPTER 28

Dogs were just things to Kyle Quinlan. He never understood how Laura attributed them with personalities or likes and dislikes. As far as Kyle could see, if you fed them, they followed you round after more food. If you kicked them, they kept out of your way. Not that he'd kick them in sight of Laura, she'd have given him a black eye, but to him they were just robots made of meat. They yapped and ate food and then crapped everywhere. And he couldn't fathom why anyone would make such a fuss about them. It was a rift between Laura and himself, his total lack of interest in animals. It also made him a little bit jealous that what had united Laura and Will Blake was their love of his pets.

So every now and then, he'd turn up at one of Laura's dog grooming salons, whichever one she happened to be visiting and he'd scratch a pug behind its ear or say something complimentary about a poodle. Laura would roll her eyes but smile, too and that gave him hope that he was winning that side of her over.

But Laura or no Laura, he nearly strangled the chihuahua he was holding when DCI Matty Cavanagh strolled into the Perky Pets salon with his trademark 'smack-me' grin on his face.

"Awright Kyle," Cavanagh said, hands in pockets, rocking on his heels. "I didn't have you down as a dog lover. You're full of surprises."

"What do you want Matty?" Laura Vexley said, stepping between Kyle and the Inspector.

Matty's eyes widened. "Just happened to be passing and thought I'd drop in. I need to pick Kyle's brains about his longstanding friendship with a certain psychopathic serial killer…"

"I'm pretty sure that this borders on harassment, Matty," Laura said. "This is a respectable business and Kyle is not breaking any laws so…"

"Let's go in the back, Inspector Cavanagh," Kyle said, handing the dog to Laura. "We can talk there."

It was cramped but quiet in the back office. A small desk and chair sat amidst a mountain range of boxes and packages. Kyle sat himself at the desk and tried to look comfortable but a large piece of cardboard fell against him and he had to push it out of the way. "What do you want, Matty?"

"I've heard a curious story recently, about Josh Gambles and you."

"Me? I haven't had anything to do with Gambles for years. He's a fucking nutter. D'you think I'd be going on prison visits to see him, the way my business interests are taking off?"

"Business is booming then? You'll have to fill me in on the details, Kyle."

"Fuck off. I'm straight and legit these days. If you think I'm not, then prove it. Now what's all this about Gambles?"

"Will Blake's brother, Jeff, you know him?"

Quinlan snorted. "Yeah, lanky streak of piss. Looks like one of my old Geography teachers. Writer or something. What about him?" A vague memory drifted around his mind of being with Jeff in the back of a pub and talking about Gambles. "Shit. Is he going to write about me?"

Matty raised an eyebrow. "I dunno, Kyle, was he? Is that why you had his house burgled?"

"Why I what?"

"You heard. His house was broken into and his laptop stolen. Nothing else was taken. Bit funny that, eh? I just wondered if you were doing Joshy boy a favour but, thinking about it, you wouldn't want him writing about your relationship with Gambles, either, would you?"

"Not particularly but then I'm not likely to go breaking into Will Blake's brother's house, am I? I'm not stupid. Have you got any evidence? No, I didn't think so. I'll save you the time. I didn't break into Jeff Blake's house and I didn't ask anyone to, either. As far as I'm concerned, Josh Gambles is dead to me. I looked out for him when we were just kids banged up together but when he killed those people and kidnapped that girl, I realised what a nutter he was."

"Fair enough, Kyle," Matty said. "I thought I'd test the waters, see how you reacted. For what it's worth, I believe you. I'll show myself out."

The door clicked shut, leaving Kyle staring at it. He pulled out his phone. "Nick? Yeah, we've got a problem. Jeff Blake. That's the one. I think we need a chat with him." He ended the call. One thing was certain, he needed to get out of this salon before he kicked something small and furry.

**

It was quite a black eye and looked even more pronounced because it was on the face of a Priest. Kath Cryer had almost jumped back in surprise when Father Lanigan opened his front door on her. "Are you all right, Father Lanigan? How did that happen?"

Lanigan gave a sheepish grin. "Let's just say, it was me who was moving in mysterious ways. I tripped over a hassock last night and ended up with this." He touched it and winced.

"You wouldn't just be saying that for my benefit, would you, Father?" Kath said, raising one eyebrow.

"I don't know what you mean, Inspector," Lanigan said, keeping his voice light and jovial.

"I mean if Terry New did that, I'm happy to go and have a word with him."

"Terry New?" Lanigan said, his face a mask of confusion. It wasn't a very good mask and Kath saw through it right away. "You think Terry New did this?"

"I know it after that pantomime, Father."

Lanigan leaned against the door frame and rubbed his forehead. "He's been under a lot of pressure lately. He's a good father to Jayden and he was a good son to Dave. I don't want to be causing him any trouble now."

"If you say so," Kath muttered. "It was Dave New I came to talk to you about, actually. What do you know about his early life, back in the Sixties?"

"Not much," Lanigan said, but there was a caution in his voice. "He played the guitar in a band, they went over to Germany, I believe. He didn't say much about it in public."

"What about in private?"

Lanigan blinked slowly and licked his lips. "You have to understand, Inspector, that in my profession, I'm not allowed to betray any confidences..."

"But surely in a case of murder rules can be..."

"These aren't rules to be bent and broken, they are solemn oaths I have made before God. Even if Dave New confessed to me that he had murdered my mother, I could do nothing about it once he left the confession box. To do so would be to break my faith with him and his faith in me and God. I can't tell you anything about Dave New that might help you infer or even guess about any sins he may or may not have confessed to. Terry New had his own reasons for being angry..."

"And what are they?"

"That's for him to tell you, not me," Lanigan said. "Nothing I could tell you would change anything."

"It might bring us closer to the truth..."

"And what will you do with that truth, Inspector? Will justice be served? Will loved ones be consoled? Or will it all just end with a report written up and stored on a server somewhere, never to be looked at again?"

"A young man has lain cold and lost in that shelter for almost sixty years. Surely we owe it to him to find out what happened to him?"

"I'm sorry, I can't help you," Lanigan said and started to close the door.

Kath held it. "Then I hope you can live with yourself, Father. A mother died not knowing what had happened to her son. Is your contract with Dave New so blessed? Telling secrets in a dark box to avoid the torments of Hell? If he was truly repentant, he would have told the world what he knew."

"I think you've said enough, Inspector," Lanigan murmured and pushed the door shut. "Goodnight."

Kath Cryer scowled at the door. "I don't think I have, mate. Not yet." Turning, she stalked back to the car.

Terry New's house was a five minute drive from Lanigan's and Kath was a bit tired of being given the run around by both of them. She pulled up and strode over to the house, banging on the door. Eventually, Terry New appeared. He looked angry at first but then he saw the look in Kath's eye. "Terry, do I have to arrest you for the assault on Father Lanigan or are you going to invite me in and tell me what the fuck is going on?"

CHAPTER 29

Kath could see flecks of tile grout and paint on Terry New's work trousers as he sat on the edge of his armchair. Sarah New perched on the arm of the chair, stroking the back of his neck as he buried his face in his hands.

"I didn't mean to thump the priest," Terry said. "It was just that when he came smarming round the house to 'see if everything was okay', I saw red."

"What is it you have against Father Lanigan? He's never harmed Jayden or anyone in your family, has he?" Kath said. "Or is it for another reason?"

Terry sighed heavily. "Look," he said, staring at Kath, "I swear down, I don't know anything about the body in the shelter. I knew my dad was in that band..."

"Arthur and the Galahads," Kath said.

"Yeah, them," Terry muttered, "I knew my dad played guitar, but he didn't talk about those days, much. Sometimes, he'd let slip that he'd played with the Beatles, but then he'd sort of clam up as though he'd said too much. Before he started going to church, he'd been very down. He was drinking a bit then. I remember him once when he'd had a skinful getting proper depressed. He was crying and saying he didn't deserve the life he'd had, but he never said why."

"He never mentioned Ernie Hughes? Are you sure?"

"Never," Terry said. "He didn't talk about the band or any other members at all apart from the name once or twice. I knew the ring had some connection with the band, but I hadn't realised that Jayden had claimed it. Honestly, I didn't know."

"Dave, Terry's dad, started going to Father Lanigan's church and it transformed him," Sarah New said. "He was so much happier and even started playing the guitar during worship. It seemed to chase those demons away."

"Yeah, until he got sick," Terry murmured, darkly. "Then he saw it as some kind of judgement. He asked me if I thought God had given him cancer as a punishment. He said that God had killed my mum for the same reason..."

"I'm sorry, I didn't realise your mother..."

"Hit and run," Terry said. "Back in the early nineties. I was only a little kid. She was crossing the road in town. Hit by a distinctive orange car but nobody was ever traced. I told him not to be daft and asked him what God would punish him for and he just burst into tears. It was horrible."

"Father Lanigan came round quite a lot during Dave's illness," Sarah said, seeing the burden of memory descending on Terry's shoulders.

"Skulking in his room, whispering things in his ear," Terry said. "That man was no good for my dad, with his 'confessional' and prayers."

"To be fair, your dad always seemed a bit calmer after Father Lanigan had been to visit," Sarah said.

"Did he?" Terry said, giving his wife a sidelong glance. "I wouldn't know, I was busy working, wasn't I?"

"Don't start that again, Terry," Sarah snapped.

"What do you think it was that troubled your father?" Kath said, trying to keep the conversation away from the domestic row that was bubbling up.

Terry shifted in his seat and Sarah leaned away from him a little. "I don't know," he said. "One thing I do know is that my dad was a kind and gentle man. I never saw him lift a hand against anyone. He raised me single-handed after we lost my mum. He wouldn't harm a fly."

**

Darkness had fallen across the city. Outside, cars swished through the damp November night and people pulled their collars high and hurried for buses and trains to take them home. With

Kath and Vikki joining them, and the sudden breakthroughs they'd just had, the etam felt galvanised. They huddled together in the Major Incident Room admiring the information on the board.

"Okay," Blake said. "Let's recap events and see if we can make any sense of it. Ernie Hughes disappears in late 1964, Arthur and the Galahads go off to Hamburg and come back two months later and never play again. It's rumoured that the manager of the band, Wayne Prosser, killed Ernie after he rejected Prosser's sexual advances. Ten years later, Wayne Prosser is murdered in a back street in Liverpool. Fifty plus years after that, a boy falls down into the shelter under Bidston Hill and accidentally discovers a body. The physical evidence suggests it's Ernie but we need more concrete proof. We also have Dave New, the Galahad's lead guitarist, on his deathbed expressing regrets for having done 'something terrible' but we can't just assume he meant involvement in Ernie's murder."

"It's quite a coincidence that the boy who found the body just happens to be Dave New's grandson sir," DC Andrew Kinnear said.

"Terry New is adamant that his father wasn't capable of harming anyone," Kath muttered, thoughtfully, "but I'm not convinced. If he knew about the body, maybe he inadvertently seeded the idea of exploring the shelter in Jayden's mind by warning him off it so much." She shrugged. "Seems like a long shot but…"

Blake nodded. "Coincidence, rumour, anecdote. We need something stronger to go on."

"Ernie Hughes had a sister, sir," DS Vikki Chinn said. "I've managed to get an address. She would be able to supply a DNA sample that would confirm the body's identity."

"Good work, Vikki. We have the names of the other two band members, too. Gary Jensen and Sam Treadwell. The latter played in a band called the Blood Beggars up until recently at least. Alex, how far have you got with locating them?"

Manikas gave a thumbs up. "I have Jensen's address and it won't be long before we track down Treadwell's, sir."

"We're getting somewhere. What about the Wayne Prosser angle? We can't dismiss the idea that he killed Ernie without looking into it more thoroughly."

"It seems like Ernie Hughes' disappearance was pinned on Wayne Prosser sometime after Prosser, himself was murdered," Kinnear said. "Which is odd, isn't it, sir?"

"Maybe the rumour was out there but people were too scared of Prosser to say anything at the time," Blake countered. "Prosser had some pretty heavy-duty friends, after all."

"Or maybe someone wanted to obscure the truth about Ernie's disappearance," Kath said. "Blame it on the dead guy with a flaky reputation. Most people are going to buy that."

Vikki looked troubled by the idea. "But who would be asking questions ten years later, Ma'am?"

"His mother for one," Blake said. "She was putting pressure on the police to keep the case open. Maybe this sister was, too."

Kinnear looked at the notes. "What about this Rapino lad, sir? The one who was imprisoned for Prosser's murder? It might be worth seeing what became of him. Leech was dismissive, said he was a junkie and probably dead by now but he might not be."

"Rapino?" Kath said, snatching the notes. "One of the early witnesses was called Rapino," She flicked through the file. "Here, Eileen Rapino. I spoke to her last week. She was a bit weird, to be honest but she was going on about her brother, Peter. There has to be a connection there, Will."

"I agree, Kath, yeah," Blake said. "Let's see what she knows about Peter Rapino and the murder of Wayne Prosser. We need to talk to the two other band members, Jensen and Treadwell."

"Sir," Manikas said, holding up his phone. "I just did a search for Blood Beggars, that's 'B-L-U-D' and 'Beggarz' with a 'z.' They're playing in Birkenhead tonight."

"Great work, Alex," Blake said. "Who fancies a bit of punk rock, then, eh?"

CHAPTER 30

The 'Green Man Bar and Kaff' was a huge barn of a place on the streets between the tunnel entrance and Cammell-Lairds shipyard. Once an old warehouse, it had been restyled into a pub, restaurant and concert venue. The brickwork had been painted with the face of an enormous Green Man, his beard and hair turning into vines and branches that twisted and crawled all across the frontage. Lurid red windows interrupted the flow but the effect was quite stunning. Posters advertised various tribute bands playing at the venue in the coming weeks. It also boasted a 'toothsome' bar meal menu, whatever that meant.

Blake shivered in the cold wind that blew up from the river. It was going dark but he could still see the outline of Liverpool across the water. "Looks like a fun place," he said to Kath Cryer as they climbed out of the car.

"They have some good acts on," Kath said. "Me and Theo came here to see a Sladed…"

"Are they a tribute band?" Blake said. "I never get that. Going to see a band that sounds like a band but isn't the original."

Kath shrugged. "It was good fun. They sounded

great, too. Just like the original..."

"But how would you know?" Blake said. "Unless you'd seen Slade back in the seventies. And even then, it'd be under completely different conditions..."

"God, I dunno, Will, it was just a night out, a bit of fun," Kath said. "I hate to take advantage of the fact that I'm acting up, but sometimes you overthink stuff that doesn't need much thought at all."

"I just don't get it," Blake muttered as they entered the bar. Inside was almost as spectacular as out. The floor was bare wood and the bark-panelled walls along with hanging plants dotted liberally around, gave the place the feeling of a forest. It being midweek and just after work, there weren't many punters. The smell of roast meat and beer mingled making Blake hungry. A bored woman leaned on the bar reading a magazine and twisting the stud in her nose.

"DCI Blake. I wonder if I could have a word with Sammy Treadwell..."

She frowned. "Who?"

"He's the drummer in the Blood Beggars," Kath said.

The woman rolled her eyes. "They aren't in trouble again, are they?" she said. "I'll have to tell Gaz the manager. He said that if they put one more foot wrong, they were out on their ear. What they done this time?"

"Do they often get in trouble?" Kath said. "What for?"

"It's the whole punk thing, isn't it? They just go too far and end up fighting or smashing bottles. It's all a bit childish if you ask me."

"They haven't done anything," Blake said, not wanting to get into a long discussion. "We just want a quick word about something else, that's all. He might be able to help us."

Blake couldn't tell if the woman had lost interest or just didn't believe him, but she pointed to a door in the corner of the room where a sign said, 'Live Music.'

"They're doing a sound check down there," she said.

The downstairs event room was a much more functional place, everything was painted black, and the open standing space made upstairs look cluttered. At one end of the room was a raised stage protected from the audience space by a metal crash barrier. A shuttered bar filled the back of the room. Blake took all this in while wincing at the squealing racket that assaulted his ears as he entered the room.

"Jeez," he muttered. "Who said punk's dead?"

"What, sir?" Kath shouted.

Three young men in their twenties, dressed in ripped tartan jeans and red skinny T-shirts thrashed away at guitars. Their hair was spiked, and chains glittered and swung in the dim light. In the background, Blake could see an older, grim-faced man pounding away at the drums. He recognised him straight away. It was the man he'd seen up on Bidston Hill when they were searching for Jayden.

Kath stepped forward and waved her arms in front of them, bringing the music to a jarring halt. She produced her warrant card. "I'm Acting DCI Kath Cryer, Merseyside..."

The nearest lad raked his fingers over the guitar strings, drowning her words and then damped them, returning the silence. He grinned at his mates.

Kath pursed her lips. "This is DCI..."

The guitar crashed again.

"...Will Blake..."

Another power chord deafened them all.

"Seriously, sunshine," Kath said, fixing the lad with a steely gaze. "Obstruction is a pretty flexible kind of offence if you want me to come up there and cuff you. I'll stick that guitar where the sun don't shine while I'm at it."

The other lads jeered at the guitarist who reddened and broke his gaze with Kath.

"Mr Treadwell," Blake called to the back of the stage. "Could I have a few minutes of your time. It's about Ernie Hughes."

Treadwell rose from his seat and Blake saw for the first time what a powerful man he was. He dwarfed the other lads who could easily have been his grandchildren. He didn't bother with a red T-shirt, instead his broad shoulders stretched a black, turtle-neck sweater and he wore tight, black jeans and Doc Marten boots. As he stepped down off the stage, Blake marvelled at his condition, given that he must be in his mid-seventies. He stood eye-to-eye with Blake, in a belligerent stance. "Yeah?" he said, "what about him?"

Blake didn't move. This man was a bully, he could see that. He used his physical presence to intimidate people, but Blake wasn't playing that game. "You've probably heard the news that we've found a body in the air raid shelters under Bidston Hill. We suspect that it's Ernie Hughes. You knew him, right?"

"I don't read mainstream media and anyway, you already know I did, so why are you asking? We were in a band together."

"Arthur and the Galahads," Blake said, Treadwell didn't even twitch. "What do you remember about the last time you saw Ernie Hughes?"

This time Treadwell's eyes widened. "Seriously?

Fuck me, that was sixty years ago, mate. I have enough trouble remembering what I did last week…"

"But sometimes, older memories are more lucid, especially in such circumstances," Blake said. "You seem pretty switched on to me, Sammy. Playing in a band like this at your age? I've got to hand it to you…"

"Yeah well," Treadwell said, allowing a tight grin. "It keeps me young doesn't it?" He relaxed a little and took a casual step away from Blake. "Look," he said, with a sigh. "Whether you believe me or not, it *is* hard to remember exact details. We played somewhere that night before we went to Hamburg, might have been Hesketh Hall in Port Sunlight, could have been Birkenhead Cricket Club, but Ernie was in a shit mood. He'd had a skinful before he came out and sounded bloody awful. I don't know what was wrong with him, but he wasn't a happy bunny. Neither were we by the end of the night."

"So you don't know why he was in a bad mood?" Blake said. "Did he say anything that might have given you a clue as to why?"

"It was usually a girl, if it was Ernie. He always had a couple on the go. There was one up in Newcastle or somewhere round there and he kept going on about her. He'd met her when Prosser sent us on a tour up there. Bloody nightmare it was but Ernie was in love."

"Were there any jealous boyfriends?"

Treadwell laughed. "There were *always* jealous boyfriends. That was my job, to see them off." He paused and grinned. "Course, it was Ernie they were after but sometimes I got lucky. Handsome by association, if you see what I mean."

Blake glanced at Kath who look disgusted.

"If you did read the mainstream media, Sammy," Blake said, "you'd know we found the body bricked up behind a wall down in the old air raid shelter, a big hole in the back of his head. We're pretty sure it's Ernie and we're treating it as suspicious."

"Really?" Treadwell said, mildly, as if Blake had just told him the test match score. "I always thought he'd just beggared off up north or something."

"You don't sound very surprised at the news," Blake said.

"What can I say, Inspector? I'm old. I've been round the block a few times. Nothing surprises me, these days."

"So you played the night before you left for Hamburg. I'm assuming you all lived near each other. How did you all get home?"

"We had to get the bus home. Can you imagine humping all that kit around on public transport?" He nodded at his drums. "It always pissed me off. So I was in a bad mood, Ernie was bladdered, and that annoyed Dave New. Hardly surprising, but we had a bit of a row at the bus stop when we got off. I remember Dave telling him to sober up for the morning as we were off to Hamburg first thing. And then Ernie staggered off down the road. We all went home."

"And that was it?" Kath said.

"That was it," Treadwell said. "We never saw him again. We went to Hamburg and ended up backing this terrible drag act, singing Beatles and Gerry and the Pacemakers stuff. We were terrible anyway but without Ernie's silky voice we were diabolical. This bird, bloke, whatever, she was worse than a drunk Ernie when she was singing sober. I guess she was quite pretty for a fella, though, he laughed. "Had the bass player fooled for a bit. The dickhead fancied her until we put him straight. She was some kind of Scouser, too, so…"

"So?" Kath said.

"Anyone who came from anywhere within a hundred-mile radius of Liverpool claimed to be a Scouser. It was cool. John Peel, you know the Radio One DJ, he was from Burton, posh end of the Wirral, about as unlike Liverpool as you can imagine but he built his radio career in the US on being from Liverpool. So I guess a Scouse drag queen would have gone down well. If you pardon the pun…"

"It didn't harm Lily Savage two or three decades later," Blake said, nodding. "And you never heard from Ernie again?"

"Never," Treadwell said.

"Didn't you wonder where he'd gone? Weren't you worried for him?"

"Worried? Do me a favour. The man had stiffed our last chance at making it big. We came back from Hamburg broken. I didn't play for years, neither did the others, as far as I know. There were rumours, of course. Someone said he was gay and went to start a new life in Hamburg, which is bollocks because Ernie was about as hetero as they come. I always thought he'd gone up north to settle down with his Geordie bird."

"What about the Wayne Prosser theory?" Blake said, raising an eyebrow.

Treadwell tensed up again. "That piece of shit? It's possible I suppose. The man was a creep and not because he was gay, either. Gay, straight, Bi, whatever, he'd still have been a fuckin' flake. He stole from us, he sent us to the worst dives imaginable, ripped us off. He was always touching Ernie up, and Ernie didn't like it. So, yeah, maybe he did kill Ernie. I don't know. He's long dead, though, isn't he? Good riddance, I say."

"You were in prison for a stretch, right?" Kath said. "GBH, wasn't it?"

"Are you kiddin'?" Treadwell chuckled. "I'm a pussycat, me. I wouldn't harm a fly. Not unless it tried to harm me first. Nah, that was Gary Jensen, the bass player. He was the one with the bad temper and no sense of humour." He shook his head. "The number of times I had to wade into a fight to save his skin. He was a fucking nightmare, all the self-control of a two-year-old."

Blake looked over at the lads in the band. They had been listening intently at first but now were getting restless, playing odd notes and shuffling around. "Well, you've got a gig to prepare for, we won't detain you any longer. We may need to talk to you again but if you think of anything in the meantime, do get in touch."

"Sure," Sammy said. "No problem."

But Blake could tell by the tone of his voice that there was a problem.

CHAPTER 31

His whole body ached by the time he got home. Like it always did. If he was honest, he was getting far too old for this game and especially for this kind of music. Most guys his age had put away their drumsticks, but he had forged on, screaming in the face of expectation and common sense. It made him feel alive while he was playing.

He got a lot of kudos for it from the young kids, especially when they found out that he'd played in the Cavern back in the sixties. A relic dredged up from the underground past, they seemed to love him for it. He even picked up a few girls every now and then. The music felt fresh and raw, but in terms of attitude he could have been playing with Arthur and the Galahads; it was all rock 'n' roll at the end of the day.

The effort of keeping up left him spent, though. If he felt alive during the performance, he felt half dead afterwards. Every joint, every muscle pulsed. On top of that, tonight he'd brought home a new worry in the form of DCI Will Blake.

They were asking questions about Ernie, Prosser and the Galahads. Those were times he'd rather not go back to. The visit from the police also meant that the village idiot, Gary Jensen would be getting a call and he just didn't know how much questioning that loser could stand up to. The world had been turned upside down by the discovery of the body but now it was closing in on him. Of course, he always suspected that the body would turn up but there was so much he didn't understand.

A new letter lay on the hall floor when he came in. It was late and, despite the pounding the evening had given him, he suddenly felt awake. It had been delivered while he was out, but he'd placed a CCTV camera in the front bay window. With any luck, he'd have caught a picture of whoever it was. That kind of knowledge gave him power.

"Game on," Sammy Treadwell muttered as he opened the letter. "Let's go."

CHAPTER 32

The great thing about the Wirral, Vikki Chinn thought, was you were never far away from the sea. There were always seagulls, big skies and the storms could be spectacular. Blakey would probably have something to say about its maritime heritage, she thought. She recalled him telling her that Admiral Nelson of Trafalgar fame had a girlfriend from the Wirral. Now as she pulled up outside a modest semi a few streets back from Hoylake promenade, she wished she lived a little closer to the sea.

She had managed to speak to Beatty Uxton, Ernie Hughes' sister, on the phone the evening before, and she had agreed to talk to Vikki. She had sounded nervous and uncertain that she could be of any help. "I was a baby when he disappeared," she had said.

It was clear that she'd been tidying the place up before Vikki arrived, the place reeked of air freshener and polish. Beatty Uxton was a stocky woman. Her round, gentle face and soft, brown eyes were framed by a dyed purple bob. She wore a chunky woollen jumper and leggings and smelt like her house. She smiled as she ushered Vikki into the immaculate living room.

"Forgive the mess," she said. "I had a whip round with the cleaner but I didn't have much chance to do anything else."

"It looks like a palace, Beatty," Vikki said, settling into an armchair. "I'm sorry to intrude on your life like this but, as you've probably heard, we've found some human remains and we're trying to establish the identity of the deceased."

"And you really think they might be my brother, Ernie?" Beatty said, looking troubled.

"It seems likely but we can't say for sure, yet. What we really need is a DNA sample from you so that we can see if it matches the remains. Would you be able to do that for us?"

Beattie looked hesitant. "It's difficult. I have so many conflicting feelings about my brother. I'm not sure how I'd cope with finding out it was him after all these years."

"I understand that, Beatty, we'd offer you full support. It will be difficult but it's our only chance of identifying him properly."

"I know but…"

"Do you remember your brother at all?" Vikki said, changing the subject in the hope of coming back round to it later on.

"I'm sorry," Beatty said, regret tinging her voice, "as I said on the phone, I was a baby when Ernie went missing. All I have are the things

Mum told me about him. That he was fun and gentle, a great singer. My dad was away at sea a lot and so Ernie was the man of the house when Dad wasn't there. Mum relied on him a lot. It broke her heart when he went away."

"Did she ever tell you why she thought he'd gone? And why she didn't contact the police?"

"At first, she thought he'd gone to Hamburg with the band. There were no mobile phones and Ernie wasn't a great letter writer, so she didn't expect to hear from him. She did go to the police, when the band came back and said he'd never been with them. The police just told her that he was a big boy and could look after himself. Mum used to say that he'd gone on the ships like his dad. Lots of lads went to sea then, apparently. They'd work for twelve months, see a bit of the world, and come back with money in their pockets. She didn't really know what had happened to him. We heard some rumours, things spread around by his so-called mates in the band."

"Why do you say, 'so-called?'"

"They just abandoned him. He didn't turn up and their first instinct was to say, 'sod him' and go chasing their dreams in Hamburg. And when they came back, one of them said he thought he might have seen Ernie over in Germany. Another one said Ernie had a boyfriend over in Hamburg. Those were different times, Vikki, it upset my mum to hear those rumours. That story even grew and it was said that Ernie went abroad on the ships, settled down with a boyfriend in LA and died of AIDS in the eighties. You can imagine what this all did to my poor old mum."

"It must have been very hard, Beatty," Vikki said, with a pained look. She wanted to give the poor woman a hug, but it was her long-dead mum who had needed the sympathy and support years ago. "Are you certain the band members spread these rumours?"

Beatty shrugged. "That's what my mum said. There was another story that he'd got a girlfriend up in Newcastle pregnant and went up there to live with her. He would have rung my mum, though, or even come back. Even out of wedlock, my mum would have treasured a grand kiddie. And, later, when their manager or agent or something was murdered. They started saying that *he'd* killed Ernie but you lot never investigated."

"Why d'you think they spread these rumours?"

Beatty sighed. "I don't know, maybe they felt guilty about leaving him behind or maybe they were angry with him for not turning up. Apparently, their time in Hamburg didn't go well. Serves them right, I suppose. What I do know is that all the different stories made things much harder for my mum. She couldn't let go and she died wondering what had happened to her precious son."

"It must have affected you, too," Vikki said in a low voice.

"Yes," Beatty said. She paused, composing her thoughts. "You know, for years, I resented this saintly brother who never was. He haunted my life, I felt compared to him all the time. There was always a part of Mum's affections shut off from me because of what happened to him. I don't know if it was because she worried about him or because she didn't dare get too close to me in case I vanished too, but we had a tricky relationship."

"This must be difficult, Beatty, but I wonder if you have any old family photographs? It gives us more background on the person we're investigating. We can see the person he was, then."

"I thought you might ask that, so I dug out Mum's family album. You can take it…"

"Thank you, we'll look after it and return it to you as soon as we can. This is very helpful, Beattie, I'm very grateful. Have a think about giving a DNA sample, too, it would make a huge difference to the investigation."

"Listen, I've been thinking as we chatted. I will give you a sample. If it is Ernie, then I'll know for certain, won't I? and then I can be sure what happened to him. How soon can we do it?"

***

The first new telephone call took Jeff completely by surprise. He was standing in the supermarket, wondering if an extra bottle of red would do any harm, given the recent events when it went off. In fact the sound of the ringtone gave him a frisson of excitement. This could be it; his agent calling with details of the final book deal. Obviously the cash advance they offered him was important but there were other details, junkets, festivals, TV appearances, travel. All of these were icing on what he hoped would be a very lucrative cake and had yet to be announced.

The voice on the other end of the line doused Jeff's anticipation like an ice-cold shower. "Thought you could shake me that easily, Jeffrey?" it hissed. "Well I'm back and it doesn't matter how much they punish me. You know, I was that close to forgiving you. That close but you ratted on me. They took my phones, Jeffrey. Wrecked my room. Do you know how that feels to have your personal space invaded?"

"As a matter of fact, I do, Gambles," Jeff said, glancing around to see if any other shoppers were near. "You know I do."

There was a pause on the phone. "I see," Gambles said. Jeff could detect no trace of the frightened sinner he'd met in the visiting room only a few short days ago. This was the old Gambles, ego the size of a planet, inflated beyond his capabilities but he was still capable of so much. "Then you had a caller, did you? I hope you realise what that means." Jeff remained silent for a second. "I know where you are Jeffrey. I'm tracking you. Supermarket, right now isn't it?"

"You can hear the announcements and rattle of trolleys," Jeff said, trying to sound brave, but his voice shook.

"You're looking at the wine."

Jeff's eyes widened. And he looked around to see if anyone was watching him. "Th-that was a lucky guess..."

"I'll be seeing you soon, Jeffrey." The line went dead and Jeff promptly blocked it. Grabbing two extra bottles, he hurried down the aisle towards the checkout, searching for any suspicious faces. How did Gambles know? Was it a lucky guess? He could have been listening to the background noise and it was a fair bet that if Jeff entered a supermarket, he'd make straight for the vino. All the same, Gambles had a way of worming into your head. Will had warned him about it.

It was cold and grey as he stepped out of the shop. Pulling his coat around his neck and trying to keep his shopping trolley under control, Jeff rattled towards his car. A black BMW drew up alongside him as he unloaded his stuff into the boot. Jeff froze, bottles in hand as the window slid down.

A bald man in a dark suit filled the driving seat. He had a kind face but at the same time, Jeff knew he was here on business. "You need to get in the back," he said.

Jeff looked around the carpark. "B-but I've got frozen stuff in the bag…"

"I'd say you've mostly got alcohol and crisps," the man said. "I watched you buy them. I'll say it again. You need to get in the back."

CHAPTER 33

Quite how DC Andrew Kinnear ended up getting to visit Eileen Rapino, he wasn't sure. Kath Cryer was all for popping out to see her but at the last moment, had some kind of meeting and had passed it onto him.

"She's as mad as a box of frogs, but you'll be fine," she had said, before disappearing off into Blake's office.

Kinnear had managed to pull the file on her brother, Peter Rapino, and it didn't make happy reading. A young boy growing up in the sixties and seventies, confused about his sexuality and made to feel ashamed, he had fled from home for the streets of Liverpool. There, he plied his trade as a male prostitute, involved in petty crime and 'immoral activity' until he murdered Wayne Prosser. He died of a heroin overdose in the eighties whilst serving his sentence.

Eileen had greeted him at the door with suspicion at first, her round, pale face peering at him through the crack. Once he'd shown his warrant card and assured her that he wasn't selling tea towels or going to steal her electricity meter, she let him in. The house struck Kinnear as cluttered but then his husband, Chris was something of a minimalist, despite having a young child who seemed to be a magnet for small plastic objects. The Rapino house had photographs, figurines, vases, bowls, tankards, statues of the Virgin Mary, and pictures of Jesus cluttering every surface.

Eileen led him to a small living room and shooed a cat off her armchair before sitting down. "Is this about Father Lanigan and the boy again. I spoke to a lady last week about it. Nobody's died have they?"

"No, not that I'm aware of, Eileen," Kinnear said. "It's about your brother, Peter. I'd like to ask you a few questions, if I may?"

"Oh," Eileen said, sounding disconcerted. "I see. I didn't expect that. He died in prison, you know. Drug overdose..." she paused, staring into space. Then her eyes snapped back into focus. "Why d'you want to talk about him?"

"I'm sorry. I thought I explained that on the phone."

"Right," Eileen said, distractedly. "I wasn't listening properly, obviously. I'm a terrible fidget and an even worse listener. Do you want a cup of tea and some biscuits? You look like you enjoy a biscuit..."

"Why not?" Kinnear said, smiling and slightly bemused by the assessment of his appearance.

"Why not what?"

Kinnear blushed. "Why not have a biscuit? I..."

"I didn't say you couldn't have a biscuit," Eileen said, confused. "What are you on about? Honestly. Are you a proper policeman? I spoke to one with a beard last week. It wasn't right..."

She disappeared, leaving Kinnear staring around the room and wondering what Chris would make of the clutter. He wondered if Eileen had kids because a lot of the family pictures were in what looked like home-made frames, adorned with beads, glitter and feathers. Eileen returned quickly with a tea tray and set it down.

"I'll be Mum," she said, pouring the tea, which hadn't really brewed yet. Kinnear watched the pale stream trickle into his cup and wondered if any number of biscuits would take away the taste of a cup of milky hot water.

"Yes, we're reviewing the investigation into Wayne Prosser's murder..."

"Peter never done it," Eileen said, without missing a beat. "Oh, there's talk around here about what happened, but our Peter was a quiet and gentle boy. He wouldn't be able to kill anyone, let alone a big fella like that Prosser. No. Somebody framed him."

"Who do you think did that?"

Eileen shrugged. "I dunno, do I? But I'll tell

you this, there are plenty of people around here with skeletons in their closet. What about that body in the shelter, eh? They're saying it's Ernie Hughes." She leaned forward as though they were being listened to by some outside source. "You can tell me, I'll keep it to myself. Did Father Lanigan do it?"

"Father Lanigan wasn't even born when Ernie Hughes went missing, Eileen," Kinnear said. "Can we get back to Peter? What can you remember about what happened?"

"I dunno, I wasn't there, was I?" Eileen said, blinking at Kinnear. "I was at home that night, watching Bonanza on telly. Do you remember Bonanza? It was cowboys and Indians. I was in love with Little Joe…"

"No, I know you weren't there," Kinnear said, rubbing his brow, this interview wasn't worth all the biscuits in the world. He glanced down at the plate and nearly groaned out loud; Rich Tea, the biscuit with 'austerity' written all over it. They always brought to mind rationing and a certain nineteen fifties greyness. "If you could just tell me what you remember about the time Peter was arrested…"

"Which time? I mean he was arrested a lot, wasn't he?"

"For the murder of Wayne Prosser."

"Horrible man," Eileen hissed.

"Let's start there, then. Why do you say Wayne Prosser was a horrible man?"

"D'you wanna biscuit. They're Rich Tea, my favourite?" The plate wobbled slightly in Eileen's hand.

They're nobody's favourite, Kinnear thought, but he smiled and took a biscuit. Either she had some kind of attention disorder, or she was stalling, he couldn't decide which. "So what was horrible about Prosser, Eileen? And how do you know? Did you ever meet him?"

"A couple of times," Eileen said. "I went out with Peter in Liverpool, he took me to some of the bars and clubs he went to." She widened her eyes. "You wouldn't believe the goings on in some of those places, honestly…"

"So what was Prosser like?"

"Like a snake," Eileen said, spraying crumbs everywhere. "The way he looked at me when Peter introduced us, ooh, it made me shiver. He was cold. Looked at me like I was a problem, like I was going to get in the way of what he wanted."

"Which was?"

"Well, you know, to get at Peter. To… to have sex with him. Look, I don't like talking about it. People judged Peter all the time, they still do, if they want to put me down. 'Ooh, your Peter, your gay druggie brother.' He had a tough time round here back in the day. He had to go to the clubs he went to meet other people like him and there were reptiles like Prosser lurking in the shadows all the time. Poor boy."

"And what did Peter think of Wayne Prosser?"

"He was frightened of him. Prosser was like a big-time gangster. Peter just did what Prosser told him. Prosser liked to hurt him. You wouldn't believe the injuries Peter would come home with, cigarette burns on his skin, bruises and cuts all over his body. And the marks round his neck, well…"

"Prosser strangled him?"

Eileen nodded. "The man was a monster. It was no wonder Peter took to drugs, having to put up with treatment like that."

"Did Peter ever talk to you about what happened the night Prosser died?"

"I visited him in prison as often as I could, but I was having my own problems then, a single parent on benefits. I was only a kid myself, really. It was hard."

"Believe me, Eileen, I'm not judging you," Kinnear said. "All we want to do is get to the bottom of what happened that night."

"Yeah, that night," Eileen said and looked into some middle distance. "It's hard to say, isn't it, sometimes? What's real and what isn't. By the time Peter was in that back alley with Prosser, he'd been on drugs for quite a while. He'd drift between fantasy and reality all the time. He'd tell me stuff that was so obviously made-up, like getting a lift through the Mersey Tunnel from John Lennon or dancing with Nerys Hughes, the one out of the Liver Birds. Making stuff up was second nature to him, too. He'd say anything to get some money out of you for his next fix. So I didn't know whether to believe him or not…" She fell silent again.

"About what, Eileen?" Kinnear said, gently.

"He told me that Prosser was choking him in that back alley and he thought he was going to die. But then he said that 'an angel in white' had appeared and stopped Prosser. He never explained what he meant, but his face lit up as he said it, like it had been real."

"Didn't he mention this in his defence?"

"The weird thing was he wouldn't repeat it to anyone else. It was like he was happy to go to prison rather than tell them about his 'guardian angel.'" Eileen fixed Kinnear with an iron stare, one that blew away any of his earlier doubts about her reliability. "What I do know is," she said, "there was another person there when Wayne Prosser was murdered, and my brother didn't do it."

***

It was probably the worst song Blake had ever heard and that was saying something. Even if Blake hadn't been sleep-deprived and weary, it would have sounded shockingly bad. There was some stiff competition out there from Blake's childhood, novelty songs that had associated dance moves that largely required participants to be legless drunk or under eight years old. Brian Wise had called into HQ and asked to see Blake on a matter of 'interest and importance.' Intrigued, Blake had found an empty meeting room and obliged him.

"After you'd gone," Wise said, excitedly, "I did a bit more rummaging around. I have quite an extensive collection of field tapes – interviews, rare recordings of bands from the sixties and the like. Anyway, something was nagging me, something at the back of my mind telling me that I had a recording of Arthur and the Galahads and sure enough, I found a copy of an old demo they did. I spent the rest of the day and half the night trying to digitise it. And here it is!" He placed his phone on the table and touched the screen.

The sound was tinny but Blake could pick out jangling guitars, a little bass and the thud of the drums. Ernie's voice was clear and bright, a little bluesy with the transatlantic accent that permeated so much music then. The tune reminded him a little of the song 'Mony, Mony' by Tommy James & The Shondells.

"Saw a little girl go riding by," Ernie sang. "All I could say was, 'My-oh-my.'"

A chorus joined in, *"It was Phiiiiiil on the filly, maaaaade me feel silly, it was Phiiiiiil on the filly, maaaaaade me feel silly."*

Blake looked at Wise, who shrugged at the words, silently.

"Long black hair, eyes of green," Ernie continued. "Prettiest lady I've ever have seen. She's the Queen of the Hill, gives me a thrill, the King don't like it but I love her still…"

The song rattled on for another minute or so, declaring the girl a princess and vowing to marry her. When the song ended, Wise beamed triumphantly at Blake. "Well?" he said.

"It's terrible," Blake said. "And what does it mean?"

"What does 'Hully Gully' or 'Tutti-Frutti' mean? I think it was just a novelty song, something that dancers could shout out the chorus to."

"I see," Blake said.

"It was a song that caused them a lot of trouble," Wise said. "Hecklers used to make up rude versions, apparently 'Filled up with willy,' was a favourite. Ernie used to get very upset. They stopped playing it in the end. You can imagine the reception it got from the record companies."

"Another source of tension between members of the band, I suppose, too" Blake mused. "Ernie would be bitter about their reluctance to play his song and they'd resent the fact that it went out on a demo."

"Exactly," Brian Wise said. "I bet they never forgave him for pushing that song through."

"I wonder," Blake said, stroking his chin.

CHAPTER 34

Gary Jensen reminded DC Alex Manikas of an elderly hobbit. He was a genial, round-faced old man with a mop of curly grey hair that was thinning on top. He wore a stained fawn cardigan and ragged slippers. His bungalow in a cul-de-sac in Prenton, a southerly suburb of Birkenhead, didn't really suggest a rock 'n' roll past, either. He welcomed Manikas in with an almost manic laugh, and huge hand gestures. "Do come in, Inspector…"

"Detective Constable," Manikas said, a little awkwardly. Maybe it was Jensen's overfriendly manner, but here was something about the man that Manikas didn't trust.

"Sorry, so sorry," Jensen said, holding up his hands. "Can I make you a tea or a coffee?"

"No, thank you," Manikas said, following Jensen into the living room. An enormous television screen dominated the room and a gas fire glowed, making it stiflingly hot. Shelves full of books and magazines made the room feel small and claustrophobic. Manikas sat himself down in an oatmeal-coloured armchair and pulled out his notebook.

"You'll have to forgive the mess," Jensen stammered. "My wife's not been well. Bad back... not that it's her job you understand. I mean, I try to do more round the house but..."

Manikas shrugged. "Looks fine to me, sir," he lied. It smelt like Jensen had been sleeping in his chair and numerous mugs and plates littered the room. A fine layer of food crumbs coated what space there was between the small stacks of crockery. "As I explained on the phone, I just need to establish a few facts about the disappearance of Ernie Hughes back in 1964."

"It was a long time ago, constable, I'm not sure I can remember anything. My memory is terrible these days. I'm sorry about that. Old age, I suppose."

"If you can try your best, sir," Manikas said, with a brief smile. "It is important. We're close to identifying the body discovered under Bidston Hill and anything you might remember will help us trace his last movements."

"So you aren't sure that it actually is Ernie?"

"It's a working theory at the moment. Almost certainly correct from the physical height and other attributes but we just need to confirm it. Anyway, when did you last see Ernie Hughes?"

Jensen bit his thumbnail. "I don't know the exact date but it was the night he went missing, I suppose. We'd played somewhere and got the bus home. Everyone was in a filthy mood with him because he'd come to the gig pissed. The whole night was a mess. Anyway, we said, 'see you,' to him and never saw him again."

"Sorry, what stop did he get off?"

"We all got off at the same stop. Top of Belvedere Road. He had a bit of a walk because he lived a few streets away from the rest of us."

"So you all got off at that stop and, what? Waved him off, 'see you in the morning,' and that was it?"

Jensen blinked at Manikas. "Yeah. That was it."

"I thought you were angry with him, and didn't you have the trip to Hamburg the next day? Surely somebody said something else other than, 'see you?'"

"I don't remember what was said exactly. I suppose Dave New had a go at him and told him not to be late in the morning. Ernie didn't really want to go. He had this bird up in Newcastle and he kept saying how much he was going to miss her."

"So Ernie wasn't sold on the idea of going over to Germany? Did that cause tension in the band?"

Jensen shrugged. "I don't know."

"You must know if your friends were arguing, sir, I mean, you've told me that Ernie was reluctant about Hamburg. Surely someone must have said something about that."

"Well, I suppose so, of course. Sammy probably took the piss out of him, said he was under the thumb. Dave would have told him he was going and that was that…"

"Dave New was quite a forceful character, then?"

"Dave was a bully," Jensen said and almost put his hand over his mouth as if realising he'd said too much. "I mean, not to speak ill of the dead."

"In what way was he a bully?"

"He just bossed us around, that's all. He wanted the band to succeed more than the rest of us, I suppose. He did a lot of the organisation and bookings before Wayne Prosser took over."

"So Dave would have been angry about Ernie being drunk that night. Angry enough to attack him?"

"No!" Jensen said, blotches of red appearing on his cheeks. "Dave wouldn't hurt a fly. Anyway, I thought it was Wayne Prosser that did Ernie in…"

"Why do you say that, sir?"

"I don't know, just something I heard. He was the kind of fella who'd do that."

"Was Prosser in the habit of hanging around Bidston late at night?" Manikas said. "Or do you think he was laying in wait for Ernie?"

"It was just a rumour I heard, that's all. You're tying me in knots." Jensen's voice had gone up an octave.

"Forgive me, sir. I didn't mean to confuse you. It's just that you mentioned Prosser and I understood that he tended to stick to the city rather than venture out into the suburbs."

"You're investigating Prosser, too?" Jensen said and licked his lips.

"Obviously, he knew Ernie, so we're looking into his movements around that time. Do you really believe he killed Ernie Hughes?"

Jensen's foot began to tap like he was keeping beat to a tune Manikas couldn't hear. "I really don't know. Prosser was horrible, he always reminded me of a wicked witch, all hunched up, with his saggy skin and his long fingers prodding you. Except he wore these posh suits and fur coats. He had a big hat, wasn't pointy though. A fedora, I think that's what they call them. Some people said he'd killed Ernie, others said Ernie had gone abroad or up north."

"Who said these things, sir?" Manikas said.

"J-just people," he said vaguely, waving his hands in the air. "Plenty of gossips around aren't there?"

"And you didn't think to look for Ernie when you came back from Hamburg?" Manikas said.

"Or even ask around a bit?"

"He wasn't really a friend," Jensen snapped. "We played music with him, but he was an outsider to our group. He'd been to a different school and lived in another street. I never liked him anyway. He thought too much of himself, always preening and combing his hair."

"But he just vanished. Weren't you the slightest bit curious?"

"Look. We weren't happy with him, all right? We'd all got excited about Hamburg. It was meant to be good money and a big adventure. We were following in the Beatles footsteps and thought we'd be famous, too. But we ended up backing some drag artist in a strip club and that was all because Ernie didn't show up. If we had come back looking for him it'd be to..." Jensen pursed his lips and looked down at his fingers.

"To what, sir?" Manikas said. "Beat the living daylights out of him?"

"Hamburg changed everything!" Jensen yelled, slapping his hand on the arm of his chair. "I didn't really want to go either but Dave bloody New pushed me into it. I never played again after that. Now I want you to go. You've upset me and I can't help you at all."

***

If the definition of madness is doing the same

thing again and again and expecting a different result, then Jeff Blake wasn't sure what to think. He had been in this situation before, bundled into the back of a black car and spirited off to meet an egotistical crime boss. Last time, it had turned out all right for him, so surely expecting it to go badly this time was misguided, right? But it seemed unlikely that he was going to be playing a round of golf with Kyle Quinlan and sinking a few pints later.

The big man who had told him to get in the car remained silent once Jeff complied and they drove up the Wirral to the leafy, exclusive village of Caldy, hangout of footballers, TV celebs and the generally well-to-do. They had pulled into a long gravel drive to an old house and the man had ushered Jeff up the stairs, through the thick, wooden door and face-to-face with Laura Vexley, Will's old girlfriend. Jeff had forgotten how tall and athletic she was, her short hair emphasised her strong cheekbones. The leggings and sweat top she wore told Jeff she was off to the gym and that she went often. She didn't look pleased to see him.

"What the fuck are you doing here?" she said, her eyes so wide, they almost popped out of her head.

"Hi Laura," Jeff said. "Good to see you, too..."

She ignored him and looked at the big man.

"What the fuck is he doing here, Nick?"

"Kyle wants a chat with him, Laura, no problem. Just a chat."

"Is this about Cavanagh in the salon the other day?" Laura snapped.

"I guess so, Laura. Like I say, no biggie…"

"Wait here. Do not move," she said and stalked off.

"Um, nice to meet you, Nick," Jeff said, giving a shrug and a grin.

"No offence, but I like to keep things strictly business until I know whether or not Kyle wants me to hurt you," Nick said.

"I thought you said it was just a chat," Jeff replied, swallowing hard.

"I just said that because," he nodded in Laura's wake, "well, you know what she's like…"

Muffled, but quite obvious yelling drifted up the hall and Nick raised his eyebrows at Jeff, who nodded and did the same. "She's worried that Kyle's going to upset my brother, isn't she?"

"You might have a point," Nick said, putting his hands in his pockets and rocking on his heels.

"It'd be a big mistake to hurt me, I suppose, what with my brother being a copper and everything."

Nick shrugged. "The trouble with Kyle is, he's

always making mistakes. That's why Laura gets so twitchy."

Jeff felt the blood drain from his face. "Yeah but…"

"Oops. Here she is…"

Laura came marching back. "All right. You can see him. Just don't say anything you'll regret, Jeff. I don't know what you want, but you're an idiot coming here."

CHAPTER 35

The room that Nick ushered Jeff into spoke of days gone by when gentlemen withdrew from the dinner table for intellectual discussion and cigars. It had a gravitas about it, with its wooden panels and portraits of moustachioed men in black suits. Sadly, the character slouched at the enormous mahogany desk looked like a reject from a reality TV show; handsome and well-groomed but lacking the dignity that this room somehow demanded. Kyle Quinlan puffed on a cigar for a second as Jeff walked across a huge expanse of carpet to stand before the desk.

"Jeffrey Blake," Kyle said, looking at his cigar. "We meet again."

"Um, yes," Jeff said and then added, "Mr Quinlan." Kyle demanded respect of sorts and Jeff was remembering Laura's advice about not saying anything he'd regret.

"You've been upsetting my old friend Josh Gambles, I believe," Quinlan said, looking up at Jeff at last. "He's been spouting off about your book. He's not a happy bunny."

Jeff swallowed hard. His mouth had gone dry, but he had to speak. "Mr Quinlan, Kyle, I-I've been working for months on that book, I can't just scrap and rewrite it. Gambles is upset because it's not entirely about him..."

Quinlan frowned. "What the fuck is it about, then?"

"It's about lots of things, life, television, me and yes, it's kind of focused on Gambles. He's the prism if you will..."

"Prism?" he snorted, exchanging a glance with Nick, who shrugged. "How's he a prism?"

Jeff scratched his ear, nervously. He wasn't very good at boiling complex ideas down into simple sound bites. His agent often said he should work on it so he could pitch books to editors at parties, but Jeff never could. "It's like my life and all the choices I made or were made for me and Gambles' life and all the choices he made or were made for him, interspersed for comparison and linked to popular TV shows of the past, music and cultural events..."

"Sounds shit," Quinlan said, he leaned forward. "You haven't got me in there have you?"

Jeff felt as though he was falling down a lift shaft, but two inspired insights struck him: one, Quinlan was afraid of the adverse publicity and two, that could be to Jeff's advantage. "It does have a bit about you in it but that's easily edited out."

Quinlan grunted with satisfaction. "Good. I

don't need the association with that nutter right now."

"The problem is, I can't shut Gambles up quite so easily," Jeff said. "He keeps getting hold of mobile phones and calling me, I block them, but the damage is done. I'm going to have to change my number at this rate and that's a pain in the arse, to be honest. If I'm going to change the manuscript, I need to be in touch with my agent and if she doesn't have my new number, well..."

"And that's my problem?" Quinlan said with a dismissive shrug.

"Gambles is unstable..."

"You must have known that when you started writing a book about him," Quinlan said. "The man had just butchered a load of people and kidnapped a young mum. What part of Gambles' crimes made you think he *wasn't* unstable?"

"No, no, I mean really unstable. Like unpredictable. A loose cannon. Gambles runs along certain lines, right? His ego is everything to him. That and his love/hate relationship with my brother. But recently, he's got religion..."

"Religion?"

"Big time, Mr Quinlan. He's been talking about Heaven and Hell and confession. He wants to be absolved of his sins."

"Fuck me," Quinlan muttered, licking his lips.

"In the past, Gambles would keep tight-lipped about almost everything he couldn't brag about," Jeff said. He lowered his voice and took the risk of leaning over the desk towards Quinlan. "Gambles is a thorn in both of our sides. If you could warn him off. Shut him up, then we'll all be happier."

Quinlan stared up at Jeff and Jeff realised how close he was to the man, he could smell his aftershave mingling with the cigar smoke. "You're right," Quinlan said at last, sitting back in his chair. "You know I thought you were going to be a pain in the arse, Jeffrey but it seems like you've done me a favour by bringing this to my attention. Leave it with me. I'll sort it."

"And Gambles won't bother me again? I can write my book?"

"With a few adjustments," Quinlan said. "You should be good to go. Gambles won't trouble you again."

"You won't be in it, I promise, Mr Quinlan," Jeff said, with a smile. "It'll be like you never had a part in Gambles' life."

"I like your thinking, Jeffrey. Nick, take him home."

***

Ian Youde was lurking around Blake's front door when he arrived home. He was wearing a hi-vis jacket and had a torch in his hand. "Sorry, Will, just doing a quick check around. Steve and Lorna down the way there had an intruder at the weekend…"

Blake felt himself colouring. "Yeah, that was me."

"Yer what?"

"Come in and I'll explain over a cup of tea."

By the time Blake had finished, Ian was grinning like a fool. "It's no laughing matter," Blake said. "I've tried keeping her in but she bolted out the house last night and wouldn't come near it this morning. Following her ended in disaster. I might actually have to leaflet the area and see if that makes a difference. Embarrassing, though."

"You see, dogs are far less trouble, aren't they, Charlie?" Ian said and gave the little Jack Russell a pat on the head. "The leafleting is the only thing you can do. If someone is inadvertently leaving the cap off some oestrogen cream and Serafina is going into the house and helping herself, then how else can you stop it?"

"What are the odds, though? It seems so random…"

"Doesn't everything with Serafina?" Ian said. "She's a force of nature more than a cat, I'm convinced of it. If weird things are going to happen, they'll happen around her."

"I'll drink to that," Blake said, raising his mug.

"Listen, I've got a couple of nephews who might be willing to bung some leaflets through local doors for a little renumeration. You get it printed and leave the rest to me."

"Thanks, Ian. I'll need to get it carefully worded," Blake muttered. "And I can think of one person who might just help me."

"Let's hope so," Ian said. "That cat thinks she's the queen..."

"What?" Blake said.

"Well, you know like she owns the place. Don't they call female cats queens, anyway?"

"I dunno, Ian, I'm calling her all kinds of names at the moment," Blake murmured but something Ian had said struck a chord. Something just out of reach and intangible.

CHAPTER 36

In contrast to the feverish excitement of their previous meeting, the team seemed subdued this morning as they gathered to plan their next move. It was quiet and missing the usual banter. They sat staring at the photographs as though willing them to start talking.

"A frustrating day, then?" Blake said, raising his eyebrows. "Alex, you don't look very happy, how was Gary Jensen?"

"Very jittery, sir, lost his temper and pretty much threw me out when I started to push him a bit. That man is hiding something. I'd say we need another go at him."

"D'you think the whole band might have killed Ernie, sir?" Kinnear said. "Dave New had a guilty conscience for the rest of his life. Whatever he did had to be serious."

Blake nodded. "That's a possibility. Sammy said Ernie was drunk and they had a go at him about that. A fight could easily have broken out."

"Gary Jensen was very cagey about what happened at the bus stop when they got back from the gig," Manikas said. "He did finally admit that words were exchanged. And the way he flew off the handle, I could imagine him having a go even now."

"So, the three of them are annoyed at Ernie, who is drunk," Kath said. "They give him a kicking and he dies. Then they hide his body in the shelter and run off to Hamburg. Nobody even knows he's missing at first..."

"Except Wayne Prosser is phoning everyone he can to find out where Ernie is," Blake pointed out.

"If Dave New did kill Ernie, he might have confessed to it to Father Lanigan," Kath Cryer said. "That might explain why the priest was so cagey about revealing what Dave confessed to."

"What about Eileen Rapino, Andrew?" Blake said.

"She was adamant that her brother didn't kill Prosser and that someone else was there the night Prosser was killed. Mind you, she also loves Rich Tea biscuits and kept going on about a TV programme called Bonanza..."

"I like Rich Tea," Kath said, huffily.

Kinnear blushed. "Sorry Ma'am..."

"Nah, I'm just messing with you, Andy," Kath grinned. "Who likes Rich Tea? Cardboard bikkies, them."

"Good for dunking, though," Vikki Chinn said.

"You can't trust them Sarge, they crumble suddenly," Kinnear said. "One minute they look fine, the next your brew's ruined..."

"But Eileeen Rapino didn't rule out the idea that Prosser might have killed Ernie, Andrew?" Blake cut in. "I mean, you didn't just go there and scrounge biscuits off her?"

"No, sir! She said Prosser was a sadist who liked to hurt her brother. Whether that makes him a murderer, I don't know."

"The thing is, sir, from a business point of view, it wouldn't make sense, would it?" Vikki said. "I mean, why kill the golden goose? Especially when you were about to send it to market, if you see what I mean. Ernie was about to go out to Hamburg, why would Prosser jeopardise all that? Plus, both Treadwell and Jensen say they were with Ernie until he wandered off home. What opportunity would Prosser have to confront Ernie, try to seduce him and then kill him? None of it works, for me."

Blake nodded in agreement. "You're right, Kath, plus we're pretty sure that Ernie's murder was premeditated. Nobody has all the materials and equipment to hand to brick Ernie's body up. Not down there. Somebody planned this. Somebody with the skills to build a wall, too. I don't think Prosser fits the bill at all."

"The band members are the obvious suspects," Kath said. "Angry with Ernie, they beat him up, realise he's dead. They have all night to go and break into a builder's yard…"

"And carry all those bricks, cement and tools, Kath? I dunno," Blake said, looking pained at having to disagree with her.

"What if just one of them wanted Ernie dead?" Alex said in a quiet voice. "What if one of them doubled back and jumped Ernie. He could have prepared all the stuff beforehand. He'd know they were all going to get off at the same stop."

"But which one of them and why?" Kath said.

"What would they think would happen if Ernie didn't show up in the morning for Hamburg, Ma'am?" Alex said, he was quite excited now, eager to get approval for his theory.

Kath shrugged. "I dunno, Alex, maybe they'd cancel it. If Ernie was dead, I guess they'd need a new singer…"

"Gary Jensen let slip that he didn't want to go to Hamburg but Dave New bullied him into it. We know that Gary has a quick temper. He burgled a house and beat the old man who lived in it almost to death. Gary said himself that he didn't like Ernie. What if he planned it all just to get rid of Ernie?" Alex sat back, smiling.

The others nodded. "It certainly makes sense. The Gary Jensen we see now isn't the same person who trod the boards back in the day," Blake said. "Dave New seemed too committed to the band to do something like that at such a pivotal time in their career. He would have had the balls to sack Ernie if he wanted to. Treadwell? I can't see a motive with him. He strikes me as a man who knows what side his bread is buttered on. I don't think he'd do anything to rock the boat just before they headed off to Hamburg."

"Except they were all young, weren't they, sir?" Kinnear said. "You do stupid, rash things when you're a teenager, don't you? Were any of them capable of planning all this? I mean, their heads were full of music, dancing, being a pop star and all that entails."

"Caution noted, Andrew," Blake said, with a smile. "I think we should have a more serious chat with Gary Jensen, all the same. Sammy Treadwell, too."

***

Hannah wasn't on the phone when Blake went up to her office. In fact she wasn't in the room at all. Blake cursed himself for not ringing first again and turned on his heel, only to bump into her.

"You all right Will?" she said, with a smile.

"Yeah, I'm fine, well, no. I... I wanted to ask you a favour."

"Come in," she said, her perplexed smile frozen

on her face. She led them into her office and Blake sat down in front of her desk.

"It's my cat," Blake said, trying to keep everything coherent. "She's very randy at the moment..."

Hannah burst out laughing. "Your cat? I'm not sure how I can help with that, Will..."

"No, no," Blake muttered, his face burning. Why was this so hard? "Thing is that my vet suspects that the cat has access to some kind of hormone cream and it's well... you know... having an effect on her."

"Who? The vet?" Hannah said, with a grin.

"Very funny," Blake said. "Honestly, at the moment, I can't sleep for the noise. If you came back to mine... well, the smell alone would put you off..."

"If I came back to yours?" Hannah said, playfully, teasing him with his own words.

"No! I meant... No! But if you did, then you'd smell it for yourself..."

"Wow, that's one hell of a chat up line, Will Blake, 'come back to mine and sniff the cat,'" Hannah laughed.

"It isn't a... I didn't mean," Blake stammered. "I want you to write a leaflet. About Serafina and the problem."

"Aaah…" Hannah said. "You're going to leaflet the area."

"I tried following her and I nearly got arrested for trespass and voyeurism," Blake said, seriously.

Hannah burst out laughing again. "I'd love to have seen that. I knew there was more to you than meets the eye, Will Blake!"

"It wasn't funny," Blake said. "Look, would you help me or not? I want it to be professional and I don't want it to give too much away either, if you see what I mean."

"Dear me, Will, you do have a tough time of it," Hannah said, with a sympathetic smile. She narrowed her eyes. "This probably requires another coffee meeting…"

CHAPTER 37

Gary Jensen had grumbled but agreed to meet them at Birkenhead station to answer further questions. Eager to find out the truth of what happened the night Ernie disappeared, Blake had decided to be there himself with Manikas. Treadwell had said that Jensen had a temper and often flew off the handle. If anyone in the current line-up of suspects was likely to attack Ernie Hughes, it was Jensen.

It was well past lunch and Blake's stomach rumbled. He was beginning to regret not diving in for a takeaway on the way over to Birkenhead, but it was too late now. They sat in the grey, air-less interview room, a table between them. Jensen struck a pathetic figure, age had ravaged him, leaving liver spots on his parchment hands and deep wrinkles on his face. His mop of curly hair looked strangely youthful on top of the crumpled wreckage that was the rest of him. Blake couldn't help thinking of Treadwell, lean and limber, fighting off any inclination of age. Clearly, Jensen had succumbed long ago, languishing in arm-chairs and slowly decaying. There may be a very good reason for that; Blake wasn't judging, all it took was an aching joint; a few months of chronic pain could slow anyone down.

There was something else about Jensen, though, an air of indignant self-pity as if he was destined for greater things but the world had wronged him in some way. Blake suspected that Jensen had spent his life coat-tailing others, hoping to steal a little of their glory not realising that his failure to flourish was of his own making. And when he came close to that realisation, he lashed out, angrily, creating a new situation to blame for his downfall.

Blake cleared his throat and leaned forward. "Thank you for taking the time to come, Mr Jensen, I'm DCI Will Blake..."

"I remember you from Searchlight. You were that copper, weren't you?" Jensen said, trying a friendly smile. "Did all the CCTV stuff..."

"I was indeed, Mr Jensen," Blake said, trying to keep the edge out of his voice. "A good while ago now..."

Jensen nodded. "Time flies." There was a moment's silence as Jensen sat staring at the table between them. "So," he said at last. "What can I help you with? I thought I'd told Constable Manikas everything I knew yesterday."

"Maybe not everything, sir," Blake said. Alex sat with his arms folded, as Blake had instructed, watching Jensen carefully. "Your relationship with Ernie Hughes, what was it like?"

Jensen shrugged. "I dunno. We were friends, I

suppose..."

"You suppose?"

"I don't know if you've ever played in a band, Inspector, but most of your time is spent playing music. We didn't write our own material, so when we rehearsed, we just suggested songs and played them until we got them right. Nobody sat around talking about their deep, inner feelings, especially not back then."

"So you just played with Ernie but never talked to him," Blake said, looking puzzled. "You must have socialised a bit."

"I told your constable, here, Ernie was a bit of an outsider. The Galahads grew up in the same street, we went to the same school, we were mates but Ernie wasn't really one of us. I mean, I got on okay with him when he wasn't drunk."

"Was he drunk often?"

"Towards the end... I mean, when he went missing. He'd have a few before coming to the gigs. A lot of the places we played didn't serve alcohol, so he'd made an effort to get bladdered. I think he was unhappy."

"What about?"

Jensen gave a bitter laugh. "Girls. I don't know how many he had on the go but there was this one up in Newcastle. Bridie or Bridgit, I dunno, can't remember, he was smitten with her. Used to talk about moving up there all the time…"

"I thought you didn't talk about your feelings, Mr Jensen," Blake noted. "When did he express this wish to leave?"

"I can't remember. When we were setting up the gear, not that he helped much with that. He was too busy either getting his hair right or moaning on to us about the fee or wanting us to write our own material…"

"He'd written one song, hadn't he?"

Jensen closed his eyes and took a breath. "Phil on the fucking filly. That was an abomination. How do you know about that?"

"An avid collector supplied us with a copy of the demo."

"Ernie and Dave liked it, they bullied me and Sammy into recording it. It was a shit song. Dave used to say it was no good because we didn't play it with any feeling but, I mean to say, how could we? It was terrible. It's not even a girl's name…"

Blake frowned. "What isn't?"

"Phil," Jensen said. "Ernie told us it was about a childhood sweetheart. He fell off her horse when he was a kid. That's how he got that limp. But Phil's a bloke's name. We just sounded like we were gay or something, which was *not* cool back in the day, I'm telling you. We got into so many fights over that."

"So you resented the song and Ernie for insisting on singing it?" Blake said.

"Yeah, I suppose so," Jensen said, licking his lips. "The only thing Ernie Hughes had going for him were his good looks and the fact that he could hold a tune when he was sober. As a person, he was a pain in the arse."

"So you didn't really like Ernie Hughes?" Blake said.

"No," Jensen admitted, glancing at Manikas as though realising he'd said something significant. "If I think about it, no, I didn't like him. But I wouldn't have hurt him if that's what you're thinking."

"I'm not thinking anything, Mr Jensen, I'm just trying to get to the truth of what happened to Ernie Hughes and how his body ended up being bricked up in an air raid shelter for sixty years."

"I don't know nothing about that…"

"You spent some time in prison. Could you tell me about that?"

Jensen's pale face coloured. "Oh, I see," he murmured. "It never goes away, does it? I did time, so I must have murdered Ernie…"

"That's not how it is, Mr Jensen, I'm just trying to get a picture of you as a person, nothing more, nothing less."

Jensen sat back, arms folded, mirroring Manikas. "Yeah, right," the old man scoffed. "Okay, I did time. After the band split up, I did a few labouring jobs, but they fell through. I was skint. I went on the rob, didn't I?"

"You broke into people's houses at night and terrorised them if they disturbed you…"

"There were one or two who woke up," Jensen said, looking down into his lap. "I'm not proud of what I did but I had a family to support…"

"Tell that to Mr Leonard Yelland," Blake said, reading from the file. "Sixty-five years old and you put him in hospital. His family say he never recovered properly."

"He wouldn't let go of me," Jensen whispered. "I had to get away, but he just clung onto me. So I hit him…"

"Trouble is Mr Jensen, you didn't stop hitting him, did you? You couldn't stop…"

"No…"

"What if I tell you what I think happened the night Ernie died? You never wanted to go to Hamburg and you hated Ernie, thought he was self-obsessed and unreliable. If Ernie was gone, you couldn't go to Hamburg. Dave and Sammy would be disappointed, but they'd come round eventually and find a new lead singer. You'd never get the blame for stealing away their big chance, Ernie would. So you planned his death."

Jensen reddened, clenching and unclenching his fists. "I never. That isn't what happened."

"You put everything you needed to brick up the body in the shelter the day before and then you waited until after the gig to jump him."

"No. You're making stuff up now."

"Or maybe you wound him and the others up to provoke a fight. Beat him almost senseless and then offered to take him home. Except you took him to the shelters instead and finished him off. Isn't that how it happened Gary?"

"NO!"

"Sammy Treadwell told me you had a temper and DC Manikas here witnessed it first-hand yesterday."

"Sammy told you that?" Jensen said, looking up from the desk. "The bastard! H-he told me to keep schtum..."

"About what, Mr Jensen?" Blake said.

Anger twisted Jensen's face. "The twisting rat," he hissed, banging a fist on the table. "He fucking well sold me out! Go on then, I'll tell you everything."

CHAPTER 38

It took a while to calm Gary Jensen down. Alex and Blake left the room and leaned on the wall, hands in pockets, pretending they couldn't hear the bumps and shouts inside.

"He really does have a temper, sir," Alex said.

"Jeez, you're telling me, Alex. He's certainly worked up about Treadwell talking to us."

"Do you think the two of them were in on Ernie's death?"

Blake shook his head. "I'm trying not to think anything at this stage, Alex. Shall we take a chance and go back in?"

Gary Jensen sat panting and red-faced, his fists in tight bunches in front of him. When he spoke, he didn't look at Blake or Manikas, he just stared at the tabletop. "There was a fight at the bus stop the night Ernie vanished," he said at last. "We'd been needling Ernie all the way home. Sammy was grumbling because he had to carry his kit anyway and Ernie, being so pissed, had dropped his snare down the stairs on the bus. Dave had been having a go at him about being unprofessional. I was saying we shouldn't go to Hamburg the next day because the idea of Ernie let loose in the bars and nightclubs of the Reeperbahn was too much to think about. Of course, I didn't want to go anyway, so I was in a bad mood about that."

"So Ernie wouldn't have been very happy," Blake said.

"By the time we got off the bus, Ernie was effing and blinding at us. Telling us we'd be nothing without him. He said that Wayne Prosser was going to make him a star, the next Billy Fury, he said. Sammy laughed at him and that made Ernie even worse. Ernie went for Sammy who backed away, but Dave stepped in and gave him a smack. For some reason, Ernie thought it was me and threw a punch my way. Before you knew it, he was on the ground, and we were all giving him a good kicking." Jensen stared off into space, silent for a moment. The telling of the tale had calmed him somewhat. When he carried on, his voice was hushed. "Then he was still. I mean like very still. He was curled up like a baby, what do they call it? Foetal position, isn't it? Dave squatted down and checked him out."

"From what you can remember, how extensive were Ernie's injuries?"

"A few cuts and bruises but nothing major. There wasn't blood pouring out of him, if that's what you mean. But then Dave said he wasn't breathing. He said he was dead."

"So, what did you do?"

"Sammy was already making a getaway, as much as you can carrying a small drum kit. I looked at Dave and we both hurried after him. We left Ernie there. It was like an unspoken agreement at first. We were never there, nothing happened, as far as any of us were concerned, the last we saw of Ernie was him walking down the road."

Blake frowned. "But who hid his body in the shelter, then?"

"I honestly don't know," Jensen said, with a shrug. "The last time I saw Ernie Hughes, he was lying on the road and I walked away. I don't know nothing about anything else."

"Do you think Sammy Treadwell or Dave New could have doubled back and hidden the body?" Blake said.

"Maybe, but they never said so, if they did. We were all in a bit of a daze," Jensen said, "the next morning, we just went through the motions as though nothing had happened the night before. I almost believed it. It was weird. I even began to expect Ernie to turn up myself. Of course, he didn't but I began to think that maybe he'd picked himself up and staggered home. Dave New might have had the wherewithal to go back, he loved the band so much and wanted us to be big. It was 1964, the death penalty was still in force. Peter Allen being hanged in Walton Prison earlier that year was still fresh in our minds…"

"All the more reason to cover it up, then?"

Jensen looked pained. "I suppose, and we were scared. I was so scared, I kind of convinced myself it never happened. Maybe Dave did hide the body. I don't know. But neither Sammy nor Dave said anything about hiding Ernie's body even once in the last sixty years."

"You three stayed in touch, then?"

"We bumped into each other every now and then," Jensen said. "We'd nod say a few words. After Hamburg, we didn't want to be in each other's company for longer than we had to. We'd fallen out bigtime over there; we ended up in a right dive backing this drag act. I blamed Dave, he blamed Ernie, Sammy blamed both of us. We slept in a tiny room in a slum with rats and cockroaches. Wayne Prosser was with us, but he seemed to be having a more comfortable time of it. We saw another side to him, I can tell you."

"What d'you mean?"

"We knew he was a twisting bastard, but he took up with this drag queen, Sasha, God he tormented her. She was in the room across the landing from us and the noises when he visited." Jensen shook his head. "Sammy slagged her off for being a bad singer but she could barely speak after Prosser had strangled her half to death. It made me sick to my stomach, treating someone like that. Anyway, our residency ended when Prosser nearly killed Sasha. She accused him of raping her too. The manager of the club threatened to call the police, but Prosser just laughed. I can't pick up a bass guitar without seeing that sick bastard leering at me with his arm around Sasha's shoulder."

"And that's why you gave up music? Stopped associating with New and Treadwell?"

"That and Ernie," Jensen said, nodding. "Dave and Sammy had no sympathy for Sasha. They said she'd brought it on herself, what with being a man pretending to be a woman and all that. Sammy hated 'queers' as he called them. Dave too, for that matter. I felt sorry for her. She found herself in that club in Hamburg because it was the only place that she could be herself and look what happened?"

"And when you got back, you never wondered about what happened to Ernie?" Blake said, feeling that Jensen was veering off on a tangent. "You never spoke to the others about it at all?"

Jensen reddened. "No. We did meet up from time to time. I started the rumour that he'd gone up north to live with his girlfriend. It just slipped out one day, when someone in the pub was asking about Ernie. Dave was furious when he found out. He said that anything like that could be traced back to its source. Turns out though, that

Sammy had been telling everyone that Ernie was gay and had gone to Hamburg after all. Dave told us that if he went down, he'd take us with him."

"So you made a pact of silence and went about your daily lives."

"We kept quiet after that but found that the rumours had a life of their own. Any time someone looked into Ernie's disappearance, they met with the 'gone to Newcastle' or the 'gay in Hamburg' story. They even grew, as urban legends do. By the eighties, everyone was saying that Ernie had moved to LA and died of AIDs. We had nothing to do with that. Maybe spurred on by this, Sammy was over in Hamburg with work or something and sent a forged letter to Ernie's mum from Ernie, telling her that he was fine and had settled down there. I thought that was cruel and I told him so." There was still a fire in Jensen's eye. "He's an evil bastard, that Treadwell. I wouldn't be surprised if he hadn't done it for a laugh. When Dave died, he insisted we meet up once in a while just so he could make sure I wasn't 'growing a conscience' as he put it."

"What did he mean by that?

Jensen shrugged. "Dave New got religion, didn't he? He was going to confess his sins to the world. Sammy put a stop to that by picking up young Jayden from school and dropping him off at home. Kind of demonstrating how easy it would be to hurt Dave's family."

"Treadwell would do that?"

"I told you, he's a nasty piece of work."

"And all the while Ernie lay there in the shelter," Blake said.

"I didn't know where his body was, I swear down. Maybe if I'd known that, I would have confessed years ago. I had nothing to lose. There's something about his body not being found that let me believe that maybe we didn't kill him. That maybe he was somewhere in the world sunning himself on a foreign beach."

"Well, he isn't, Gary," Blake said. "We won't detain you further but obviously, we'll be considering charges once the investigation is concluded. We need a word with Sammy Treadwell, too."

"Don't we all," Jensen hissed through gritted teeth.

CHAPTER 39

Superintendent Martin sat back in his chair, grinning. As far as he could see, the case was closed, killers identified. No doubt he could see a clear, uncomplicated weekend just around the corner, Blake thought. A round of golf, maybe, a nice Sunday roast at the local carvery with the wife. Blake almost didn't have the heart to break it to him.

"Obviously, this wasn't a victimless crime, Will, but it seems like Treadwell and Jensen being brought to justice sends out a clear message that it doesn't matter how long ago your crimes were committed, we'll catch you."

Blake kept a straight face. He knew what Martin meant, this crime happened so long ago that neither Blake nor Martin could have done anything about it. But they'd caught their villains. Public confidence was important and so were the 'optics' of the whole incident but at the same time, all Blake could think about was the murder of a young man with his whole life ahead of him.

"There are a number of loose ends that need tying up, sir," Blake said at last, watching the satisfied grin slide from Martin's face.

"What kind of loose ends?" Martin said, eyeing

Blake with suspicion. "I know you, Will, you'll pick at this case until everything unravels and we're back to square one."

"We need to speak to Treadwell and interview the pair of them under caution. No doubt their versions of events will differ. They may even try to blame each other. I just don't think we're home and dry, yet."

"I knew you'd do this, Will. It doesn't have to be complicated. Just a gang of lads losing their tempers and then covering up their crime."

"It's just that some things don't add up, sir," Blake said. "I just don't think Jensen has what it takes to kill a man in cold blood, sir. There's a difference between what he did to Ernie as part of a group and actually planning the death of an individual, isn't there? Besides..."

"Please, Will..."

"As far as Jensen was concerned, they left Ernie Hughes lying on the roadside. How did he get bricked up in an air raid shelter?"

"It could easily have been Dave New or Treadwell. Right now, all we do know is that the band set upon poor Ernie Hughes and kicked him to death unless Treadwell tells us a different story..."

"Maybe..."

Martin pressed his fingertips against his temples so hard, Blake thought his head would burst. "What do you mean, 'maybe?'"

"I mean, sir, how would you move a body from the roadside to the shelter. It's a fair walk with a dead weight..."

"There were three fit young men in that band, Will."

"Even so, sir, shifting a body without detection would be very difficult. What if Ernie was coming round, still dazed but able to walk? Someone guides him to the shelter and then finishes him off with the hammer."

Martin looked troubled. "That would imply someone planned Hughes' death well before the night..."

"They must have done, sir, surely. Did Sammy Treadwell and Dave New just happen to stumble upon the bricks and fresh mortar to seal the body up with? Those supplies must have been down there already."

"That doesn't mean it couldn't have been one or all of the band, does it?" Martin sighed. "But it has to be based on the truth. We can't convict an innocent man. Go on then, Will, tie up your loose ends. Please, just keep it low key..."

"Don't worry, sir, you know me."

***

As agreed, Blake called up to Hannah Williams'

office as soon as he could and they headed into town. "Where are we going this time?" Blake said, pulling a worried face. "The Cavern? The Blue Angel?"

Hannah laughed. "I thought we'd just find a quiet table at Leaf. You've been there, haven't you?"

"Of course," Blake said. "Anyway, I can't think of a better place than Leaf to design a leaflet..."

"That's verging on dad humour, Will," she said, giving him a pained look. "You should be ashamed..."

"So, this leaflet," Blake said, squashing down the tiny dagger of ice in his heart at the memory of being a dad. It had been brief and tragic. He didn't want to dwell on that now. "It has to be simple and quite generic."

"Like your good self," Hannah said.

"Cheeky."

Hannah stopped in the street. "Why don't you leave the leaflet to me, Will? Let's go somewhere else. Somewhere more exciting."

***

Only a glimmer of streetlights reached this part of the hill. A thick blanket of cloud shrouded any moonlight and so the darkness in amongst the trees was total. It didn't bother Sammy Treadwell. He arrived a good hour before the allotted time and his eyes had become accustomed to the dark. Now he stood in the shadow of an old venerable oak tree, waiting. The letter had been different from the others he'd received; written on scrappier, lined paper pulled from a pad. There had been no stickers and the handwriting was much more erratic. It told him to be there at ten-thirty in the evening with a simple, *'Curious to know what I know? Meet me at the air raid shelter vent, Thursday 10:30pm. Come alone. All will be revealed!'* Even that message demonstrated a writing ability absent in the previous notes.

It had struck Sammy as curious that the note arrived a full day and night before the assigned time. If it was him planning this meeting, he'd spring it at the last moment. As it was Sammy had plenty of time to go up to the hill during the day and spec out the best places to hide. If this was some kind of trap, then Sammy would be ready and would know the terrain. He wasn't stupid.

So here he was. Police tape fluttered in the breeze and the night seemed particularly black where the brickwork of the vent stood.

He shivered. Not that he was scared. He couldn't wait to meet this joker who'd caused so much trouble with the letters. If it was Terry New, he'd have him, that fat bastard was all bluster like his dad used to be. Sammy didn't have any money to be blackmailed, anyone would know that, so it wasn't certain what the letter-sender was expecting from him. Maybe whoever it was would give him a sermon and beg him to repent. Sammy would give them a good hiding. He grinned in anticipation and cracked his knuckles theatrically.

Then the night exploded into red. The force of the blow was so sudden and so strong that it sent him staggering from his hiding place towards the vent. It felt as though a band of iron had been strapped tightly and painfully round his head and a warm liquid trickled down the back of his neck. He tried to lift his arm to touch whatever it was, but he couldn't move it. A second blow made vomit rise in his mouth and a strange coldness enveloped him. Then he felt firm, hands push into the centre of his back, propelling him forward on jelly legs.

He grunted as his face slammed against the vent wall, blinking at the rush of cold air that came up from the darkness. Why wouldn't his arms work? What had hit him? His tongue felt huge in his mouth and tasted of blood. The hands slid down and gripped his ankles and suddenly he was upended, sliding through the hole in the vent cover.

Then he was weightless. There was a last flash of pain as his shoulder clipped something metal and hard, then blackness.

CHAPTER 40

A shaft of golden morning sunlight pierced the grilled windows of the prison chapel and warmed Josh Gambles as he knelt at the low altar rail. It wasn't a huge room, but it was quiet and an air of peace permeated it. It smelt like a church too, musty, a little bit of polish in the air, the sweet scent of flowers. Not that Josh had been in many churches. Maybe if he had, he wouldn't have done the shocking things he did. Was that all it took? To walk into a building every week and hear the word of God?

The last church he'd been in was a crumbling ruin that he used to imprison a terrified woman. He was never going to harm her, she was merely bait, something to create a sense of urgency for DCI Will Blake. He stopped and looked up at the cross on the altar. She had escaped. Maybe God had given her the strength to do that.

A wretchedness filled his chest, weighing his stomach down as surely as if he had a ton of lead in there. He was worthless. Truly a sinner. Ashamed. But what was it the poet William Blake had said? "Shame is pride's cloak," Gambles muttered. "I can never be redeemed after what I've done and if I think I can, then I'm as arrogant as when I didn't care about the people I killed."

He thought of Hell, the fires, the ovens, to burn eternally. Constant pain. Unremitting foulness, drowning in excrement forever and ever. Is that what a loving God would want for him? He deserved no less. "A-and I'm not just saying that," he muttered to the cross. Surely God would look into his heart and see the truth; that he really did regret his actions.

Maybe realising what his life could have been was part of the redemption. He could have channelled his admiration of Will Blake into striving to become a police officer, or a social worker. He could have just run a proper fan club. There were myriad things he could have done to turn away from the path that led to the deaths of those innocent people. He could see that now. Maybe it was also part of the punishment, a little Hell on Earth. A little Hell inside his own head. Would that make him Satan, then? A tear trickled down his cheek as he became aware of a huge presence kneeling at the altar rail beside him. He looked to his left.

The man who had joined him was enormous. A pile of muscle and sinew squeezed into a prison uniform. Josh frowned, wondering if he'd seen this man around before. Perhaps he was new. Now that he thought about it, Josh realised he didn't really pay much attention to his fellow prisoners anyway, other than to keep an eye out for attacks. This man was bald, rings of neck fat about his collar. His jowls gave him a hang dog expression and his tiny snub nose finished the look. His huge hands were crossed at the altar rail as though he was about to take communion.

He gave a sidelong smile. "Have you said your prayers, Josh?"

***

The harsh rasp of a body bag zip was not the sound that Blake had wanted to hear so early in the day. He'd woken up on Hannah Williams' couch, fuzzy-headed and wondering why his phone was buzzing so insistently.

The night before was a blur, they'd been to a pub, a Cuban restaurant in an old church, more pubs. Blake had primed Ian Youde to check on Charlie and Serafina and then just gone with the flow. He found himself back at Hannah's chic flat in Toxteth, marvelling at the art on her walls, the stripped floorboards and retro furniture. It was like something out of a design magazine and made him blush to think of his own, run-down mausoleum of a house. "That was fun," Hannah had said, sipping her coffee.

"It was," Blake admitted. "Probably not wise on a school night but I think this case will wrap itself up, eventually. I just don't know how far we can get with it. At least we can use Ernie's sister's DNA to establish the identity of the body and give her some peace of mind."

"Are you ever off duty, Will Blake?" Hannah had said, grinning and throwing a duvet at him. "You're welcome to stay over or get a taxi home. It's quite late though. You should get out a bit more, mate."

Will had smiled back. "I had a great time and yes, you're right. I should." He'd settled himself down on the sofa and slept soundly until the shrill ringtone shattered his peace.

Now he watched white clad scene of crime officers searching the undergrowth around the air vent on Bidston Hill and sighed. He relaxed for one moment, one evening of enjoyment and this happens.

Jack Kenning stooped over the pale blood-stained head of Sammy Treadwell as it poked out of the bag. He didn't need to do that; Blake would have taken his word for it but the man had a theatrical streak. "Another hammer blow to the back of the skull," he said, "and then pushed down the vent, I'd imagine. He was lying at the bottom, limbs broken by the fall. Dead before he hit the ground."

"Thanks for that, Jack. I've a lovely image to mull over during the day," Blake said. He scanned the area around the vent. "Any sign of a weapon?"

"An old claw hammer, wooden handle, no apparent identifying labels. Dropped by the vent,"

Jack said. He nodded at the dark hole in the concrete plug that had once sealed the shaft. "Mallachy is down there, he looks gloomier than usual, so I suppose they've found very little. Bushes under that tree are bloodstained and crushed back there. We think that the victim was struck from behind and then pushed across the clearing and down into the hole."

"Time of death?"

"Council workers found him this morning, quite early. They were preparing to seal up the hole. The body's cold, rigor mortis is easing, so I'd hazard a guess and say between ten and eleven last night. Obviously, we'll get more detail back at the lab."

Blake nodded. "I'm impressed, Jack. You usually hedge your bets more than that."

"Maybe it was the note in his pocket, telling him to meet a mysterious someone up here at ten thirty last night that swung it for me," Kenning said, with a toothy grin.

"Really?"

"Something about meeting up here if he wanted to know what the letter writer knew, something like that. It's been bagged. We'll get an analysis of the paper and ink, handwriting that sort of thing. Quite exciting, very Agatha Christie, eh? A poison pen letter?"

Blake shook his head. "There's nothing exciting about any of this, Jack, it's just grim." He pulled out his phone and called Kinnear. "Andrew, can you get round to Sammy Treadwell's house, there should be a forensic team there soon. See if they've found any letters. Oh and get Manikas to arrest Gary Jensen on suspicion of murdering Sammy Treadwell. We need to talk to him again."

Chapter 41

If Gary Jensen had looked haggard yesterday, an early morning call from Alex Manikas arresting him on suspicion of murdering Sammy Tread-well had aged him by a few decades more. The man's eyes were red, his curly mop of grey hair looked lank. Everything about Jensen drooped as though he felt totally defeated by the world.

Blake, still recovering from his night out with Hannah, rubbed his brow and looked at Gareth Cornell, Jensen's solicitor, who looked equally crumpled but probably because he couldn't find a suit to fit his skeletal frame. The only person in the room who seemed chipper and ready to face the long day was DC Manikas who sat next to Blake, regarding Jensen coolly.

"You do understand why you're here, Gary?" Blake said, leaning on the table between them. "Can you tell us where you were last night between the hours of seven and one in the morning?"

"I was at home all that time," Jensen said, glancing at Cornell. The poor solicitor had obviously advised Jensen to give a no comment response to every question but Jensen was red around the cheeks already.

"And your living room window, DC Manikas here, observed that it was boarded up when he came to arrest you. How did that happen?"

Jensen glanced at his solicitor. "No comment."

"Your knuckles are bruised, Gary," Blake said. "You been in a fight?"

"No comment."

Blake shrugged. "Suit yourself, Gary but after what you said at the station yesterday, I have to inform you that you're our prime suspect. It doesn't look good. If you've been anywhere near Sammy Treadwell, the DNA evidence will give you away."

Jensen had a hunted look about him. "I-I can't bloody win, can I?" he snapped at the solicitor. "I'm stuffed, either way."

Cornell shuffled awkwardly in his seat. "Gary I... "

"Let's get the bruises out of the way first," Jensen snapped. "Okay, yes, I had a fight with Sammy Treadwell last night but I didn't kill him."

"Right," Blake said. "What time was this?"

"About eightish," Jensen said, flexing his hand and looking down at the bruises. "He came round to mine to check I was keeping quiet."

"About what?"

Jensen gave a bitter snort. "Everything. You know, Ernie, the band, Hamburg. Anyway, I told him to piss off. I said I was sick of being pushed around by him. He thinks he's hard but he's an old man like me and I decided to show him that. So I smacked him one, in the face."

"Did he retaliate?"

"He was going to, but I hit him again before he could think about it. He was so shocked, he didn't know what to do. Then I threw him out and shut the door on him. He bricked my bloody windows."

"And then he left?"

"Yeah. He said he'd be back, that it wasn't over, but he's full of shit." Despite his haggard features, there was a levelness in Jensen's voice and a steely glint in his eye that disturbed Blake. He realised that people underestimated this man all the time. Maybe Blake had too.

"What did you do after the brick was thrown?" Blake said. "Weren't you tempted to follow Treadwell? After all, you'd just given him a good thumping and thrown him out."

"No," Jensen said. "I was knackered after that. And the neighbours were looking by then. I didn't want any more of a scene."

"So he throws a brick through your window and you do nothing? I find that hard to believe, Gary," Blake said. "A man with a temper like yours..."

"I don't care what you believe or don't believe, Inspector, when you get to my age, you'll know what it's like. Temper or not, I had to have a sit down after that fight..."

"The trouble is, Gary, your DNA is all over Treadwell's body and there were specks of his blood in your hair..."

"From the fight, I'm telling you. I wouldn't have the first idea how to kill someone, let alone the strength these days..."

"Did Treadwell ever say anything about the letters he received?"

"Letters about what?"

"A letter was found on Treadwell's body, telling him to be at the air raid shelter on the night of his murder..."

"Well, there you go, then," Jensen said, throwing his hands in the air. "Do you think I ran after him once he'd bricked my window and handed him a letter?"

"There were other letters found in Treadwell's house; short ones, hinting that the writer knew something and that Treadwell should confess."

"Like a blackmail type thing?" Jensen said, paling. "Someone who knew about Ernie?"

Blake leaned forward. "What if you sent those letters, Gary? What if Treadwell cottoned onto the fact that it was you and came round to confront you?"

"Then he wouldn't have gone up on the hill if he knew it was me, would he? And he never said nothing about any letters."

"The neighbours heard the window break but they didn't see anyone in the street," Manikas said. "Are you certain it was Treadwell who did that?"

"Why would I lie about that?"

"You're no stranger to lying to cover up a murder, are you Gary?" Blake said. "You spread all kinds of rumours. Even pinned Ernie's death on Wayne Prosser. Why not wriggle out of this one by muddying the waters?"

"No," Jensen snapped. "Sammy Treadwell came to my house and attacked me. I defended myself and he ran off after breaking my window."

"Or did you arrange to meet Sammy up there, ambush him and then hurry home, having broken your window already to give the impression of an argument?"

"Oh, come on! Listen to yourself. That's bollocks!"

"Is it, Gary?" Blake said, firmly. "Nobody else saw Sammy Treadwell at your house. I'd say there's a pattern here. You had a fight with Ernie Hughes but didn't kill him. You had a fight with Sammy Treadwell but didn't kill him. Can you see why I'm suspicious? You were the last person to see Treadwell alive and I'm dubious about the whole fight story, to be honest."

"I never killed him!" Gary Jensen said, tears glistening in his eyes. "The horrible bastard was about the nearest thing I had to a friend. And that's saying something."

"I think I need time with my client," Gareth Cornell said. "He's obviously upset and I want to remind him of his rights and a best course of action."

"Feel free," Blake said, sitting back. "There's plenty of time. It's not like he's going anywhere until we've got to the truth."

***

The team seemed to share Superintendent Martin's sense of frustration at the news that Blake wanted to look further into certain aspects of the case. They sat in the Major Incident Room, staring at the board which seemed to have taken a life of its own. Photographs, maps and diagrams jostled for position with each other in a confusing morass that no longer gave any clarity.

"The letters that were found in Sammy Treadwell's house trouble me," Blake admitted. "There's something about them that brings to mind that terrible song that Ernie wrote about his childhood sweetheart."

"Maybe it's because the letter paper was heavy

weight and scented, sir," Kinnear said. "You know, connotations of an old-fashioned romance."

"Connotations," Kath Cryer said. "Get you."

"It could be, Andrew," Blake said and shrugged. "Can't get away from it that's all."

"It is a pretty awful song, sir," Manikas said. "Bit of an earworm as they say."

"Just a bit of fun, wasn't it?" Kath Cryer chipped in. "No worse than Agadoo or Baby Shark. People just like novelty songs, don't they?"

"What about the building materials, sir?" Vikki Chinn said. "Like you said, they must have been placed in the shelter with a view to bricking Ernie's body up. Maybe somebody remembered a lot of activity up there on the days leading up to Ernie's disappearance. I mean, it's a long shot but..." she shrugged.

"It's worth looking into. Or it might be that they were taken from some building site nearby."

PC Mark Robertson raised his hand. "I'm over there later this afternoon, sir, I could have a chat with Pippa Fearon, she seems to be a bit of an authority on the history of the hill. If there was any construction work done, surely she'd remember."

"Thanks, Mark, that would be great. Any news on the hammer used to kill Treadwell?"

"Not much, Will," Kath Cryer said. "Other than it's old and a little bit rusty. Whoever used it wore gloves and there's no other traces of DNA on it. The only thing they would say is that it looks to be about the same age as the lump hammer used to kill Ernie."

"Jeez," Blake muttered. "I don't know if that's useful or just deepens the mystery."

"Oh, and forensics also say that Treadwell's DNA is all over the house brick thrown through Jensen's window."

"Which would suggest that Jensen wasn't lying when he said that he had an argument with Treadwell earlier in the evening," Kinnear said, gloomily. "And I thought we had our man."

"Did the house searches reveal anything else?"

"No, sir," Vikki Chinn said. "Nothing significant. Treadwell had a small stash of dope but nothing that points to the past. Unlike Dave New, both men seemed to have purged their lives of anything to do with Arthur and the Galahads."

"Maybe Dave New felt more guilt, sir," Manikas said. "That might explain why he kept some of the band artifacts. He couldn't throw them away because he couldn't let himself forget."

"Perhaps," Blake said. "Treadwell seemed to be able to move on easily enough or maybe all his anger at the world was a product of his guilty conscience. Jensen just seemed to hide away from the past. I don't think he ever recovered, which is why I don't think he killed Treadwell."

"Who did then?" Kath Cryer said, with an edge of irritation in her voice. "You know the Super is going to see his arse if we let Jensen off the hook without a good reason."

"We focused on the band a lot, sir," Vikki said, "but maybe we should have thought more about the audience. Didn't Treadwell say that he spent a lot of time seeing off jealous boyfriends? Could it have been someone who saw Ernie as a love rival who killed him?"

"That's possible, Vikki," Blake said. "To do that, though, you'd need to live locally and have access to building materials. But if someone other than the band members killed Ernie, why blackmail and kill Treadwell?"

Vikki nodded unhappily.

"We still haven't really eliminated Wayne Prosser from our list of suspects, for the murder of Ernie sir," Kinnear said. "I know Prosser didn't venture across the water much but it's still possible that he killed him. The phoning up every other call box routine might be a good cover."

"Good point, Andrew. I hate to say it, but we need to go back over the evidence one more time. I'm sure the answer is there somewhere. Whoever killed Sammy Treadwell lured him up to the vent shaft with the promise of an answer to the mystery of Ernie's death. That suggests to me that Sammy didn't know what had happened to Ernie's body..."

"But that Sammy could identify whoever it was who moved Ernie from the bus stop after the band had beaten him up," Kath said, slowly. "Will, if it isn't Jensen, then who is it?"

Blake shook his head. "I don't know, Kath. I'm going to work my way through those files again until I figure it out. Come on people, back to the drawing board."

CHAPTER 42

Hannah Williams peered at Blake over the top of a pile of paperwork. Blake smiled apologetically. "Sorry, Hannah, I'm still snowed under. The words are beginning to run into each other, to be honest..."

"Then take a break, mister. This is the second time I've popped down to see if you're up for a coffee. I've got to go now," she said. "You should come out, even if it's just for a bit."

Blake sighed. "I don't know..."

"Look, sitting there staring at the same file for hours on end won't solve anything. Maybe a walk and a warm drink will loosen things up..."

"You make me sound as though I'm constipated," Blake said, grinning more freely.

"Well you are, sort of, aren't you?" Hannah said. "There's too much information going through your head. Step back from it. Let things go through your system..."

Blake wrinkled his nose. "Can we change the metaphor? I've a feeling it'll end badly."

"You see what I mean though, right? Come on, half an hour might make all the difference," she laughed, looking out into the main office. "Your team might appreciate the break, too."

"I'm not taking them to the coffee shop," I might buy them a drink when the case is solved but..."

Hannah shook her head, smiling. "Come on."

The family photograph album that Beatty Uxton, Ernie Hughes' sister had loaned them lay open on the desk where Blake had been flicking through it. Ernie's, square jawed, flawless face stared out at him from the picture. He was sitting at a table, presumably at some kind of family get together or maybe a works do. There were people laughing and chatting in the background, someone leaning out of the frame into another conversation. A young woman rested her hand on his shoulder, her face blurred and half in shadow. "She looks kind of familiar, but I can't place her," Blake muttered, still hovering at the edge of his desk.

"She'll be there when you get back, Will," Hannah said. "And you'll have fresh eyes."

"You're right," Will muttered. "I'm going round in circles, here. Twenty minutes won't harm anyone."

They walked in silence for a while, Blake letting the cold November breeze blow the stuffiness out of his head. Shoppers bustled around them as they strode through the Liverpool One shopping precinct. Blake didn't care where they drank and let Hannah lead him. He watched the light glimmer on the rain-slick pavements. The official Christmas lights hadn't been switched on yet but the shop windows more than made up for it with baubles, tinsel and fairy lights wrapped around mannequins and displays.

Music drifted out of one shop doorway, Paul McCartney was simply having a wonderful Christmastime. Blake wondered what the young McCartney have made of that. On a darker note, he couldn't help thinking of the number of years that song had played while poor Ernie Hughes lay lost in the darkness.

"I can't stand that song," Hannah said.

Blake pulled a face. "It's a Christmas song, isn't it? What d'you want, misery and navel-gazing?"

"The lyrics are so inane."

"Ha! I'll play you Phil on the Filly when we get to the coffee shop, then you'll know inane lyrics..."

"Phil on the what?"

"Filly, you know a young female horse. It's the song Ernie wrote about his childhood sweetheart. Jensen was telling us that Ernie fell off her horse and broke his leg."

"Phil? Was she a Philomena or a Philippa?" Hannah said. "Philippa more likely. Sounds posher than Philomena, that's a more working-class catholic name..."

Blake stopped in the street. "Jeez," he muttered.

"What is it?" Hannah said, looking back at him.

"The horse, queen of the hill." Blake said quietly. "Gives me a thrill, the King don't like it but I love her still. She said her father kept her away from the local boys…"

"Will, are you all right?"

"Never better, Hannah, the walk was a great idea, I just realised who the woman in the photo album is," Blake said, pulling out his phone. "Kinnear? Get as much background as you can on Pippa Fearon…"

CHAPTER 43

Technically speaking, PC Mark Robertson had a couple more days to go before he hung up his handcuffs and retired but he had a few days in lieu, and he fully intended to take them, so this was his last ever house call. He'd left it until the end of the day; visiting a posh old lady in a big old house seemed a fitting way to round off a long career and contrasted with his first day when he'd found himself raiding a brothel above a dry cleaner's shop in Hoylake.

This end of the hill was quieter than the Observatory end and, as he drove along Eleanor Road, he began to wonder quite where Pippa Fearon's house was. The dwellings here were large with spacious drives and gardens but Mark knew that a few properties that stood on the actual side of the hill were virtual mansions.

Darkness closed in where a row of streetlights had failed but his headlights picked out a faded sign marked: *The Skerries* at the side of the road. It was hard to see anyway, being tucked in the undergrowth. The gates to the property were shut and Mark wondered if he shouldn't have left his visit until the next day. Pippa wouldn't be expecting him because the number she gave was unobtainable and he had been unable to forewarn her. She was a robust old bird and probably wouldn't mind the unannounced intrusion. If she did, well, he'd go away and leave it to someone else. Tomorrow, it wouldn't be his problem.

He pulled up the car and climbed out. The autumnal smell of leaf mould and wood smoke on the air made Mark smile. This was his favourite time of year. Somewhere a firework went off, then three more. His smile slipped; the yearly pyromania that seized the nation's teenagers took the shine off it a little, he had to admit. Still, next year, he might spend October and November in New England, enjoy the leaves changing colour and leave chasing scrotes with small explosives to someone else.

The old wooden gates slumped on their hinges. Mark pushed at one and it opened with a shuddering creak, the base gouging up a pile of soil, old gravel and dead leaves as it went. He peered up the dark drive to the silhouette of the big house. No lights seemed to shine in the windows or at the doors. What was left of the gardens had reverted to sapling woods and the spindly trees leaned over the path just daring Mark to walk forward.

"You going up to the Witch House, mister?" a young voice said, making Mark jump and turn quickly. Two lads wearing a dark hoodie and riding one BMX, stood watching him from the road.

Mark recognised them as Zach and Liam, the boys who found Jayden when all this madness began.

"What do you mean, 'Witch House?'" Mark Robertson said, with a laugh that sounded a little too shrill.

"Haven't you seen her? The woman who lives there? She's dead old," Zach said, his eyes wide.

"A being 'dead old' makes you a witch, does it?"

"No, she's fuckin mental too. Nobody goes near that house."

"Oi," Mark said. "Watch your language. You need lights on that bike, and I don't want to see you giving him a backie on it, okay?"

"Whatever," Zach said. "It was nice knowing you, mister."

"Wheel it!" Mark called after the two lads as Zach kicked it forward and Liam jumped on behind him. "So much for community policing." He turned back to the gate and started to walk up to the house. A quick chat, write a few notes up back home and drop them off at the office tomorrow. It couldn't be easier.

***

It was dark in the living room when Jeff's front doorbell woke him up. At first, he wondered where he was and why he couldn't see. Then the book slid from his face stopping on his belly. He stared around the room, taking in the wine glass on the table next to his armchair and the huge bag of kettle chips he shouldn't have been eating. He groaned and sat up, noticing the time. It wasn't all that late but he'd certainly started that bottle too early in the day. Still, he deserved a celebration; his agent had phoned to let him know there was 'something of a bidding war' going on between two big publishers and he should open the bubbly. Plus, Gambles hadn't phoned again since the incident in the supermarket. Jeff had opted for a bottle of red instead and settled down with his first book Quixote Junction, rereading it with a relish he'd never experienced before. The doorbell rang again

"Hello, Jeffrey, mind if I come in?" Laura Vexley said, sweeping past him into the hall. "Did I wake you up?"

"Laura, erm, I didn't expect you. What do you want?"

"I just thought I'd congratulate you," Laura said, flashing a brief smile.

Jeff grinned, the wine still making him feel mellow and slowing his thoughts. "Thanks, Laura, that's very kind of you... wait, how did you know about the book deal? Any announcement is embargoed for a good few weeks yet until..."

"I don't know anything about a book deal and

I don't care though I suspect you might. I just came round to let you know that you got what you asked for."

Jeff frowned. "What?"

"Your wish has been granted, Jeffrey. Your best pal Josh Gambles is dead."

Jeff felt his throat tighten. "Dead? How? When?"

"Obviously details are sketchy, but our contacts inside say it looks like he was strangled to death in the church chapel earlier this morning. Seems like *someone* got to him."

"Got to him?" Jeff repeated. He suddenly felt dizzy and leaned against the wall. "Wait a minute. What do you mean, my wish has been granted? I never asked for him to be killed."

Laura shut the front door. "Once more for the microphone, Mr Jeffrey Blake, famous author with a new book deal. What the fuck did you think would happen if you told Kyle Quinlan that Gambles was blabbing about their past?"

"I-I don't know," Jeff could hardly breathe. He couldn't believe it. Josh was dead. It was surreal. "I didn't want him to murder Gambles. Just have a word with him…"

"Have a word," Laura said. "Fuck, Jeff, how naïve can you be? Kyle doesn't 'have a word' with people. He snuffs them out. He did that to Gambles on your request..."

"Mine?" Jeff stammered, trying to sound outraged but realising he just sounded guilty. "I never asked him to..."

"Oh, behave, Jeff," Laura snapped, "You wanted him out of your hair. He attacked you in the visiting room, didn't he? He didn't want you to write your stupid book. So you came to Kyle asking him to solve your problem. But you have to be careful what you wish for. You're at least guilty of conspiracy to murder now."

"No. I never wanted that," Jeff said, slumping onto the bottom step of the stairs. "I never asked Quinlan to kill Josh. Never."

"Listen Jeffrey, Whatever you wanted, it's happened. Josh Gambles is dead, and no amount of handwringing will bring him back. His murder looked like suicide, but the police aren't stupid..."

"The police?" Jeff squeaked.

"They're going to be looking into this, Jeffrey, and they will come and talk to you, it's inevitable. You must be clear in your mind that you are not going to say *anything* about meeting Kyle or me at any point. Is that clear?"

"Or what?" Jeff said, the wine making him momentarily reckless. "Suppose I do tell them what went on between us? I'm innocent. Why should I suffer?"

"You aren't innocent, Jeffrey, you never were. You've been dipping the nib of your pen in the blood of those victims ever since you agreed to work with Gambles. That's why you should suffer, because you should never have started writing the book and you should never have finished it. At some point, you should have realised how fucked up your relationship with Gambles was. As for what happens if you do say anything to anyone, it's quite simple. You've seen what happens to blabbermouths."

"I'll tell Will."

"He won't be able to protect you, believe me, I know. Look at Gambles. He was in prison, supposedly safe. It's a cliché but, one day, when you least expect it, you'll see someone walking towards you and you'll know your time is up. It'll be painful, too."

Tears stung Jeff's cheeks. He tried to tell himself that they were for Josh Gambles, but he knew self-pity when he felt it. He looked up at her. "What happened to you, Laura?" he said.

"I took back control," Laura said, folding her arms. "I stopped running from my past and decided to live life on my terms. I was living a lie, Jeffrey, the lie you tell yourself. That if I ignore the bad things in life and get educated, get a job, then I'll be a good person. But I was living off stolen money, I just fooled myself that I'd escaped."

"But …"

"Look at you Jeff, all cut up about a murderous psychopath who butchered people and ruined so many other lives along the way. Or are you more concerned about yourself? It excited you to play around in the shallow end of the criminal world, didn't it? Now you feel sullied by it, contaminated, even. It's pathetic."

"But there have to be rules…" Jeff said, thrashing around for something sensible to say.

"You sound like your brother now, Jeffrey. Another one quick to judge. At least Will plays by the book. People like you bend the rules to suit yourself; a little coke at dinner parties, ignoring where it comes from and lamenting the decline in the rule of law. Writing about the escapades of sick psychopaths, making a living from death and suffering."

"Whereas you don't?"

"I know where my money comes from and what it costs. The strong eat the weak. People like you despise people like me because you're scared. Scared of your own hypocrisy. Anyway, I'd love to stay and chat all evening but it's been a long day. Just remember, you can keep quiet, enjoy your success with this book, I'm pretty sure Gambles' death will only make it more popular. Or you can say the wrong thing and we will eat you alive.

Goodbye Jeffrey, I hope we don't meet again."

CHAPTER 44

Blake had already made his excuses to Hannah and was heading back to the office when Kinnear rang back. He sounded worried.

"Sir, I just spoke to Beatty Uxton, Ernie Hughes' sister and she remembers her mother talking about Pippa Fearon very well. In fact her exact words were, 'that mad woman.' Apparently, Pippa was very possessive of Ernie, obsessed with him. At first, Ernie quite liked it but then she became aggressive towards other girls who showed any kind of interest in him. She said that Pippa's father kept her locked up in the house a lot of the time, more for the safety of the local teenagers. When Beatty was about ten, her mother heard that Pippa had been sent to some kind of institution 'for her health.' The rumour was that it was some kind of asylum."

"Jeez," Blake muttered. "What did Pippa's father do, any ideas?"

"Funnily enough, sir, he was the Hughes' land-lord. That's how they met. He built properties and some he rented out. Self-made man..."

"With a ready supply of tools and materials on hand to brick Ernie up..."

"Vikki checked the Niche database and she has a mention," Kinnear said. "Pippa assaulted the Chair of the Bidston Hill Preservation Society. Something about the Chair wanting the shelters to be opened as a tourist attraction. She was opposed to the idea. Violently."

"We better get round there," Blake said. "Wait. Wasn't Mark Robertson meant to be paying her a visit?"

"That's what worries me, sir. I've tried to call Mark but he's not responding."

Blake was in the carpark by this time and climbing into his car. "Get some back up over to Fearon's house and ping me the address. I'm on my way."

***

Mark Robertson's car sat just by the gateway to The Skerries, Pippa Fearon's house, although Blake nearly missed it due to the streetlights being out on this stretch of road. For a moment, he wondered if Pippa had sneaked out in the dead of night to deliberately damage them. He shivered as he got out of his car but he didn't have time to worry. He could hear sirens in the distance and Mark was in the house with a suspected double murderer. Or were there more victims? Even as he ran up the path, the case of Wayne Prosser was tumbling over in the back of his mind. The rent boy, Peter Rapino had said he'd been saved by a guardian angel, was Pippa Fearon his saviour?

It was hard to pick out any details of the house other than it was old and very large. It loomed over Blake in the darkness and he could feel its presence. Leaded windows reflected what little light got through the low, grey clouds and the dense foliage on the surrounding land. Blake glimpsed some mock Tudor timbers and a bit of red brick but what struck him was the overwhelming sense of decay.

He passed a garage next to the house and shone his torch in. The light reflected off the windscreen of an old car, dull and dusty after sitting for years but Blake could see the bright orange paintwork in his torch beam. The rest of the garage looked empty.

As he approached the house, he saw holes in the glass, and peeling paint on the frames. Ivy had colonised most of the walls, leaves shivering and hissing at him in the breeze. The front door stood ajar, and Blake pushed it open gingerly. It groaned ominously and he noticed leaves piling up in the hall as though it never really closed.

Conscious that two victims had already been hit in the back of the head with a hammer, Blake eased himself into the hall and pressed himself against the wall. The place was cold and smelt of damp. A dim light glimmered in the back room at the end of a long corridor.

"Hello?" Blake called in a low voice. "Miss Fearon? Mark?"

Silence.

Blake crept down the hall towards the light, glancing behind him now and then in case of ambush. He came to the door and listened. At least one person was inside, he could hear heavy breathing. Pushing the door open, he inched over the threshold.

A single candle guttered on a scrubbed pine kitchen table, creating a bubble of light that reflected off an old Aga stove and a few cracked plates on a dusty Welsh Dresser. Pippa Fearon, sat at the table as though awaiting friends who were coming for tea. Except Pippa held an old service revolver in her long, thin hand. Blake froze.

"Inspector Blake, do come in and sit down," Pippa said.

"Is that an order or an invitation?" Blake said, hovering by the door.

"Probably an order but we do so like the veneer of respectability and manners, don't we?"

Blake took a few steps towards the table. On the floor in the shadow lay a body. It was very still. "Mark? are you okay?"

"I liked his sense of humour," Pippa said. "In the

face of adversity and all that but he tried to take the gun."

"Pippa, we need to call an ambulance. Can I check he's all right."

"If you want a bullet in the head, be my guest. Otherwise, sit down."

"You know you can't get away, don't you? We know you killed Ernie Hughes and Sammy Treadwell. Back up is on the way. You must have heard the sirens."

"Why would I want to get away? This is my home. I'm not going to leave here."

"What do you want?"

Her eyes flashed and Blake saw real misery in her eyes. "I want Ernie back. I want him here, with me."

Blake shuffled to the chair in which he was expected to sit but remained standing. "But Ernie's dead, Pippa, you know that," he said, gently.

"I know that. I killed him, didn't I? I knew where he was. I could go up on the hill and be with him any time I felt like. No more Daddy locking me in, no doctors or so-called 'nurses' pinning me down and medicating me. Just me and him up on the hill, like it was meant to be."

"You killed him to keep him from going to Hamburg," Blake said, glancing over to Mark's still form. "Was that always the plan?"

Pippa nodded. "I was going to surprise him when he came back from singing with the band, lure him away to the shelters with the promise of," she gave a strange, coy smile and inclined her head, "well, you know what…"

"And then you were going to kill him?" Blake said, trying to comprehend her plan. "But if you loved him so much, how could you do that?"

"Ernie was weak, Inspector, a child running after the next new toy he saw. I knew where he belonged. With me. He was mine. Nobody else's."

"So you lay in wait, but then the band started to beat him up."

"I nearly ran out to save him but then, I thought, why not let them do the work for me? And they did, they beat him senseless. He could just about walk with my help. So we strolled in each other's arms to the shelter. It was blissful. I had all the materials prepared…"

"He lay there, lost for sixty years, Pippa," Blake said. "Nobody knew where he was."

"I knew," Pippa said. "I spoke to him every day."

"Not every day," Blake said. "Your father sent you to a hospital, I believe."

"You haven't sat down yet, Inspector. Please do so. This was my father's revolver from the war but it's in good condition," she said, looking hard at Blake. "Don't let its age fool you into thinking it's not deadly."

"Can I at least check Mark's pulse, Pippa? He's a good man. Days away from retirement. A grand-father…"

Pippa paused, then waggled the gun. "Quickly, then you sit."

Blake knelt down. Mark Robertson groaned a little. It was hard to see in the candlelight but he seemed to be bleeding from the shoulder.

"Here," Pippa said, throwing some old cloth napkins down from the table. "Pad it with this, then on your seat, young man."

Blake stuffed the cloth in between Mark's torn flesh and his shirt then sat down. "It must have been hard, being separated from Ernie for so long during the seventies."

"I don't remember much about that," Pippa muttered. She shook herself. "Golly, Inspector, are you always such a glumster? Let's talk about how we're going to get Ernie back here where he belongs."

Blake gave her a pained look. "Pippa, other offi-cers are on their way. Once they realise you have a gun, there'll be an armed response unit here in minutes. Put the gun down. I don't want you to get hurt and I want to get Mark to safety."

"They won't hurt me as long as I have you here, will they?"

"Then let PC Robertson get to hospital," Blake said. "I'll stay and we can give your demands to the officers outside and we can negotiate from there."

Pippa rolled her eyes. "They aren't demands," she said. "You make me sound like some kind of terrorist. They are requirements." She looked hard at Blake. "No. It's a trick. We'll tell them I want Ernie brought here to the house when they arrive. As long as Ernie's nearby, I'll be happy."

Mark moaned and muttered something.

"Please, Pippa," he said. "You don't want his death on your conscience, do you?"

"I doubt his death will trouble me much," Pippa said, sitting back. "You get to my age and you see all kinds of death, some of it fair, some of it totally unjust. Bright young things snuffed out in the prime of their lives, dark, fat corrupt beasts gorging on prime steak and claret and sleeping like pigs in muck." She pointed the gun at Blake. "It's an unjust world, Inspector."

CHAPTER 45

Pippa lapsed into silence for a while. She looked at Blake but he couldn't fathom what was going on in her mind. "When you were a child, did you ever poke a stick in an ant nest, just to see what would happen?"

Blake nodded, glancing down at Mark. The constable was breathing heavily and Blake didn't like the sound of it. He had to keep Pippa talking while he thought of a way to disarm her or at least get her away from the kitchen and Mark. "I suppose most kids have at some point."

"That's what I've done with the Galahads," she said staring into the darkness that surrounded them. "Stirred things up for them every now and then. I hated that band. The Galahads! There was nothing even remotely gallant about any of them. Ernie would never let me go to the dances they played at; he said they were ruffians and common. Half the time I couldn't get out anyway because my father would lock me in my bedroom. It felt like the band was stealing him away from me. And when Dave New and Wayne Prosser hatched this Hamburg idea, I hated them even more."

"Then why take it out on Ernie?"

Pippa's eyes flashed and her mouth became a tight line. For a second, Blake wondered if he'd overstepped the mark. "Because they had control of him. He did what they told him. Dave New was a nasty bully, I knew that much. So I set him free from them. It was just Ernie and me then. But then watching them living their lives, growing older, marrying, having children, it made me want to hurt them."

"Then what stopped you?"

"Oh, I did my best," Pippa said. "A rumour here, a sly comment to a prospective girlfriend there. Gary Jensen never understood why the girl of his dreams stood him up. It was because I told her what he was really like. The woman he married in the end married him out of desperation. She despised him from the outset."

"You set out to mess up their lives? That's…"

"Crazy? The doctors said I was cured. I don't know what of, there's no cure for love is there, Inspector?" She stopped and thought for a second. "I suppose there's no cure for hate, either then, it being the other end of that spectrum, wouldn't you agree?"

Blake shrugged. "I suppose so," he said, more to keep her mollified. He glanced down at Mark again.

"I didn't stick to gossip and poisoned words, though," Pippa said wagging the gun at Blake.

"Dave New's wife had an unfortunate accident."

"Hit and run," Blake murmured in horror.

"I enjoyed that funeral. I think Ernie did too, when I came up to the hill and told him about it. I mean who did they think they were, carrying on as normal? Of course, the whole cancer thing. That wasn't me."

"Dave thought it was a punishment from God."

"Maybe it was," Pippa said. "But when Dave New died, I realised I'd been wasting my time. I went to his funeral, you know. And I saw his grandson, and his son weeping behind the coffin. Father Lanigan banging on about what a fine, Christian man he was. Jensen and Treadwell even put in a brief appearance at the back of the church but didn't linger. I did. I stayed to the bitter end. I even shook his son's hand and said how very sorry I was."

"Why was it a waste of time?"

"It was pointless, wasn't it? I mean, Dave New was a saint in the eyes of his family. I could have killed his grandson but that would just have generated even more sympathy for him. And the other two, well, what a pathetic pair. Jensen rotting away in his armchair, walking up to the bookies in the same stained pants every day. And Treadwell, still cavorting around with youngsters, screaming his hatred at the world. Pathetic."

"So you started sending the letters to stir things up between the remaining band members," Blake said.

Pippa looked puzzled. "I only sent one letter, Inspector. Someone else knew something. Interesting. I only sent the one note to bring Treadwell to the vent."

"But why start killing again? Why now?"

"Because you took Ernie away. Because Treadwell or Jensen could have identified me. They always thought they'd killed Ernie but they left the body. They'd have worked it out and then where would I be?"

"Right here, only perhaps without a gun? I really think we need to get Mark an ambulance, Pippa. He's innocent."

Her face twisted. "He's not innocent. He was there when they found the boy and Ernie. I saw him. None of you are innocent. You took my Ernie from me. I want him back. Why are you talking so much? Are you trying to trick me?"

Blake held up his hands, trying to calm her but the gesture seemed to have the opposite effect and she raised the pistol. The instant he saw the pistol hand lift, he threw himself to one side, landing on a hard quarry-tiled floor. The gun went off, but Blake was quick on his feet and sprinted down the corridor. "Stop!" Pippa screeched and Blake knew he wouldn't make it to

341

the door. Instead, he pitched to the left into the shadows. Blue lights from outside strobed the hall, giving him glimpses of doorways, cupboard and windows.

He could hear Pippa's footsteps coming nearer and, his heart thumping, he hurried up the stairs. The gun went off again and Blake heard wood splinter close by but he didn't stop to check how close. The sound of gunshots would have alerted a need for armed response. They'd have to wait for that before they came in and Blake would have to play hide and seek at least until Pippa's remaining four shots had been wasted. Assuming he could.

Blake peered into the nearest bedroom, it had two doors inside. Pippa was halfway up the stairs. "Wayne Prosser tried it on with my Ernie, you know," she called. "He told me but I was so proud because he fought him off. It was me he loved really. Me."

Silence fell and Blake could imagine the tall, gaunt woman on the landing, listening intently. Every floorboard seemed to squeak. He crouched behind a large double bed, not daring to move.

"And them, the Galahads, his so-called friends," she hissed, "they spread rumours about him, told all kinds of lies. Only I knew the truth." A creak told Blake she was moving again. He hurried over to a small door in the corner of the room. It opened with a clunk that made him wince.

There was a flurry of movement outside and Blake slammed the door behind him, managing to slide the bolt at the top and throw himself back before another loud bang rang in his ears. The door shook with the impact and the smell of gun smoke filled it. More blue lights flashed through small windows behind him and he realised he was in some kind of servants' corridor that gave access to the bedrooms. It occurred to him that Pippa would know this too and use a door from one of the other bedrooms to access the corridor. It was straight and narrow; if she fired a shot she could hardly miss. The question was, which way would she go? Left or right? She had the advantage here, she'd grown up in this house, knew it even in the dark, he imagined. He was discovering it for the first time. All he had to do was get himself cornered and it would be game over.

For a second, indecision gripped Blake and he stood frozen to the spot, listening to his heart thump wildly. For the first time since he was a child, he was genuinely scared. Primal urges to run from or confront the old woman wrestled against his attempts to control his breathing and stay focused.

A click echoed further down the passage and Blake hurried away in the other direction. It didn't matter that his feet thudded on the bare floorboards, Pippa knew where he was. He wrenched open the next door and threw himself in just as another gunshot exploded through the house.

"Four," Blake muttered. Slamming the door behind him and bolting it. The room left him stunned. From the slivers of light and the flash of the police cars, he caught glimpses of a room plastered in photographs of Ernie Hughes. Some had been blown up to poster size, others were small. They clearly varied in age, the older ones having been faded by sunlight and curled by the damp. An altar-like table sat beneath one large picture of Ernie posing with his guitar, his lip fixed in an Elvis sneer. Dead candles lay scattered across the tabletop.

The door rattled. "Pippa," Blake called. "You don't want to hurt me. We can still bring Ernie here, bring him home. If you shoot me then it won't happen."

"I'm sick of men telling me what to do, lying to me and then going behind my back," Pippa called through the door. "You're all so stupid. Be honest, for once. You aren't going to bring Ernie back here, are you, Inspector?"

Blake flinched and ducked instinctively as the gun went off again, sending splinters of wood flying into the room but the door held. Pippa's footsteps faded off down the passage outside and

Blake glanced around for another door. She had one shot left, after that, he was confident he could overpower her but until then, he had to keep moving.

The house groaned and complained at all the movement around it, giving away Blake's location. Pippa seemed light on her feet and Blake found it hard to pinpoint where she was. He stepped out onto the main landing again and froze.

She stood, a stark, scarecrow silhouetted against the large picture window that looked out from the end of the landing at the top of the stairs. The flash of blue from outside made it hard to discern her features.

"I suppose it was going to happen one day," she said. "Someone would have found Ernie, wouldn't they? I just wish it had been when I'd gone. That fool at the Conservation Society was trying to start a campaign to open up the shelters, make them safe. A tourist attraction. Can you believe it? We fell out over that, I can tell you."

"Pippa..."

"It's so hard, dying, isn't it?" She said. "I mean, it's easy enough to be killed; you could step in front of a bus and that would be it but if you're waiting to die. Waiting and waiting. Waking up each new morning and wondering when it will be the last one. I've wanted to die ever since Ernie went, just never had the courage. Can you believe that? Brave old Pippa. She can kill others but not herself."

"Nobody needs to die, Pippa…"

"If only Ernie had been a little bit stronger, less inclined to get distracted by a silly ponytail or a giggling swish of skirt," Pippa said. "We could have been together forever."

"But you can't change people, Pippa. You think you can, but they are who they are. You either love them for that or let them go."

Pippa blinked at him. "You sound like you mean that, Inspector."

"I do," he said. "Ernie was a showman, wasn't he? He sang and danced. He loved the admiration. It was who he was. He was never going to settle down." Blake paused. He was talking about Ernie but he could have been talking about Laura. She would never change, either. It was time to let go of that. "Come on, put the gun down…"

But before she could reply, the front door crashed open and armed response officers exploded into the hall below, bellowing and shouting orders. Bright lights shone up into Pippa's face, making her look frail and drained of colour.

"Armed police!" someone yelled. "Put the

weapon down or I will shoot."

Pippa looked directly at Blake, her face lit up in the spotlight. "It's hard to die, Inspector," she said, "but not to be killed." Turning back to the officers at the bottom of the stairs she pointed the gun at them.

Two shots rang out and Pippa Fearon crumpled to the floor. The gun fell from her grip and bounced down three stairs before coming to rest. Leaning against the wall, Blake slid to the floor.

CHAPTER 46

A weak autumn sunlight filtered through the thin clouds, making the street looked washed out and pale. Blake sat in the passenger seat of Alex Manikas' car. Manikas sat looking puzzled and slightly worried, too.

"I'm sorry to drag you out on your day off, Alex, but I think this will be useful."

"That's okay, sir, a bit cloak and dagger but why have you brought me here, to Suzi Elston's house?"

"I just wanted to have a chat with her unofficially," Blake said. "And I wanted you to be there, too."

"Are you okay, sir?" Alex said, looking hard at Blake. "I mean, you had a shock last night being chased around by Pippa Fearon and..."

"Yeah, I'm fine. I didn't get much sleep once I'd debriefed the world and his wife. I can't say I'm happy about Pippa's death but what else could anyone do. I think she was determined to end it that way once she was in a corner. The clock started running the moment you uncovered Ernie's body. Anyway, I can't rest until I've tied up all the loose ends. Follow me."

Blake led him to Suzi's front door and knocked. It was still midmorning, and a few car washers were craning their necks to see what these two strange men were doing. "I bet Gloria Parsons is filming us," Alex said. "This will make her day. So much gossip for her to spread around the neighbourhood."

The door creaked open and Suzi Elston peered out at them over a pair of reading glasses. "I'm sorry to trouble you Ms Elston," Blake said, flashing his warrant card. "You know DC Manikas, of course, I wondered if we could have a moment of your time. It won't take a moment."

"I don't really…" she began.

"It's about Hamburg," Blake said. Making Alex blink in surprise.

Her face fell and she shuffled back into the hall without comment, leaving the front door open.

"It was Ernie Hughes wasn't it?" Suzi said, sitting in her living room, hugging herself and rocking back and forth. Alex had gone into the kitchen to make a cup of tea for them all.

Blake nodded. "It was. The discovery of his body brought up your name, too, I'm afraid. Then a shrewd guess led us back here. We couldn't find any records of your mother having a daughter. Not that we did an extensive search and often that kind of information is hard to dig up. People move, change name. Some people go to Germany and call themselves Sasha Schatzi."

Manikas came in with a tray of tea mugs. "I found some biscuits, too," he said. "I hope you don't mind…"

Suzi Elston smiled, taking a mug from the tray. "Schatzi means 'darling or 'sweetheart.' It's quite cheesy but then so was my act. Most of the time I passed as a woman in the clubs and around town. George Harrison asked me out, you know. He was drunk of course, but I thought, 'I'll take that compliment, thank you.' I hadn't transitioned then. 1964 was hardly the time for it. I was still Sidney Elston, on paper at least. But over there, I could be myself."

"Was that your plan when you left the Wirral? To go to Germany?"

"Not at first. I just wanted to get lost somewhere big. London was the biggest place I knew. I met plenty of people down there. Some of them lovely," Her face darkened. "Others less so."

"Did you meet Wayne Prosser before you went to Hamburg?"

"I went to Hamburg to get away from bloody Wayne Prosser," Suzi said. She put a hand to her mouth. "I'm sorry. I tend to keep… painful memories buried deep. None of this is easy to talk about, Inspector…"

"Will," Blake said. "Call me Will. Prosser treated

you badly."

"He treated everyone badly," Suzi said, "but, yes, he beat me, tormented me. I was a virtual prisoner in his flat for months. Only let out for good behaviour. In the end, I ran away yet again." Her smile came back. "And I rediscovered myself in Hamburg. I realised for the first time that there was nothing *wrong* with me, I'd just been trying to fit into the wrong environment. Karl, the manager at the club I worked in said I 'blossomed.' Of course, my Liverpool connections and accent helped." She held her head up. "I was the Merseybeat Queen." Her voice soured. "Then the Galahads showed up. With Prosser in tow."

"That must have been a shock for you, given your personal history with the man…"

"He took up where he left off. Karl tried to intervene, but Prosser wasn't scared of him. The Galahads weren't much help. Gary was kind to me but the other two," she shook her head. "The way Prosser abused me stopped me from singing. I nearly lost my voice all together. Then one night, I tried to stand up to him. He put me in hospital. Karl brought some friends up to Prosser's flat and they threw him out. Sent him packing. But I took a long time recovering from that, both physically and mentally."

"And when you recovered, you came back to England, didn't you?"

Suzi nodded. "Eventually. I was undergoing surgery after that and was in and out of hospital. Karl was very kind and sent money to help me with the bills. I missed my mother but my father was still on the scene and even though I'd heard he was ill, I couldn't bear to face him. I worked down in London but made brief forays up here…"

"And Peter Rapino?"

Suzi flinched a little at the mention of his name. "The poor boy," she whispered. "He'd fallen prey to an older, more debauched Wayne Prosser. I saw them together at the Lisbon pub in town one night and I knew he would end up dead. I met him alone once or twice and tried to warn him away but it was no good. All Wayne had to do was buy some drugs and Peter went trotting after him."

"But you saved him, didn't you?"

"Am I under arrest?" Suzi said, looking from Alex to Blake and back.

Blake sipped his tea. "That depends on what you say next."

Suzi gave a long sigh. "I was there when Prosser died but I didn't kill him. I'd been doing a show at a private club in Liverpool, a sort of burlesque thing and they wanted a drag act, so I obliged. Anyway, after the show we all piled down to the Lisbon and that's where I saw them. Peter looked terrible, spaced out of his mind and Prosser was almost carrying him out of the pub. I knew what would happen to him. I knew the look in Prosser's eyes."

"You thought he intended to kill Rapino?" Blake said.

"I knew it," Suzi said, fiercely. "I followed them out. Peter had pulled a knife on Prosser but he was shaking like a leaf. Prosser would have taken the blade off him easily, but I just appeared around the corner. Prosser hadn't seen me for what? Ten, eleven years. He looked like he'd seen a ghost. For a moment, he didn't know what to do but that was all Peter needed. I watched him kill Wayne Prosser and I tell you, I'm glad I was there to look him in the eye and tell him he wouldn't be missed."

"Peter called you his Angel in White," Blake said. "Like you saved him by striking the blow."

"I was there, Inspector. I know what I saw," Suzi replied. "Peter Rapino killed Wayne Prosser and I'm glad that the poor boy did. I saved him from being killed but he did the killing. I went to visit him in prison a couple of times, but he wasn't coping well. I was one of the few people at his funeral, too. Me and his sister, Eileen. I keep in touch with her. She's a simple soul, full of gossip."

"And after the funeral you went home to care for your mother."

A calmness returned to Suzi, tears welling in her smiling eyes. "Mum knew who I was straight away. She hugged me and called me her precious daughter. I was always her child and always loved. She knew who I was before I did. I nursed her to the end, and I have few regrets. So you can do what you want with that story. You can arrest me, put me in prison, I don't care…"

"I don't think we'll be arresting anyone today, Suzi," Blake said, with a smile. He craned his neck at the tray and plate of biscuits. "I'll have one of those Hobnobs and another brew, if that's okay. I'd love to hear about the Reeperbahn in the sixties, though. You must have some tales to tell."

***

He should have been grinning like a fool, dancing around the restaurant but Jeff Blake listened grimly as his new editor gushed excitedly about the book. She was called Sophie, she was 'psyched' to be working with him, apparently, but, to be honest, he didn't care anymore.

"It's just such a rich vein, Northern, gritty, but with heart, too," she said and then lowered her voice. "And I mean, I shouldn't say it, really, but the news of Gambles' murder… well… that's brought him right back into the spotlight. This is going to be massive. We have to get you in at Hay, Edinburgh, oh and there'll be all the crime festivals too, can't miss them out. Imagine, rubbing shoulders with the likes of Rankin and McDermid!" She put her fork down and grinned. "Ooh, I'm so excited, I need a wee. Excuse me!"

Jeff watched the young woman totter off between the tables. "I can't do this, Ursula," he said, turning to his agent.

Ursula sat back in her chair and put her napkin on the table. Her long earrings sparkled as she shook her head. "We didn't bring her all the way up here just to tell her that the deal is off, Jeffrey. That's insane. This is what you wanted, isn't it?"

"But so quickly after his death, I just…"

She stared at him through her pointed glasses, with her short grey hair and tight mouth, she reminded him of a severe schoolteacher. "It's a quarter of a million quid, Jeffrey. Nobody gets that kind of money these days unless they're hosting a quiz show or they shagged a Royal."

"It's just that I… I…" Jeff looked at her desperately. He'd once read in a folklore book about people who believed the fairies could 'tongue-tie' victims so they couldn't speak about them. It felt like that now, like Laura Vexley had somehow cursed him with her threat. But it was cowardice, plain and simple.

"You what, Jeffrey? Is there something you want to tell me?" she said and looked at him quizzically. In a moment of weird paranoia, Jeff wondered if she was somehow in league with Quinlan and Laura. That they had somehow tipped her off about his role in Gambles' death and told her to make sure he published or else.

"No," he said, looking into his wine glass. "No. It's just bad timing that's all."

Ursula leaned forward. "It's not bad timing, Jeffrey. It's fucking *brilliant* timing. That foul little man's death is the best thing that happened to us. I can't believe you're even thinking of him. This book could be huge and the only thing who can screw things up is *you*. They will throw a shitload of cash at this and if you cock-up, you'll be ghosted by every publisher in London. In the world, even. You'll never write again, understand? Never. So put your 'fuck me' face on and schmooze the shit out of this situation or you and I are parting company. Sophie!" Ursula stood up as the editor returned. "Tell Jeffrey about who you met in the green room at Hay this year, he'll be so jealous."

Sophie grinned and tucked a strand of blonde hair behind her ear. "Next year Jeffrey, it'll be *you* they're all bragging about having met," she said. She shivered. "What's it like, having that kind of personal rapport with a serial killer?"

Ursula looked pointedly at Jeff, who grinned. He felt hollow, like he was trapped inside a shell of a man who looked like him but wasn't. Trapped deep inside this shell, he was screaming. "Well, it's... scary first of all. You think of all the terrible things he's done. You look at his hands and the inevitable realisation crosses your mind," he stopped and stroked his chin. "At the same time, though, you see a human being, a lost child and you wonder, how did it all come to this?"

Sophie bit her lip. "Incredible," she murmured. "You know, such a multi-faceted person could be viewed in so many ways. I mean... is there a follow-up book we could do?"

"It's such a rich vein," Ursula said, "I'm sure we can explore that and film tie-ins, real-life documentaries." She raised her glass. "Here's to Josh Gambles, our deepest thanks and rot in Hell!"

Jeff grinned and raised his glass and inside, he screamed to be let off this ride.

CHAPTER 48

She liked the sound of scissors snipping through cardboard and she liked the smell of glue, too. Making stuff was what kept her sane. Snipping and gluing and doing. It stopped her thinking about Peter and Wayne Prosser. Or about the garage man who used to let her ride in his orange car until Pippa stopped him. Or about that night when she was just six and she'd heard a noise and looked out of her window. She'd seen Sammy Treadwell, Dave New and Gary Jensen kicking Ernie to bits in the street. They should have owned up, but they never did.

Since Sammy had been murdered, she'd been at a bit of a loss who to send her letters to. She'd prayed really hard, though. And God had answered her prayers. Not just her one prayer but all of them.

She'd never liked Father Lanigan and had been praying for him to go away. He was too young to be a priest and he obviously didn't like Rich Tea biscuits. So she'd been praying to get rid of him. And she'd been praying hard for someone new to write to.

And there they were one evening. Wrapped in each other's arms.

She'd come in early to do her praying, but the door was locked, so she'd gone round the back and that was where she saw them.

He was a priest and should know better than to hug and kiss anyone, let alone a married woman.

So she was snipping and gluing and doing. All she needed now was Sarah New's postal address and she could get going. It was nearly Christmas and Eileen Rapino had a lovely, bright Rudolph sticker to use.

CHAPTER 47

The one flaw in Blake's leafletting plan, as far as he could see, was being able to judge whether it had worked or not. Serafina's behaviour could change and he wouldn't know if that was because someone had realised that she was sneaking into their house and stealing their hormone cream somehow. It could be coincidence, or it might not work at all. If most people were like him, they put leaflets straight into the recycling without glancing at them.

Hannah had done a stunning job on the leaflets. A picture of a Persian cat not unlike Serafina filled the middle of the flyer. Blake smiled at the note and started to read. 'A strange request!" It began. "Recently my cat has begun to display some unusual behaviour. You may have been disturbed by the noise! My vet believes that my cat may have access to hormone cream or gel. If you use such products, could you check that the lid is secure or that they are put away. Hopefully, if she stopped ingesting the hormones, she'll be okay!"

There was a 'any more information box and Blake's name and address, which he thought was only fair. He called Hannah. "They look great," he had said. "Thanks. How did you know what Serafina looks like and how did you get my address?"

"You aren't the only detective around here, Will," Hannah said, laughing. "I asked your team, it didn't take much. Andrew Kinnear would sell his grandmother for a Jammie Dodger and Kath Cryer is a veritable fount of information."

"Are you sure there's no cost?"

"Nah. Called in a favour from my mate who works at a printer's. It was ten minutes' work, honest."

"I owe you another coffee sometime. Possibly even a meal."

He'd handed the money over to Ian Youde's nephews, two older teenagers who didn't really look that keen on the job and they'd taken them away. Youde vouched for them and said they were hard workers but for all Blake knew they could have binned the leaflets once they were up the road.

Now he stood in front of the wardrobe mirror scowling at his suit. Something was wrong with it, but he couldn't work out what. He turned and looked at the back. All fine. He sniffed at the arm and wondered if Serafina had sprayed it with her own exquisite odour. He couldn't tell. He was so inured to the stench around the house that unless someone told him he stank of cat pee, he wouldn't know.

"Sod it," he muttered. He was going to be late for Mark Robertson's retirement party at this rate and he didn't want to miss that. As he hurried down into the hall, he glimpsed a fluffy tail vanishing into the cupboard under the stairs.

"What are you up to now?" Blake muttered, opening the cupboard door wider. It was one of the many jobs that needed doing in this house. Years of overpainting had left it unable to close, and it needed resetting on its hinges. It was always hanging open.

In the dim light, all Blake could see was Serafina's tail and backside. She grumbled as he lifted her out. He set her down and noticed a smudge of white on her nose just before she licked it off. "Don't tell me," he said to her and looked back inside the cupboard.

It smelt musty and damp in the darkness of the cupboard. Blake didn't think he'd taken anything out of here or disturbed this space since his mother disappeared. Underneath a pile of old boots and shoes, he found a cardboard box, one side broken down and open. He set it down on the hall floor and pulled at the lid. Mice had gnawed at the cardboard at some point and, it seems at the contents, too.

The box was full of old packets of tablets, bottles of cough mixture and tubes of all kinds of lotions from pile cream to skin softener. Blake vaguely recalled emptying the bathroom cabinet in a frenzied attempt to clear the house of his mum's presence. He must have shoved everything into a box and then, uncertain how to dispose of the contents, he stuffed it under the stairs. Everything felt a bit sticky and in amongst it all was a tube that had split, its innards dolloped in a greasy pile. Gingerly, he picked up the tube with finger and thumb. It was hard to read the branding, but he could see the words 'oestrogen cream.' Blake groaned out loud. It must have been his mother's from some time in the past. It was enough that Serafina reminded him of his mother without the cat dredging up snippets of her personal past for his delectation.

"Jeez." He dropped the tube back into the box and picked the whole thing up. Serafina meowed at his ankles as though begging him to put it down. "It must smell of mice," Blake said to her. "A kind of mice cream that makes you randy." He shook his head. "Sorry, girl, I'm sure it's not good for you and I need my sleep."

He dumped the box in the wheelie bin and made sure the lid was closed, then climbed into his car. After all these weeks, trying to figure out where the problem lay, it was right on his doorstep. Closer, even. Wasn't that always the way? He shook his head, imagining how he might explain this to Youde, or Hannah. His eyes widened. Or what if a neighbour came along, begging forgiveness and explaining the ins and outs of their hormone therapy.

"Jeez," he muttered one last time and started the engine.

***

Everyone had gone inside the Pollard Inn, where Mark was holding his retirement do. Everyone except Hannah Williams who stood in her coat, staring intently at her phone. Blake parked up and hurried over.

"Were you waiting for me?" he joked.

Hannah gave a smile. "I was just checking my work emails," she said.

"Really?"

"Oh, okay, I didn't want to end up sitting next to someone really dull, you know."

"I'll take that as a compliment," Blake said. "Come on, we better get inside."

"People will talk, us arriving together," Hannah said, linking arms with him.

"If they're talking about us, they're giving some other poor bugger a break," Blake said. "Come on."

The warmth of the room hit them as they entered, and Blake made his way with Hannah to a large table that had been commandeered by the team. "Room for one more?" Blake said, nodding to Hannah. Kath dragged another chair over and soon they settled down.

"Did you sort your cat out sir?" Kinnear said, slathering a bread roll with too much butter. Chris, his husband slapped his hand and took the knife off him.

"A long story, Andrew but yes, I think I got to the bottom of it," Blake replied. "Probably best not contemplated over food…"

The tinkling of a fork on glass saved Blake from having to elaborate. He looked across the room to see Mark Robertson standing with a glass. He had one arm in a sling and looked a little pale but otherwise had made a full recovery. "I wasn't going to make a speech," he said, his voice quiet so you had to listen. "I could tell you all kinds of stories, some that would make you laugh, some would make you shudder. I think we've all been there, haven't we? I could bang on about what needed fixing in the police force and ramble on until you begged for mercy. But, even though it's my retirement, tonight is about you lot, too. Who go out in rain, sleet and hail, or baking heat to make a difference. You lot who I always knew had my back. And I want to single out one person tonight. Will Blake. I'm pretty sure I wouldn't be here," he looked around at his table, "with my wife and kids, if it weren't for you." His voice was thick with emotion. "I just wanted to thank you, in front of friends, family and fellow officers. There was a moment in that house when I thought I was going to die with my boots on instead of hanging them up, Will. You saved my life."

Blake felt his face blaze. He half stood and gave a wave, uncertain what else to do. Hannah gave him a nudge and he stood up. "Mark, thank you. You're too kind. I think I did what anyone here would do. I know people here who have literally taken a bullet for their colleagues, so I'm in good company. And I know I'm always in good company with you Mark, with your local knowledge, patience and good humour. In one sense, I wish you weren't retiring because we'll all miss you. But enjoy yourself, you deserve it. Just don't drop by too much with your holiday snaps, it kind of rankles after a while, you know?" he picked up his glass. "To Mark."

The room burst into applause and Blake sat down. "That was shite," he whispered to Hannah, under his breath.

"Yeah, it was," she said, smiling "stop fishing for compliments."

Blake grinned and watched his team, Kath bitching about the soup, Manikas pouring wine and watching some of the single female officers as they passed the table, Vikki Chinn, slapping Kinnear's hand when he reached for another bread roll. Tasha Cook had a glazed smile fixed on her face as Ian Ollerthwaite filled her in on the latest updates to the new train layout in his loft. Family. Not the only one he had but the best he could wish for.

The End

ABOUT THE AUTHOR

J. E. Mayhew

Jon Mayhew lives on the Wirral with his family and has done all his life. A teacher for many years, he enjoys traditional music and plays regularly in cei-  lidh bands and sessions. Jon is also an award-winning author. His dark chil- dren's books are published by Bloomsbury.

Made in the USA
Las Vegas, NV
15 November 2021

34517207R00217